Too Rich and Too DEAD

CYNTHIA BAXTER

BANTAM BOOKS

TOO RICH AND TOO DEAD
A Bantam Book / April 2009

Published by Bantam Dell
A Division of Random House, Inc.
New York, New York

This is a work of fiction. Names, characters, places, and incidents either
are the product of the author's imagination or are used fictitiously.
Any resemblance to actual persons, living or dead, events, or locales
is entirely coincidental.

All rights reserved
Copyright © 2009 by Cynthia Baxter
Cover art © Robert Ginsti
Cover design by Marietta Anastassatos

Bantam Books and the rooster colophon are registered trademarks of
Random House, Inc.

ISBN 978-0-553-59036-4

Printed in the United States of America
Published simultaneously in Canada

www.bantamdell.com

OPM   10 9 8 7 6 5 4 3 2 1

PRAISE FOR CYNTHIA BAXTER'S

Murder Packs a Suitcase
An Independent Mystery Booksellers
Association Bestseller

"A new series that capitalizes on Baxter's trademark
humor and ingenuity... Pack a virtual suitcase and
accompany Mallory on her assignment from hell...
A perfect choice for the Elaine Viets fan."
—*Mystery Scene*

"Perfect train or plane reading... [a] very
promising series." —*Connecticut Post* Forum

"With a character as appealing as veterinarian
Jessica Popper in her Reigning Cats & Dogs series...
Baxter will have you hankering for another excursion
with Mallory." —*Richmond Times-Dispatch*

"Thoroughly entertaining... The mystery is well-
plotted, the culprit a surprise and the tie-in
to Mallory's old life will leave the reader
wanting more." —*FreshFiction.com*

"Author Cynthia Baxter has conjured the varied
flavors of the Sunshine State to deliver a mystery
packed with orange punch. Go ahead, take a sip."
—*RomanceReviewsToday.com*

ALSO BY CYNTHIA BAXTER

The *Murder Packs a Suitcase* Mystery Series
Murder Packs a Suitcase

The *Reigning Cats & Dogs* Mystery Series
Dead Canaries Don't Sing
Putting On the Dog
Lead a Horse to Murder
Hare Today, Dead Tomorrow
Right from the Gecko
Who's Kitten Who?
Monkey See, Monkey Die

And coming soon:
Murder Had a Little Lamb

To Tama,
who also can't sit still

Too Rich and Too DEAD

Chapter 1

"I travel a lot; I hate having my life disrupted by routine."
—Caskie Stinnett

Whoa! Who's *that*?" Jordan asked, leaning over to pick up the newspaper he'd just knocked off the kitchen table en route to the refrigerator. "She's really hot!"

Mallory Marlowe glanced up from the coffee mug that up until that moment had been the focus of her attention. She assumed that the female who had aroused such a strong reaction in her eighteen-year-old son would turn out to be a member of the Star-of-the-Month club, some actress or singer who was as well known for flaunting her curves as she was for her talent.

So as soon as she saw the face staring back at her from the front page of the *New York Times* Style section, she gasped.

"Oh, my gosh!" she cried. "I *know* her!"

" 'Carly Cassidy Berman,' " Jordan read aloud. "She invented some magic potion that makes people young again. Or so she claims."

"Let me see that."

Mallory reached for the newspaper, still wondering if somehow she was mistaken. Yet there was Carly Cassidy, staring right back at her from page one, wearing the same cat-that-ate-the-canary grin she'd worn when she'd been crowned Homecoming Queen. In full color, no less.

"You really know her?" Jordan asked as he retrieved a carton of orange juice from the refrigerator.

"I sure do," Mallory replied. "We went to JFK High together. Everybody knew her. In fact, she was voted Most Likely to Succeed."

"Cool." Jordan plopped down in the seat opposite hers. "She looks amazing—for somebody your age, I mean. Maybe that crazy potion of hers really works."

Mallory had to agree that that was a definite possibility. From the picture, it looked as if wrinkles, not to mention cellulite, had failed to stake a claim during the past two and a half decades. In fact, Carly didn't look much older than she had in high school.

True, her hairstyle had changed. Gone were the long, silky tresses that as a teenager she was forever flipping over her shoulder. While her hair was still just as blond and still just as silky, these days it was cut into a complicated set of layers. It curved around her face in such a flattering way that it looked as if a stylist had meticulously arranged each individual strand.

Her face had also changed since her days of shouting "Who's your worst en-e-my? John F. Kenn-e-dy! Go-o-o, Bulldogs, go!" on the football field every Saturday. But while her girlish prettiness was gone, it had been replaced by a womanly beauty that was at least as striking.

All in all, there was no mistaking that the woman pictured on the front page was indeed Carly Cassidy, apparently now known as Carly Cassidy Berman. After taking a strong sip of her coffee, Mallory began to read.

Enterprising Entrepreneur Bottles the Waters of the Fountain of Youth

Can drinking a magic potion twice a day turn back the hands of the clock? Carly Cassidy Berman thinks so. So do the thousands of believers who have been scrambling to snatch Berman's creation, Rejuva-Juice, off the shelves at health food stores all over the country.

They've also been flocking to Berman's chichi spa, Tavaci Springs, its name derived from the Native American Ute tribe's word for "sun." She opened it less than a year ago in tony Aspen, Colorado, well known as an enclave of the financially and physically fit. Local residents and visitors alike not only endure a six-month wait for a reservation; they also pay upwards of fifteen hundred dollars a day for the privilege of staying at this mountain hideaway that combines the rustic elements of a former silver mining town with an array of touchy-feely New Age accoutrements. The hefty price tag enables guests to imbibe unlimited quantities of the pricey potion, as well as to indulge in facials, massages, body wraps, and even mud baths that incorporate the same ingredients that reportedly make Rejuva-Juice "plastic surgery in liquid form."

But fans of Rejuva-Juice say it's much more than Botox-in-a-bottle. Its devotees insist that it also significantly increases both their energy level and their mental powers.

The secret, according to the elixir's creator, is the unique ingredients, which Berman claims have never before been available. The determined entrepreneur spent two years traveling around the world, trekking to remote villages in such locales as the Himalayas in Nepal, the rain forests of South America, and the tropical islands of the South Pacific. Her mission was to learn about the herbs, roots, and other substances that primitive peoples have used for centuries to improve their well-being and increase their life span.

As for the formula used to make this magical potion, the wizard behind it has no intention of divulging it.

"That's a secret I'll take to my grave," jokes Berman, who is forty-five but looks at least a decade younger, making her a walking advertisement for her product's effectiveness. "Some of Rejuva-Juice's components are already well known, such as açaí berries and goji juice. But others, the ones that really make it so amazingly effective, were never available in this country before. That is, until I spent two years slogging through mud and climbing mountains and paddling down rivers to reach the most isolated spots in the world. I was determined to track down these miracle ingredients and bring them back home with me."

Mallory stopped reading long enough to take another sip of coffee. Oddly enough, it suddenly tasted like some of that mud Carly Cassidy had slogged through en route to fame and fortune.

She skimmed the rest of the article, which interwove experts' dismissals of Rejuva-Juice's purported benefits with quotes from some of its die-hard fans, including a few movie stars who were household names. When she reached the end, she sighed loudly and folded the newspaper in half, coincidentally removing Carly's face from view.

Mallory did her best to muster up good feelings about her former acquaintance's success. After all, she had nothing against her, aside from the mild case of envy that suddenly reared its ugly head, momentarily making her feel as if she was back in high school.

Involuntarily, she glanced down at her ratty pink bathrobe, a gift from her daughter long before she'd even started college. In fact, she seemed to remember that it dated back to the time when Amanda still believed in Santa Claus. As if the robe's fraying cuffs and threadbare chenille weren't depressing enough, she was also wearing the bottom halves of what had once been her son Jordan's pajamas. After the seam had ripped along the thigh, he'd deemed them too shabby to remain part of his working wardrobe. Mallory's standards weren't quite as high.

As for the T-shirt that completed her outfit, it had once belonged to her husband. Her reason for hanging onto this particular item was rooted more in emotion than practicality or laziness. Less than two years had passed since David had died. The shock of learning that he had plummeted from the balcony of a high-rise hotel had been bad enough. But her subsequent discovery that his death might have been the result of foul play—and her realization that she would never know the whole truth—haunted her at least as much.

Stumbling upon an exciting new job just a few months earlier had also gone a long way in helping her get her life back together. She'd never expected to find herself writing travel articles, much less writing them for a well-respected lifestyle magazine like *The Good Life*. But when a friend at the local newspaper here in the New York City suburb of Rivington recommended her for the job, she suddenly found herself embarking upon a whole new chapter of her life.

Mallory realized that all things considered, she'd been fortunate. Yet as she sipped her coffee, she couldn't help comparing her own life to Carly Cassidy's. She supposed it wasn't surprising that the two of them had ended up going off in such different directions. After all, they hadn't exactly started out their lives in the same way. The outstandingly pretty, perky, and popular Carly had not only been Homecoming Queen and captain of the cheerleading squad, she had also been class president during both their junior and senior years. And the year their hometown had held its first and only apple festival, she had been chosen Miss Red Delicious. Mallory, meanwhile, hadn't even made it into the semifinals for Miss Granny Smith.

She had to admit that according to her recollection, she hadn't really minded. Mallory was one of those people who never felt particularly comfortable being in the spotlight—even when surrounded by a dozen other varieties of fruit.

In fact, the long-ago apple festival highlighted how different the two of them were. It was no wonder Carly had built a spectacularly successful career based largely on her natural flair for glamour and self-promotion.

It occurred to Mallory that she might try getting in touch with her one of these days. Even though they hadn't exactly traveled in the same circles, catching up on old times might be fun. She also welcomed the opportunity to satisfy her curiosity about what Carly's life was really like—the glowing *New York Times* report aside.

She was adding "Google Carly Cassidy Berman" to her mental To Do list when Jordan picked up the newspaper and commented, "I think it's cool that you know somebody so famous—and so hot."

"Who's hot and famous?" Mallory's daughter asked as she bounded into the kitchen.

"That's for me to know and you to find out," Jordan replied, his sister's arrival instantly causing him to regress at least ten years.

Unlike eighteen-year-old Jordan, whom no one could ever accuse of being a morning person, Amanda was as sunny as the bright yellow paint on the walls. While Jordan wore nothing but a pair of baggy blue-and-white-striped boxer shorts, Amanda was fully dressed in a crisp white T-shirt and black sweatpants that actually looked good on her tall, willowy frame. Her little brother's dark blond hair stuck up in a hundred different directions in a way that screamed bed head, but she had brushed her long, straight auburn hair and pulled it back into a neat ponytail.

This had turned out to be one of those odd years in which spring break for both Amanda's and Jordan's schools, Sarah Lawrence and Colgate University, was the same. And Mallory had been relishing the past few days. She had even enjoyed the familiarity of their harmless bickering, a remnant from their childhood that told her things were slowly getting back to normal.

"I have a right to know what you two were talking about," Amanda insisted. She grabbed the newspaper away from her little brother, crying, "Let me see!"

"Hey, I was reading that!" Jordan insisted, scowling.

"Oh, go—go eat breakfast or something." Studying the front page with a frown, Amanda added, "I can't believe you think this Carly whoever is hot. She looks old enough to be your mother."

"*Thank* you," Mallory breathed into her coffee mug.

In a louder voice, she added, "It just so happens

that Carly and I are the same age. We went to high school together."

"You mean you two were friends?" Amanda asked.

"Not friends, exactly," Mallory replied. "More like acquaintances."

"Hey, maybe she has a daughter my age," Jordan commented, lifting the carton of orange juice toward his lips.

"Jordan, don't drink out of the carton!" Amanda shrieked. "That is so gross!"

He shrugged. "I'm the only one who drinks this stuff. What difference does it make?"

And then, as if to demonstrate to his older sister that there was absolutely no reason to conform to the arbitrary rules of society, he chugged down half the contents without coming up for air.

Having lost that round seemed to fuel Amanda's determination to win the next one.

"The woman in the newspaper isn't the only person from that high school who's famous," she insisted. "So is your own mother."

"I'm hardly famous, Amanda," Mallory countered.

"Of course you are!" her daughter exclaimed. "Millions of people all over the country read your column. And *The Good Life* has a very sophisticated audience."

Mallory was about to thank her daughter once again when Amanda turned to her, wearing a sweet expression that could mean only one thing: She was about to ask a favor.

"By the way, Mother," she said, her tone so syrupy that Mallory wished she'd made pancakes for breakfast, "when I woke up this morning, I realized that classes start up again in only four more days. I was thinking that maybe I'd drive to Connecticut and stay overnight at Lora's. Would it be okay if I took your car?"

"How is Mom supposed to manage without a car?" Jordan retorted. "Stuck out here in the middle of suburbia while you go off with your dorky friends!"

"Maybe she's going on another travel assignment," Amanda replied archly. Focusing on her mother once again, she asked, "When *is* your next trip, Mother?"

"Yeah, Mom," Jordan said, wiping his mouth with the back of his hand, Neanderthal-style. "Where are you going next?"

"Good question," Mallory replied. "Which reminds me: I'm supposed to call Trevor this morning."

She'd barely gotten the words out before her cell phone, left out overnight on the kitchen counter, began to hum.

"Is that mine?" Jordan asked, glancing around frantically.

"No, I think it's mine," Amanda said, dashing across the kitchen for her purse.

"Actually, I believe it's mine." Mallory reached over and grabbed her phone, then checked caller ID before answering.

"Good morning, Trevor," she greeted the magazine's managing editor before he'd even had a chance to say hello.

"Good morning yourself," he returned congenially. "I hope it's not too early to call."

"Not at all," Mallory assured him. "In fact, my kids and I were just talking about you."

"Nothing too terrible, I hope," he joked.

"Actually, they were asking me where I was being sent next."

Trevor let out a deep, booming laugh. "You make it sound like you work for the CIA."

"*The Good Life* sends me to much better places," Mallory assured him. "No spies, no microchips, and no cyanide tablets."

"Not to mention that your job description includes some pretty nice perks," Trevor kidded. "Staying at the best hotels, eating at fancy restaurants, going on endless sightseeing expeditions—all in the name of research, of course." He sighed. "In my next life, I think I'll come back as a travel writer."

"No one appreciates how hard we travel writers work!" Mallory shot back in the same teasing tone. "I once had two massages in the same week."

"Poor baby!" Trevor cooed.

"Actually, at the second spa, the massage therapist asked me when I'd last had one. I actually fibbed and told her it was three months ago."

"In that case, maybe I should put a cap on the number of spa treatments per trip."

"I didn't say I *minded* getting two massages," Mallory insisted. "Although I'm not sure I can say the same about the eight pounds I've put on since I started writing for the magazine."

"The demise of your girlish figure is *my* fault?" Trevor asked with feigned indignation.

"Not yours, exactly. More like the fault of all those wonderfully generous chefs in those afore-mentioned fancy restaurants. They always insist that I sample every appetizer and every dessert on the menu. Then there are those who look positively crushed if I say no to the wine pairings..."

"I'm definitely putting in my application to be reincarnated as a travel writer," Trevor said, laughing. "And if I have to start wearing a bigger belt, so be it."

"At least it's for a good cause." Her tone more earnest, Mallory added, "I really do take my job seriously. If *The Good Life's* readers are going to look to me for advice on where to spend their hard-earned vacation dollars, I want to be sure they get the whole story. And that includes the bad as well as the good."

"In that case," Trevor said, "I think you'll appreciate your next assignment."

"I'm all ears."

"This time, you've got a choice." Trevor paused to clear his throat. "We had an editorial board meeting late yesterday afternoon, and we came up with a new concept for the next issue. We're looking for an article about a destination that's famous for one particular type of activity. But we want to answer the question of whether it's possible for any visitor to have fun there—even one who doesn't enjoy whatever it is that put it on the map."

"Sounds interesting," Mallory commented.

"We thought of a couple of possibilities," he continued. "One of them is Nashville. We'd want to answer the question, Can someone who doesn't like country music still have a good time there? Another idea is Alaska. The question would be, Can an indoor person have an enjoyable vacation in the wilds?" He paused before asking, "What do you think?"

"Interesting angle," she commented thoughtfully. Her eyes drifted over to the folded-up newspaper on the table. "But given the theme, how about Aspen?"

"Aspen?" Trevor repeated, sounding surprised.

"That's right." She did some fast thinking. "How about finding out if it's possible for somebody who doesn't ski to have fun in Aspen?"

"I take it you're not a skier?"

"Hah! I'm one of those people who puts skiing in the same category as riding a motorcycle over the Grand Canyon."

"Aspen, huh?" Trevor was silent for a few seconds, as if he was mulling over the idea. "I don't know, Mallory. We did a piece on top ski resorts last winter. Even though Aspen wasn't the main focus of the article, I kind of feel we've already covered it."

"But not Aspen for nonskiers," she insisted. "I bet there's lots to do there for people who have no intention of setting foot on a ski slope." She hesitated before asking, "Have you ever heard of a spa called Tavaci Springs?"

"Yes, as a matter of fact—even before I read about the woman who founded it in the *Times* this morning. Carly something."

"Carly Cassidy Berman," Mallory said. "How about an in-depth interview with her, something that goes beyond all the PR fluff? I could write about how entrepreneurs like her choose Aspen as the location for their businesses because of its wealthy and sophisticated clientele. And a top-of-the-line spa like Tavaci Springs is perfect because it gives people who visit Aspen something else to do besides skiing or snowboarding."

"Hmm." Mallory's heartbeat quickened as she waited to hear Trevor's response. "Of course, you'd have to get this Carly Berman to agree to speak with you. Honestly, I mean."

"I think I can do that. It just so happens that she and I went to high school together."

"No kidding!"

Mallory smiled. She could hear from his tone how impressed he was.

"I think you may have something there, Mallory," Trevor said thoughtfully. "The timing is certainly right. Since it's April, ski season is probably winding down. It would be kind of interesting to see if there are enough other things going on there to interest nonskiers. I know Aspen hosts a film festival and a few other special events throughout the year, but I'm more interested in what's available on a year-round basis. Attractions, restaurants, maybe some outdoor activities . . . and the spa, of course. The fact that you're friends with the woman behind Tavaci Springs would be a real bonus."

Not *friends*, exactly. Mallory gulped like a Looney

Tunes character, hoping she hadn't just promised more than she could deliver.

"Yes," Trevor said, still sounding as if he was thinking out loud, "focusing on Aspen could work. How soon would you be able to go?"

As soon as I buy some fashionable new clothes, get a facial, and find a really good hairstylist, Mallory thought gleefully.

Not to mention guzzling all the Rejuva-Juice I can get my hands on.

Chapter 2

"When preparing to travel, lay out all your clothes
and all your money.
Then take half the clothes and twice the money."
—Susan Heller

Ten days later, as Mallory stood at the baggage claim at the Aspen/Pitkin County Airport, waiting for her bag to emerge, she couldn't help noticing that her fellow travelers' suitcases and carry-ons bore a disproportionate number of Burberry, Coach, and Fendi labels. Or that parked outside next to the runway were so many private planes that she felt as if she'd just arrived at the Lear Jet factory store.

For the first time, she fully understood that she was about to experience a place that was like no other.

Not that she hadn't seen her share of conspicuous consumption in New York City. But here, it was much more concentrated. After all, the airport was small. In addition to the single runway, it consisted of only a one-story brick and glass terminal. Inside, it was outfitted with little aside from the three basic amenities every airport should have: a restaurant, a bar, and a gift shop.

At least as striking was the fact that instead of being surrounded by towering skyscrapers that were the symbol of commerce and wealth, all around her were the magnificent Rocky Mountains, their craggy gray peaks zigzagging across the pale blue sky. She'd expected to see mountains, of course. But she'd had no idea how bowled over she'd be by how huge they were—or how beautiful.

As she glanced at the well-heeled men and women around her, Mallory was glad that before coming she'd made time to get her hair cut so that it now included some layers. She'd also managed to pick up a few Eileen Fisher separates for less than half price at Nordstrom's Rack.

After retrieving her suitcase, she stood apart from the crowd, her eyes darting around the airport as she tried to spot the public relations representative who had arranged her trip. But while she had exchanged endless e-mails with the woman who handled publicity for the city of Aspen, she knew nothing about her. Based on the fact that her name was Astrid Norland, Mallory expected a stocky woman in clogs with blond braids curled around her ears like two gigantic cheese Danish.

So she was totally unprepared for the tall, model-thin blonde she suddenly noticed striding toward her, her smile communicating that she knew exactly who Mallory was. The woman could easily have passed for Heidi Klum's sister—except for the fact that she was much prettier.

Instead of clogs, Astrid wore caramel-colored knee-high boots with stiletto heels. They happened to be the perfect complement to the rest of her outfit: an ivory ski parka lined with what looked like real mink and a pair of skintight chocolate brown leather pants.

"You must be Mallory," she said warmly as she approached, her voice tinged with the slightest accent. "I'm Astrid. Welcome to Aspen!"

Mallory didn't know her Scandinavian accents very well, but she would have bet her laptop that this one was Swedish. In less than five seconds, she'd also surmised that Astrid was as personable as she was gorgeous. Not unusual for women who chose to go into the public relations field, she knew, aside from the fact that this particular one struck her as *exceptionally* personable and *exceptionally* gorgeous.

"Pleased to meet you, Astrid," Mallory said. "Thanks for picking me up."

"No problem."

As Astrid waved her hand in the air, Mallory caught sight of ten perfectly manicured nails. They were thickly lacquered with a dark nut-brown polish that struck her as more Manhattan than mountaineer. Now that she was up close, she also saw that Astrid's large blue eyes were fringed with lashes so long, dark, and dense they looked like awnings, and her cheekbones were sharp enough to cut through some serious Swedish ice.

"Need any help with your bags?" Astrid asked

cheerfully. Gesturing toward the airport entrance, she added, "We don't have far to go. My car is parked right out front."

"Thanks, but I'm fine," Mallory replied. "I'm actually pretty good at getting in and out of airports. It comes with the job."

"I envy you," Astrid commented with a sigh. "I've thought of leaving PR and doing some travel writing myself. But I love Aspen too much." Flashing a smile, she added, "Which is why I'm so glad that my job is to make other people love it, too."

"I've only been doing this for a few months," Mallory admitted, "but I really like going to new places all the time. I find something to love in each one."

"But you're going to like Aspen best of all," Astrid insisted.

Mallory laughed. "I'm absolutely ready to be convinced."

As she fell into step with Astrid, Mallory suddenly felt strangely short. Astrid had to be at least six feet tall. Of course, the spiky heels on her soft leather boots added a good two or three inches. She wondered what kind of traction those things got in the snow.

Like Astrid's wardrobe, her vehicle was top-of-the-line. Mallory was no car expert, but she knew an especially expensive Mercedes when she saw one. This one was powder blue with chocolate brown leather upholstery that looked as if it had been cut from the same bolt as the sleek leather pants Astrid had been poured into.

After they'd both settled into the front seat, Mallory cracked open the window so she could breathe in some of that fresh mountain air. Even though back in New York spring was shouldering its way in, here at nearly eight thousand feet above sea level the air was delightfully crisp and cool.

"Now that you're here," Astrid said once they got on the road, "let me give you a short course in Aspen's history. Aspen one-oh-one, I call it. The first thing you need to know is that this area is called the Roaring Fork Valley. The Ute Indians, the original inhabitants, called these magnificent peaks 'Shining Mountains.' It was a pretty peaceful place until the summer of 1879, when prospectors found a major silver lode here. One of the biggest in the world, in fact. They set up a camp they called Ute City, but the name soon changed to Aspen after all the aspen trees.

"Aspen would have remained a small mining camp if it hadn't been for Jerome Byron Wheeler," she continued as she veered onto Highway 82, heading toward town. Even though traffic was minimal, the nonchalance with which she darted between lanes left Mallory gripping her seat. "He was president of Macy's department store then. Of course, there was only one Macy's in those days, back east in New York City. Wheeler was a real innovator, and he made silver mining profitable by building a working smelter to reduce silver ore along with a tramway to transport the ore down to the smelter.

"Anyway, thanks to Wheeler and all that silver, by 1893 Aspen's population had grown to twelve thousand. The town was booming, with a hospital, two theaters, an opera house, four schools, and three banks. It also had six newspapers and its own small red-light district."

While Mallory was finding Astrid's history lesson interesting, she was much more fascinated by what she saw out the window. Not long after they circled through a roundabout, signs of civilization began to appear in the form of pleasant, relatively modest houses along tree-lined streets. From the looks of things, they were driving through the outskirts of the greater metropolitan Aspen area.

But the attractive houses looked like the toy-sized ones underneath a Christmas tree compared to breathtakingly beautiful Aspen Mountain, which loomed more than three thousand feet above the entire town. Even though it was April and the trees and grass at ground level were decidedly green, the imposing mountain was still covered with snow. Yet there wasn't a single skier in sight. As she'd learned from the research she'd done over the past week and a half, the mountain always closed around April 1.

"Everything was great until 1893," Astrid continued, "when silver crashed because the federal government decided to return to the gold standard." She careened around the curves in the road with such confidence that Mallory assumed she was also an expert skier. "The town just about died. By 1935, there were only seven hundred residents. But all that changed in the mid-thirties when a group of international businessmen swooped in and saw the area's potential as a ski resort. They formed the Aspen Ski Club and hired a Swiss avalanche expert named André Roch to create a racecourse on Aspen Mountain.

"During World War Two, the Army's Tenth Mountain Division trained nearby, and many of the soldiers enjoyed skiing in Aspen in their free time. One of them was a man from Austria named Friedl Pfeifer. After the war, Pfeifer joined forces with Walter Paepcke, a businessman from Chicago, and his wife, Elizabeth, who was a patron of the arts. While the Paepckes were mainly interested in developing the area as a cultural center, Pfeifer remained committed to building a ski resort that was as good as the ones in Europe.

"Aspen Mountain opened in 1947, already boasting the longest ski lift in the world. But Paepcke's vision was also very much alive. In 1949, he orchestrated a major event called the Goethe Bicentennial Convocation in honor of the great writer's two hundredth birthday. Programs in music, dance, theater, and art were held, which attracted creative people from all over the world."

Astrid's voice was filled with pride—or at least a good PR rep's imitation of it—as she concluded, "Aspen was on its way to becoming an international center for both skiing and the arts. It also became a desirable spot for celebrities looking to build their dream vacation home. Our local citizenry has included Donald Trump, Kevin Costner, Don Johnson, Goldie Hawn, Jack Nicholson... And let's not forget John Denver. In fact, you might want to check out the John Denver Sanctuary, near Rio Grande Park, while you're here. It's one of our most popular attractions for both skiers and nonskiers. There's also the John Denver Memorial Grotto on Aspen Mountain. Of course, you'd need to be on skis to see that."

A hidden competitive streak in Mallory suddenly made her want to show Astrid that she wasn't the only one who'd done her homework. "Speaking of skiing," she said, "there are four different ski mountains in the Roaring Fork Valley, aren't there? Including Aspen, I mean."

"That's right," Astrid replied. "Aspen Highlands and Buttermilk opened in 1958, and Snowmass opened ten years later."

Glancing over at Mallory, she added, "But of course you're different from most travel writers in that you're not interested in Aspen as a skiing destination."

Mallory nodded. "That's right. I plan to write about everything *but* skiing."

Astrid nodded. "Well, I'm here to help you see and do whatever you need for the article you're writing. I've set up visits to a few of the places we e-mailed about, but have you had a chance to decide what your top priorities are? We want to make sure you see everything you need to see."

"I've actually come armed with a list," Mallory said. "The Wheeler Opera House, the Cooking School of Aspen, a shopping tour, maybe some spa treatments..."

Astrid glanced over, looking surprised. "It sounds as if you've done quite a bit of research."

"I try to come to every new destination prepared," Mallory replied. "Even though I'm new to the job, I've learned that the more I know before I arrive, the more comprehensive I can make my article. These research trips are pretty brief, never more than five days. Some have been as short as three days. But I'm supposed to come away from my whirlwind tours a virtual expert, the last word on what to see and do—as well as what to avoid."

"I imagine you use the Internet to do most of your research," Astrid commented.

"That's very helpful," Mallory said. "But I also read two or three guidebooks. The idea is to show up with a list of places I want to investigate. I also plot out a rough schedule. I figure out which items on my list are physically close together so I can minimize travel time. And I have to keep track of the hours the various places are open and which days they're closed." With a shrug, she added, "The last thing I want to do is to show up somewhere I think would be perfect for my article only to discover that it's open every day of the week except that one."

"I know exactly what you mean," Astrid agreed. "When I plan press trips for visiting journalists, I do the same thing. The organized ones like you who've figured out what they want to do in advance usually get much more out of their trip."

"Speaking of which," Mallory added, "there's one place that's not listed in most guidebooks that I want to be sure to see. In fact, it's critical to the article I'm writing. It's a spa called Tavaci Springs."

"Of course. You mentioned that in your e-mail. I've got an interview set up with the owner on Thursday."

Unable to resist the urge to sound like an insider, Mallory said, "Actually, she and I went to high school together."

Astrid's eyebrows shot up so high that they disappeared into the ring of mink that framed her face.

"Carly Berman?" she repeated, her voice wavering. "You know Carly Berman?"

Mallory looked at her quizzically. Was she just imagining it, or did Astrid actually sound alarmed?

"That's right." Even though she suspected she already knew the answer, she added, "Do you know her, too?"

"Yes, as a matter of fact." By now, Astrid had regained her composure. "Pretty well, in fact. That's why I was so surprised. Goodness, what a small world!"

"Since I won't be visiting Tavaci Springs until Thursday, I might give Carly a call before then," Mallory mused. "I could probably contact her through the spa, but do you happen to have a number where I could reach her directly?"

"I believe I do." As she stopped at a red light, Astrid flipped open her red metallic cell phone and punched one of the buttons again and again, miraculously doing no damage to her long, perfectly manicured fingernail in the process. "What I mean is, I should have it, since I have the numbers of pretty much all the businesses in Aspen. The public relations department works closely with the Chamber of Commerce, so I need to be able to get in touch with anybody. I can even give you the Bermans' home number. It's area code nine-seven-oh . . ."

After punching Carly's numbers into her own cell phone, Mallory glanced up and saw that they'd arrived in the center of town. From the maps she'd studied, she already knew the streets were laid out in a grid. But she wasn't prepared for the fact that most of the buildings were made of red brick, giving the town a somewhat rustic look. One of the central streets, East Hyman Avenue, was closed off to traffic and paved with more red brick. Large sections in the middle of the Hyman Avenue Mall were planted with trees or flowers, creating an inviting pedestrian walkway.

"I'll just take a quick drive around to help get you oriented," Astrid said. "Over there is the ice skating rink. It's right across the street from the Rubey Park Transit Center, which has convenient bus service to the other ski mountains. That big hotel over there is the St. Regis, one of the largest hotels in Aspen. Now we're coming to the base of Aspen Mountain . . ."

Mallory was already dazzled. Aspen was clearly a ski town, but one with way more style than she'd ever expected. Not only were the streets crammed with luxury boutiques and real estate offices; she knew from her research that the tiny community also boasted something like eighty restaurants.

"Here at the other end of town," Astrid continued as she turned down a street that took them away from the mountain, "you'll find the Aspen Art Museum and Rio Grande Park, where the John Denver Sanctuary I mentioned before is located. I know all this doesn't mean much to you now, but I promise it won't be long before you know your way around.

"Your hotel is also at this edge of town," she said, turning left onto East Main Street. "I arranged for you to stay at the Hotel Jerome because it's Aspen's most historic hotel. Jerome Wheeler opened it in 1889."

Mallory already knew all about the Hotel Jerome. From her research, she'd learned that Wheeler's dream had been to construct his own version of the great hotels of Europe, even though Aspen was still very much a raucous mining town. The Hotel Jerome was one of the first buildings west of the Mississippi that was fully lit by electricity. It also featured hot and cold running water, indoor plumbing, and a relatively new invention: the elevator.

Mallory loved the fact that being a travel writer enabled her to visit locations that up until now she'd only heard about. Besides, as a travel writer, she was generally treated better than any ordinary tourist. The staff at the hotels, restaurants, and attractions on her itinerary knocked themselves out to make sure she came away with a positive impression of their establishment. They showered her with first-class treatment, something she hadn't exactly become used to during the two decades she'd played wife, mother, and reporter at a small-town weekly. After all, her daughter wasn't the only one who understood that whatever Mallory wrote for *The Good Life* would be read by nearly two million people. Moneyed people, for the most part, as well as people who liked to travel.

"During your stay," Astrid noted, "be sure to check out the J-Bar, which has been an Aspen institution forever. It started out as a bar, but it became a soda fountain during Prohibition. You must try its signature drink, the Aspen Crud, which is basically a milkshake made with bourbon. It's supposed to represent the J-Bar's history as both a saloon and an ice cream parlor. But wait a few days before you do. Aspen is roughly five thousand feet above sea level, which means drinking anything alcoholic before your body has had a chance to get acclimated is guaranteed to give you a splitting headache."

Advice worth following, Mallory thought, resolving to keep as far away from any form of firewater as she could. It was just as well, since she was already warming to Aspen and she didn't want to dull her experience.

"You must also see some of the other luxury hotels here during your stay," Astrid insisted. "Tonight, you're free to do whatever you please. If you decide to rent a car, the front desk can arrange to have one delivered to the hotel. But for tomorrow evening, I've booked dinner at Montagna. It's the restaurant at the Little Nell, Aspen's only ski-in, ski-out hotel. I know you're here to find out how much there is for nonskiers to enjoy, but you'll still appreciate the fact that there's a ski concierge who provides guests with slopeside services. That means storing skis overnight so guests don't have to lug them around, as well as warming their boots in the morning."

"Now there's a concept," Mallory commented. "Skiing with warm feet. It's almost enough to get *me* out there—at least on the bunny slope."

She was certain she detected a hint of condescension in Astrid's smile. She resolved to keep her anti-skiing jokes to a minimum.

"I've also arranged for you to have a facial and a massage at the St. Regis, the hotel I pointed out to you before," Astrid added as she pulled up at the front door. "You'll be doing a site visit of Tavaci Springs, of course, but I wanted you to experience the Remède Spa, as well, since it's really something special. I hope you don't mind."

Mind? Mallory thought, her head already spinning. Enjoying leisurely dinners and being pampered at hotel spas is what my job is all about. I don't blame Trevor for being envious.

"You'll find a copy of the itinerary in your room, and I believe we have each other's cell phone numbers," Astrid said as she opened the trunk of her Mercedes and stepped back to allow the hotel bellman to retrieve Mallory's suitcase. "I'm sure you'd like some time to get your bearings, but feel free to call me if there's anything you need."

After thanking Astrid once more, Mallory followed the bellman and her suitcase into the Hotel Jerome's lobby. Her eyes immediately widened, and sentences began forming in her head.

"Entering the lobby of the Hotel Jerome is like stepping out of a time machine," she thought, reminding herself to jot down her thoughts as soon as she reached her room. "Visitors will instantly be transported back to the Wild West—or at least to Colorado's most successful silver mining town during its heyday in the 1890s. Ornate dark red wallpaper covers the walls, thick Oriental carpets cushion the wooden floors, and the old-fashioned lampshades and overstuffed couches are edged with silk fringe..."

She also made a mental note about the exposed wooden beams crisscrossing overhead and the large black marble fireplace on the back wall, topped with a huge mirror and flanked by a matching pair of mounted deer heads. She half expected the Unsinkable Molly Brown herself to flounce into the room and belt out a song.

The décor of her room was much more traditional. She didn't mind, since there was definitely something to be said for modern touches such as Internet access, digital TV, and a fully stocked minibar. Still, the wallpaper had a homey, old-fashioned pattern, the drapes were made of flowered fabric, and the thickly padded upholstered chair was paired with a matching ottoman. If old-fashioned translated to pretty and comfortable, that was fine with her.

After she kicked off her shoes and hung up her clothes, Mallory sank into the upholstered chair and pulled out her cell phone. Yet even though she'd thought about little besides getting in touch with Carly ever since she'd read the article about her in the *Times,* now that it was finally time to do so she was actually nervous. She suddenly felt like an uncertain fifteen-year-old again—one who'd gotten through high school by doing as little as possible to call attention to herself.

Looking her up will probably be fun, Mallory told herself firmly. Besides, you promised Trevor an in-depth interview. It's pretty much what got him interested in Aspen in the first place.

Still, none of that helped keep her heart from pounding as she heard the buzzing of the phone at the other end of the line.

It was followed by a familiar sounding "Hello?"

"Carly?" Mallory began in a strangely high-pitched voice. Not only did she feel fifteen; her voice made her *sound* fifteen. "This is Mallory Marlowe—although I used to be Mallory MacGregor. I don't know if you remember me, but we went to JFK High together—"

"Mallory MacGregor?" Carly exclaimed. "Of *course* I remember you! You were the girl who liked to read!"

Mallory told herself she was just imagining that Carly made it sound as if she was the girl with leprosy.

"That's me," she replied cheerfully.

"How *are* you, Mallory?" Carly squealed. "And *where* are you?"

"I'm fine—and I'm in Aspen. I read the article about you in *The New York Times* a few days ago, and it just so happened that I was coming here on business. I recently started doing travel pieces for a magazine called *The Good Life*. In fact, I've got a visit to Tavaci Springs scheduled for Thursday, but I figured I'd look you up as soon as I got here, just to say hello—"

"I'm so glad you did!" Carly sighed. "Boy, we had some great times back in high school, didn't we?"

Mallory wasn't sure how to respond. True, she'd had some wonderful times during her teenage years. But none of them had remotely had anything to do with Carly or her crowd. In fact, some of the best times she could recall had been related to that weird pastime she liked to indulge in: reading.

"Those were certainly the days," she finally said, noting there was a good reason why meaningless clichés hung on for so long.

"But now you're here in Aspen," Carly went on. "I'd love to see you! You simply must come over. How about tonight? Are you free for dinner?"

"As a matter of fact, I am."

"Great. Do you have a pen? I'll tell you where I live. It's less than a half-hour drive from the center of town."

"I'm afraid I don't have a car yet," Mallory explained.

"In that case, I'll send one. Which hotel are you staying at?"

When Mallory hung up a few minutes later, she was stunned. While she had been hoping for a congenial reception, she hadn't expected Carly to embrace her as a long-lost friend. Yet that was exactly how she was acting.

In fact, Carly's reaction made her wonder if Rejuva-Juice had one more miraculous power: rewriting history.

Chapter 3

"I think that travel comes from some deep urge to see the world, like the urge that brings up a worm in an Irish bog to see the moon when it is full."
—Lord Dunsany

While Mallory hadn't exactly understood what Carly meant by her offer to send a car, she assumed she meant a taxi—or maybe a vehicle from one of those private car services that were so popular with high-powered Manhattanites.

She found out how wrong she was when a sleek silver Rolls-Royce slid in front of the Hotel Jerome precisely at the designated time. Just as she was telling herself, "No, it couldn't be," a chauffeur in a dark uniform climbed out and said, "I'm Carly Berman's driver. Are you Mallory MacGregor?"

Close enough, Mallory thought, settling into the spacious backseat. As she ran her fingers over the velvety soft leather upholstery, she reflected on how easily she could get used to this.

The late afternoon sun was low in the sky as the

chauffeur whisked her out of Aspen. As they drove along a winding road they picked up right outside of town, the smattering of buildings quickly gave way to wide fields. Just beyond were scenic foothills that quickly morphed into majestic mountains. Mallory couldn't resist the urge to crack open the window. She leaned her head back against the seat, closed her eyes, and breathed in the cool, pine-scented mountain air.

They rode for at least fifteen minutes before the car turned down a side road, one that no one had bothered to pave. As they bumped along, Mallory assumed the road was deliberately left in such poor condition to deter prowlers. Either that or the man she thought was a chauffeur was actually a kidnapper who was driving her to his secret cave, albeit in high style.

She decided the first scenario was the more likely explanation when she finally spotted a rustic building nestled in the foothills. Because it was made of wood and stone, it blended right in with the craggy rocks, brush, and occasional smatterings of wildflowers.

At first, she was disappointed. From a distance, Carly's house didn't look all that impressive.

It wasn't until the Rolls got much closer that she saw how huge it was. It sprawled across the rugged terrain, in some places spiking up three stories high. The exterior was largely glass, with huge windows everywhere. The clever interplay of indoors and outdoors extended to the numerous decks and balconies, as well as a large stone patio that overlooked a rock garden.

Now that she saw how much her destination for the evening resembled one of the rustic mountain lodges she was accustomed to seeing in John Wayne movies, Mallory hoped the outfit she'd finally decided upon wasn't a mistake. The loose-fitting black pants and jacket she wore with an iris blue silk blouse suddenly seemed so urban, especially compared to, say, a cowboy hat and chaps.

Still, the chauffeur is wearing a uniform, she reminded herself as she walked toward the front door, the gravel crunching beneath her feet. And the housekeeper who opened the door even before she'd had a chance to knock was dressed in a black dress and a crisp white apron that was more Kensington High Street than OK Corral.

My choice of clothes is fine, she decided with relief, grateful to Eileen Fisher for serving her so well. At least I got that part right.

"Good evening," she greeted the housekeeper pleasantly.

At first glance, it was difficult to discern the woman's age. While her chubbiness gave her cheeks a smooth, almost childlike appearance, her dark hair, pulled back into a single braid that hung down her back, was streaked with gray. She wore two gold chains around her neck, one with a large gold cross dangling from it and a second with the name "Juanita" written in script.

"I'm here to see Carly," Mallory added when the woman failed to respond.

"Mees Berm, she ees expecting you," the house-keeper finally replied, acting as if making polite conversation wasn't part of her job description. "Oh, and welcome to Casper Ranch." Muttering as if she were talking to herself rather than to Mallory, she added, "I always forget I'm supposed to say that. One more rule Mees Berm make me remember."

O-kay, Mallory thought. Aloud, she asked, "Casper Ranch? Is that Casper as in Casper the Friendly Ghost or as in Casper, Wyoming?"

"Ees C-A-S-S-B-E-R," Juanita explained crossly. "Cass-Ber. Ees a combination of Meester and Mees's last names—Cassidy and Berm. Mees Berm, she make eet up." She rolled her eyes, as if looking toward heaven for understanding. "She theenks giving a place a fancy name makes it more high-class or something."

"I see." Mallory wondered if Carly's house-keeper's deliberate mispronunciation of her employer's last name was due to her faulty English or one more way of asserting her independence. Or would scorn have been a more appropriate word?

She kept her questions to herself as she followed Juanita inside, noting that the house's interior was as impressive as its dramatic exterior promised. The cavernous living room's A-Frame configuration was emphasized by exposed beams made of uneven dark wood that looked as if it had been stolen from Abe Lincoln's birthplace. The same shape was echoed in the tremendous windows that dominated three of the walls, each of them five-sided so that their tops also formed peaks. All that glass did an effective job of making the spectacular landscape part of the décor. At the moment, the scenery happened to include the pale yellow sun setting against a darkening blue sky streaked with oranges, pinks, and purples that in any other context would have looked downright garish.

If I lived here, Mallory thought, I don't think I'd ever leave this very spot.

That feeling was reinforced by the furnishings, which like the room itself were striking enough to be featured in a glossy design magazine. They incorporated an array of amazing textures: the ragged gray stones of the fireplace that jutted up between two of the gigantic windows, two Three Bears-style chairs made from rough-hewn wood but softened with buttery leather cushions in a deep shade of red, a long comfy couch upholstered in shaggy white fabric that reminded her of a polar bear.

As she stepped farther inside the room, a poodle suddenly stuck its head up in the air. Mallory realized that even though the dog was in plain sight, draped comfortably across the couch, its fluffy white fur had caused it to blend in with its surroundings so well that she hadn't even noticed it. But the dog noticed her, leaping off the couch and bounding toward her enthusiastically.

"Get away, Bijou!" Juanita insisted crossly. "Bad dog!" But aside from glaring at the animal, she made no move to rescue Mallory.

"It's all right," Mallory assured her. "I love dogs." She bent down to let the poodle lick one of her hands while scratching her behind the ears with the other.

Mallory was still admiring the house that Rejuva-Juice built, along with the pet she suspected had been chosen because her fur matched the décor, when she heard a familiar voice cry, "Mallory? Is that really *you?*"

Mallory turned and saw Carly loping toward her. Her long strides, unencumbered by ridiculously high heels, sent the silky fabric of her brightly colored print dress swirling around her knees as if she were a dancer.

Mallory's first impression was that the Carly Cassidy of today was a considerably more sophisticated version of her earlier self, her youthful exuberance replaced by cool elegance. In fact, Mallory decided that the photograph in *The New York Times* hadn't done her justice. While the flattering shot had made it seem Carly hadn't put on any weight en route to her forties, in person she actually looked slimmer than she'd been in high school, if that was humanly possible. Somehow she'd managed to fend off the effects of both the years and the carbs, both of which had taken their toll on the waists, hips, and thighs of most of the other middle-aged women Mallory knew.

Her hazel eyes were bright, and she simply exuded energy. Just as the *Times* had claimed, Carly Cassidy Berman was the best possible advertisement for Rejuva-Juice's effectiveness.

"It's *so* good to see you again!" she cried, sweeping toward Mallory with her arms spread wide. Bijou jumped out of the way, as if the savvy poodle had just realized that a tidal wave was approaching.

Mallory braced herself for a big bear hug—which left her totally unprepared for the kiss on each cheek she got instead.

"How long has it *been?*" Carly squealed once she'd stepped back. "I've always been much too busy to make it to any of the reunions, so we probably haven't seen each other since—wow, could it really be graduation?"

No doubt, Mallory thought, still amused by Carly's warm reception. After all, it's not as if either of us went out of our way to keep in touch afterward.

"I think you're right," she replied. "I don't remember us running into each other since then."

"No matter how long it's been, it's great that you're here now." Carly suddenly froze. "You're not going to tell anyone how old we *really* are, are you?"

Mallory chuckled, then stopped herself when she saw she was serious.

"But you look fabulous, Carly!" she insisted. "Maybe you should tell people you're actually ninety—but that Rejuva-Juice keeps you looking so young!"

Carly let out a merry, high-pitched laugh. "Mallory, you're so funny! I should hire you as my marketing director." Her smiled faded. "Seriously, let's not mention our age to anyone, okay?"

Mallory blinked. "Of course not."

Carly's smile returned. "Now let me take a look at you." She ran her eyes up and down Mallory as if she were appraising a used car. Which was exactly what Mallory felt like as she stood there, enduring her scrutiny. In fact, once again she traveled through a time machine, back to gym class—and a very vivid memory of Carly and some of the other girls clustered in the locker room, eyeing her and tittering. When she'd glanced down self-consciously, she'd discovered she was wearing two different colored socks. Somehow, in tenth-graders' eyes, that was the equivalent of forgetting to put on any clothes at all.

Still, there was such a thing as good manners, and Mallory expected Carly to come up with a line about how terrific Mallory looked, too. Something about how she hadn't changed a bit since their days together at JFK High—or at least that she hadn't changed *much*.

Instead, Carly drew her perfectly lipsticked mouth into a straight line, then actually allowed a second line to appear on her face—this one smack in the middle of her forehead.

"I'll be sure to send you home with plenty of Rejuva-Juice," she said earnestly. "Fortunately, there's finally something to help all of us face the ravages of time."

Mallory opened her mouth in astonishment. But before any words of protest managed to make their way out, Carly shrieked, "Juanita? Pack up a case of Rejuva-Juice—no, make that two cases—for my old friend. And make sure you get her address so it'll be waiting for her when she gets home."

Old? Mallory thought crossly, not at all confident that Carly was referring to the length of their acquaintance.

"Now come sit down," Carly insisted, perching

on the couch and patting the seat cushion next to her. "Tell me all about what you've been doing for the last, oh, however many years it's been. I want to hear about everything: husbands, children, careers, whatever."

Mallory sat down on the couch and folded her hands in her lap. When she realized that that particular posture might make her look prim—and, heaven forbid, possibly even *old*—she instead draped one arm across the back of the sofa.

"Let's see," she said thoughtfully. "I suppose I should start with the reason I'm here. I recently embarked on a brand new career as a travel writer."

"How exciting!" Carly cooed. "Do you travel to exotic spots like Paris and Cairo and Dubai?"

"Actually," Mallory replied, clearing her throat, "so far I've stuck to U.S. destinations. My first trip, back in January, was to Orlando. My mission was to find out whether the 'old Florida' still exists, and I went to places like alligator farms and the Ripley's Believe It or Not museum—"

"I'm sure that whoever you work for will eventually come up with some *interesting* places for you to visit," Carly cooed, reaching over and patting her knee. "Things are already looking up, aren't they? After all, you were lucky enough to get sent to Aspen!"

Mallory forced a smile. Good old Carly, she thought. Even after all these years, she hasn't lost her talent for putting someone down while making it sound as if she's trying to be nice.

"I actually enjoyed Florida," Mallory told her.

"The other places I've covered, too. And it turns out that I'm actually a pretty decent writer. At least that's what my editor seems to think. He likes the fact that I—"

"What about your personal life?" Carly interrupted. "Are you as happily married as I am?"

"I was."

"Divorced?"

"My husband, David, passed away almost two years ago."

"Poor Mallory!" Carly exclaimed. "I am *so* sorry. So you're all alone now?"

"Not exactly. I'm lucky enough to have two of the greatest kids in the world. Amanda is twenty. She's a junior at Sarah Lawrence. And my son, Jordan, is a freshman at Colgate. They've both had kind of a rough time since their dad died, but they're strong and independent and I know they'll do just fine. I'm really proud of—"

"They say children are a blessing," Carly said vaguely. "Personally, I never had an urge to be a mother. Somehow, it just doesn't fit with how I see myself. Instead, I've made my marriage my focus.

"In fact," she went on with a deep sigh, "I can't even *bear* to think about the possibility of something happening to Brett. I can't imagine how I'd ever manage without *my* adorable husband."

"It's been tough," Mallory admitted. She wasn't sure if Carly was being sympathetic or once again playing a game of one-upsmanship.

"Well, I'm glad that you'll at least have a little male companionship at dinner," Carly said brightly.

Winking, she added, "It just so happens we have a special guest joining us tonight. And who knows? Maybe you two will hit it off."

Once again, Mallory was uncertain of Carly's motivation. She was still trying to decide if her attempts at playing matchmaker were well-meaning or simply insensitive when she added, "Speaking of dinner, I'm afraid we have to eat dreadfully early." Her eyes sparkling, she added, "I'm giving a talk at the Wheeler Opera House tonight, and I can't keep my public waiting! By the way, Mallory, you *must* come!"

Mallory forced a smile. While she remembered Carly having had a big personality back in high school, it seemed to have ballooned into one of rock-star proportions.

But she hadn't forgotten for a moment that she was here on a mission. And while she had yet to broach the subject of an in-depth interview, she hoped that seeing Carly in action would add one more dimension to her article.

"Ah, here come the menfolk," Carly announced abruptly.

Two men had just ambled into the room, each clutching a martini glass. It was hard not to focus on the taller one. He was lean and unusually well-built, as if he treasured his gym membership card as much as his platinum American Express card. His navy blue cashmere sweater flattered his frame, as did the dark jeans that looked as if poor Juanita had actually ironed them.

Yet even more riveting than his fit torso was his

face. The man was dazzlingly handsome, with well-proportioned features, bright blue eyes, and what looked like a year-round tan. When he smiled—something he appeared to do easily and often—he revealed two rows of perfect, dazzlingly white teeth. From his thick, gleaming silver hair, carefully styled into place, Mallory suspected that he was in his mid-fifties, implying that he had enlisted the aid of a cosmetic dentist somewhere along the line to obtain the million-dollar-smile effect. And given the Bermans' taste in cars, he might even have spent that much.

"Brett, my love, I'm dying for you to meet my good friend from high school," Carly gushed, sweeping toward him. She linked her arm in his and gazed into his eyes adoringly. "This is Mallory MacGregor—oops, sorry, I mean Mallory Marlowe. Do you believe that Mallory and I have known each other for—well, I'm not even going to tell you how many years!"

Mallory smiled wanly. All this talk about the passage of time was making her feel ancient. "Nice to meet you, Brett."

"Pleased to meet you, too," he boomed, his eyes sweeping over her as he reached out to shake her hand. Not surprisingly, his handshake was as hearty as his voice. "It's always a treat to meet one of Carly's friends."

"And this is Gordon Swig," Carly said, gesturing toward the man standing next to her husband.

Gordon wasn't nearly as tall, as lean, as young, or as handsome as Carly's husband. In fact, the short, slightly balding man in a dark brown jacket and khaki pants seemed about as far away from Brett Berman on the Impressive scale as anyone could get.

But there was an even more striking difference between the two men. While Mallory got the feeling Brett was assessing her, looking her over in the same way his wife had, Gordon was smiling at her in a warm, friendly way that she decided made him much more appealing than the taller, better-looking man beside him.

"Gordon is only in town for a few days," Carly noted.

Not a very revealing introduction, Mallory noted. But she just smiled and said hello.

"Can I get you a drink, Mallory?" Brett offered congenially. "Gordon and I are having martinis."

"Nothing for me," Carly chirped. "I never drink before one of my public appearances."

"But I do." Brett grinned wickedly. "And hopefully you do, too, Mallory. So what'll it be?"

"A glass of wine might be nice," she said. Remembering Astrid's warning about the devastating effects of alcohol at high altitudes, she added, "But please, just a little. I only arrived a few hours ago."

"I've got a Colorado wine that'll knock your socks off." Brett swooped an open bottle off an end table with a top made of slate. "It's from Desert Moon Vineyards in Palisade. Their clever marketing people came up with the name Altitude Bordeaux Blend. Now tell me: how could a wine with a charming name like that hurt anybody?"

Carly glanced at her watch. "Oh, my! It's getting

late. I've got a show to do! I told Juanita it was cru-
cial that tonight of all nights she serve dinner on
time—" She took off across the room, screeching,
"Juanita?"

Whatever she said apparently did the trick. Less
than five minutes later, Mallory found herself sitting
in the dining room with the Bermans and their other
out-of-town guest. Just like the living room, the dining room was lined with nearly wall-sized windows.
They offered spectacular views even though by now
the colors of the glorious sunset had faded, leaving
in their wake a cobalt blue sky strewn with twinkling
stars.

The long dining room table and the fourteen
chairs surrounding it were made of the same rough-
textured wood as the Papa Bear chairs in the living room. Overhead, centered on the ceiling, was
a chandelier large enough to illuminate the entire
room. It looked as if it was made of real tree
branches that had been cleverly intertwined, the narrow twigs at the end of each studded with tiny, twinkling white lights. And there was one more element
of what Mallory was starting to think of as in-your-
face rustic: an imposing pile of rocks in one corner,
with water cascading over them to create an impromptu waterfall.

"Now isn't this nice," Carly remarked pleasantly.
Her voice instantly becoming gruff, she barked,
"Juanita? Do you think you could bring in the first
course before hell freezes over? And could you get
Bijou out of here? She's underfoot, as usual."

Whatever happened to please and thank you? Mallory wondered.

But she was less worried about her hostess's abrasiveness than she was about what that aforementioned first course might be. Surely a couple who'd built their fortune on a health tonic that they claimed was second only in effectiveness to bottled water from the Fountain of Youth carried their obsession into every other aspect of their lives as well. *Especially* food.

So as Juanita appeared from the kitchen, scowling as usual but this time bearing a large platter, Mallory nearly pulled a neck muscle in her efforts to see what she was going to be forced to eat in the name of politeness. Brown rice and veggies? Some tofu concoction that she would have to choke down with more of that dangerous headache-inducing wine than she cared to drink?

"I hope you like lobster," Carly said before she'd had a chance to identify the whitish blobs on sticks that were piled high on the plate Juanita slammed down on the table.

Lobster? Mallory thought with relief. And then: In *Aspen*?

After all, this wasn't exactly a seaside town. In fact, if geography had anything to do with menu planning, she figured that tonight's dinner was much more likely to revolve around mountain goat and snow cones.

"These are actually lobster lollipops," Carly went on to explain. "One of the chefs in town, Matthew Zubrod at DishAspen, came up with them. He calls them lobster corn dogs, but I think of them as lollipops. At any rate, I practically had to get down on my hands and knees to get him to give me the recipe."

"Interesting image," Brett observed. "In fact, if I didn't trust you completely, I might be thinking that—"

Fortunately, at that moment Juanita came sashaying out of the kitchen once again, swinging her abundant hips. From the way she carried herself, it appeared that she and not Carly was the true queen of the manor.

"What is it, Juanita?" Carly asked crossly.

"Sorry to interrupt, Mees Berm," the housekeeper began.

Mallory observed that she didn't look the least bit sorry.

"There ees a phone call for you. That woman again—Sylvie Snow-something or whatever her name ees. She keeps calling and calling—"

"This is not a good time," Carly said archly. "Take that Snowdon woman's number and tell her I'll get back to her."

"She ees not so good at taking no for an answer," Juanita grumbled.

The frosty look on her employer's face must have made an impression even on her, because she quickly added, "But I tell her again."

"What's all that about?" Gordon asked once Juanita had strutted off, muttering under her breath.

Carly sighed. "Let's just say that when you're a 'have,' the 'have-nots' never give up."

Mallory was curious enough that she wished Gordon would pursue the issue a bit further. But being a good guest, and probably one who hoped to be invited back again, he just nodded and returned to his meal.

"Anyway, where were we?" Carly asked congenially. She'd gone back to playing the perfect hostess without missing a beat.

"You were painting a mental picture for all of us," Brett replied, his expression changing to a distinct leer. "You on your hands and knees, doing whatever it took to get some chef to give you his recipe—"

"That's right," Carly said, clearly determined to ignore her husband's innuendoes. "The story behind the lobster lollipops. I finally got Matthew to share his recipe with me, but not until I'd convinced him that I'd never tell it to a soul. I promised I'd take it to my grave—along with the recipe for Rejuva-Juice."

The exact same line she'd used with the *New York Times* reporter, Mallory noted. She got the feeling it was something she said all the time.

"We have the lobster flown in directly from the Caribbean," Brett noted as he bit into one of the lollipops. "A tiny island called Barbuda, a few miles off Antigua. It's the only place in the world where this particular variety is found. Unfortunately, the locals ship most of them to France. Damn frogs manage to get the best of everything. But I managed to talk them into overnighting us a few of the buggers once a week."

Dr. Atkins's dream, Mallory thought as she reached for a delicacy that was solid protein—and one that in the past twenty-four hours had logged even more frequent-flyer miles than she had. Of course, this poor unfortunate creature would never have a chance to redeem them.

Still, when she took her first bite, she decided the trip it had made was worth it. The moist, tender morsel tasted like butter in crustacean form.

"It's expensive, but I can't resist indulging my man," Carly cooed. "Lobster is one of Brett's favorites."

"It's true," he admitted with a chuckle. "I'm afraid my wife spoils me something awful. She's the one who insists that even mountain folk like us should enjoy lobster once a week. Even if it costs us more than the payments on the Rolls."

"Oooh, you know you deserve it!" Carly cried, her voice ascending a few octaves as she lapsed into baby talk. "You deserve anything your widdle heart desires." Winking conspiratorially at Mallory, she said, "Brett's the love of my life. Number three—but at least I finally got it right! Didn't I, Mr. Huggy-Poo?"

Mallory forced a smile, even though she would have been tempted to retch if the lobster lollipops hadn't looked so darned tempting. This was one of the countless times in the past few months that she desperately wished David was with her. She could just picture the expression that would have been on his face as they'd exchanged horrified yet amused looks over the dinner table.

"The Bermans' guests always eat well," Gordon commented. "Maybe that's why I can't keep away."

"Gordon lives in L.A.," Carly explained. Fortunately, she was back to talking like a grownup.

"Goodness, you didn't fly in just for dinner, did you?" Mallory burst out before she could stop herself. She already felt like a hayseed, largely because she generally thought of lobster as a special occasion food that could only be served with champagne and a cake that had words written on it.

"Not this time," Gordon replied.

To hide how impressed she was that anyone she'd graduated with knew someone who *ever* flew to Colorado all the way from California just for dinner, Mallory took another bite of the succulent, perfectly cooked lobster. As if the meat itself wasn't something out of a seafood-lover's fantasy, the delicate sauce dripping off it raised the concept of appetizers to an entirely new level.

"To be perfectly honest, the food is just a bonus," Gordon went on. Smiling mysteriously, he added, "I actually have an ulterior motive for allowing Carly and Brett to wine and dine me."

"And here I thought you simply enjoyed our company, Gordo," Brett said with a smirk.

Mallory glanced around the table, suddenly feeling as if she'd found herself on the outside of an inside joke.

"Are you in the—uh, a similar type of business, Gordon?" Mallory realized she didn't know exactly how to refer to the industry in which Carly had made her name. Health food? Vitamin supplements? Beauty aids?

Snake oil?

Carly answered for him. "Gordon is in a much more glamorous line of work. He's a film director."

"Really!" This time, Mallory figured she was entitled to sound impressed. "What kind of films?"

"The big-budget Hollywood kind," Brett boomed before his guest had a chance to respond. "Tell her the titles of some of the movies you've made, Gordo."

"I'm sure Mallory isn't interested in hearing my life story," Gordon said dryly, staring into his glass. "She's just being polite."

Mallory was surprised to see a slight flush rise to his cheeks. From what she'd heard, directors had the largest egos in Hollywood—no small distinction in a place like Tinsel Town where egos routinely grew bigger than the Hollywood Bowl. So she couldn't imagine why Gordon would be the least bit reluctant to dazzle her with his list of film credits.

"This is no time to be modest, Gordo my man!" Brett insisted. "Here, I'll do it for you." He rattled off the names of a half dozen movies. She not only recognized them; she also remembered that they had starred such big-name actors as Burt Reynolds, Jill Clayburgh, Ryan O'Neal, and George C. Scott.

It took her a second or two to realize that while all the actors who had starred in Gordon Swig's movies were famous, their superstardom dated back at least thirty years.

Which meant Gordon Swig was—for lack of a more graceful word—a has-been.

"How exciting!" Mallory remarked graciously. "I've seen every one of those movies."

"Then you must own a DVD player," Gordon replied with a sardonic smile.

"Gordon's gotten into some other things in more recent years," Carly said, answering the awkward question, "So what have you done *lately?*" that hung in the air.

Fortunately, Juanita chose that moment to make another grand entrance.

"How ees lobster candy?" she asked, putting her hands on her broad hips and glancing around the table expectantly. "Ees good?"

"Lobster *lollipops,*" Carly corrected her. "And they were excellent, as usual."

Juanita's eyebrows shot up as if receiving a compliment from the lady of the house was as much of a rarity around here as Dress-Down Friday.

"Then I bring out the next course," she said as she began collecting plates.

What next? Mallory wondered. Lamb flown over from New Zealand—in first class?

Even though she was off by a few thousand miles, she wasn't disappointed that the evening's entrée turned out to be elk. True, it was so local that she could picture the main course while it was still on four legs, frolicking on the mountainside with those goats she'd been imagining not long before. But she'd already learned that the cuisine chez Berman was, indeed, worth flying in from L.A. for.

"So what about you, Mallory?" Gordon asked pleasantly as he passed her a massive plate piled high with slabs of meat. "What brings you to Aspen?"

"I'm a travel writer." Mallory realized that even after four months on the job, she still surprised herself every time she said those words. "I'm doing an article on Aspen for a publication called *The Good Life*.

"In fact," she said, nervously glancing at Carly, "I'm hoping that Carly won't mind being the main focus. I want to write about why entrepreneurs who target an upscale clientele choose Aspen as the location for their businesses, as opposed to Beverly Hills or Palm Beach or Greenwich. We have a meeting at Tavaci Springs set up for Thursday, and I'm hoping she'll agree to an in-depth interview that goes a bit beyond the usual questions and routine answers."

"Sounds fascinating," Gordon said, nodding. "And perfect for *The Good Life*. It's a magazine I know well. In fact, it's gotten me through many an otherwise boring plane ride."

"That's because Gordo's flying coach these days, instead of in his own plane," Brett wisecracked.

Carly cast her husband a dirty look. Gordon pretended not to notice either the comment or the expression.

"And I assume your article is geared toward skiers...?" he commented.

"Actually, I'm targeting nonskiers." Mallory patted her mouth with her napkin. She'd suddenly found herself the focus of everyone's attention, and the last thing she wanted was to be caught with elk juice dripping down her chin. "I'm trying to find out if a visitor can have a good time in Aspen without setting foot—or ski boot—on a mountain."

"And what's your conclusion so far?" Gordon asked.

"Mallory only got here this afternoon," Carly explained, sounding a tad cross. Mallory wondered if it was because she hadn't been the center of attention for at least three minutes. "She just checked into the Jerome a few hours ago. And I haven't given her a chance to do any sightseeing. As soon as she called me to say she was in town, I insisted that she come to dinner. She's coming to tonight's presentation, too."

Smiling at Mallory prettily, she added, "As for that interview, I'll make sure I set aside enough time on Thursday to give you whatever information you need. I'd be happy to be the focus of your article."

"What a surprise," Juanita mumbled before picking up the last of the plates and vanishing back into the kitchen.

Surprisingly, Mallory didn't share Juanita's cynicism. In fact, she couldn't have been more pleased.

I got what I came for, she thought happily. Even more important, I got what I promised Trevor.

She knew, of course, that her next challenge would be getting Carly to let down her guard. She hoped to get past her defenses and uncover something more about what made this successful Aspen entrepreneur tick. Her ups and downs, any personal demons that may have plagued her along the way, events in her past, both positive and negative, that had gotten her to this point...

It could have been the wine—or perhaps just her burgeoning confidence—but at the moment Mallory felt completely confident that she'd be able to deliver.

Maybe Carly was voted Most Likely to Succeed, she thought with satisfaction. But this onetime classmate of hers isn't doing too badly herself.

Chapter 4

"All journeys have secret destinations
of which the traveler is unaware."
—Martin Buber

Rather than gathering around the fireplace for brandy, the evening's after-dinner activity consisted of the Bermans and their two guests taking the Rolls into downtown Aspen for Carly's eight o'clock presentation at the Wheeler Opera House.

Brett drove, insisting that there was no reason why his chauffeur should have all the fun. He parked the elegant silver car half a block away from the theater, maneuvering it so that it took up not one but two parking spaces.

As the foursome headed toward the entrance—Carly taking the lead with her husband trailing after her, Mallory and Gordon lagging a few paces behind—Mallory was shocked by the size of the crowd streaming inside. Scores of men and women, almost all of them old enough to remember when

Eisenhower was president, pushed their way into the small lobby on the first floor. They chattered away, exhibiting the same excitement they'd probably felt when they'd seen the Stones in concert for the first time—or in some cases, Frank Sinatra. It wasn't until that point that she realized just how popular Carly was. Or at least her claim that she had the ability to restore youth.

"I'm going backstage," Carly informed them when they reached the double doors that opened onto the small lobby. "I have to do my breathing exercises before I go onstage."

"I'll come with you," Brett offered. "We need a few minutes to go over the introduction."

As Carly charged off toward a back stairway with Brett in tow, Mallory turned to Gordon.

"In that case," she said, "we might as well go inside and find seats."

"If you don't mind, I think I'm going to bow out," he replied, glancing longingly at the door. "I've seen Carly's dog-and-pony show before. Besides, she's not the only one who's putting on a show tonight. So are the Nuggets." Smiling sheepishly, he explained, "I'm kind of addicted to basketball."

"What about your car?" Mallory asked. "Isn't it still at the Bermans'?"

"I'll catch up with all of you later," he said with a wink. "That way, Carly will never even know that I spent the evening watching the Lakers take on her home team instead of watching a rerun of the Rejuva-Juice story."

"Have fun," she told him, not letting on that she

was disappointed that she'd be sitting in the audience alone.

As she trudged up the stairs with all the other attendees, once again Mallory noted that, not surprisingly, Carly's audience consisted largely of individuals who had reached a point in their lives at which old age was no longer an abstract concept. But even in the case of those who appeared to have glided into middle age only recently, most had put at least some effort into looking younger than the number of candles on their last birthday cake would indicate. The women had colored their hair to banish the gray, and a few wore perpetually surprised expressions that said they were no stranger to facelifts. While fewer men were in the crowd streaming upstairs, the ones who'd turned out for the evening tended to be unusually trim, as if their way of warding off the ravages of time was by befriending a Nautilus exercise machine.

But she forgot all about the audience as soon as she walked into the opera house. It was much bigger than she expected, and considerably more grand. The thick velvet on the seats was a rich shade of red, as were the carpets and the curtain on the large wood-framed stage. Exposed beams covered the ceiling, which was painted the same deep blue as the walls. In back was a curved balcony bordered by a low wooden balustrade, its distinctive look a reminder that the theater had originated back in the days of the Wild West.

After Mallory found a seat, she remembered that she still had her guidebook in her purse. Opening it to the page she'd marked with a bright orange Post-it and labeled "Local Sights," she skimmed the section on the Wheeler Opera House.

Like the Hotel Jerome, it had been built by Jerome Byron Wheeler. It opened in 1889, bringing culture to a town that was only ten short years away from attracting the very first prospectors. The interior included a grand stairway with a gleaming wooden balustrade, a retiring room for ladies, and hand-painted frescoes on the walls and ceiling.

The theater also featured state-of-the-art lighting, including an elegant handmade chandelier constructed of hammered brass and silver. It was covered with more than thirty lights, each one shielded with a flower-shaped shade. The curtain, made by a well-known opera house scenery painter from Chicago, was designed by two New Yorkers and featured the Brooklyn Bridge spanning a river crowded with ships from all over the globe.

During its first five years, the Wheeler presented concerts, lectures, vaudeville shows, and Shakespearean plays. But after the silver crash of 1893, Wheeler went bankrupt. What hurt most was losing his crown jewel: the opera house. It remained standing, but its productions became considerably more modest. Instead of concerts and plays, it hosted events such as town meetings in which locals no doubt bemoaned the fall of their beloved town.

Then, in 1912, two major fires ravaged the Wheeler. While electrical problems caused the first, the second, which occurred only nine days later, was attributed to arsonists. The flames were so intense that they melted the famous chandelier.

It wasn't until the 1960s and 1970s that the opera house was restored, and a crystal chandelier was added. In 1984, more extensive restoration was completed, and the Wheeler Opera House was finally returned to its former glory. Once again it became an important cultural center, featuring a variety of performances just as it had in its original glory days: opera, ballet, concerts, Broadway plays, films, and lectures, including the one that Carly Cassidy Berman, one of Aspen's brightest stars, was giving tonight.

Mallory tucked the book back into her purse and glanced at her watch. When she saw she still had some time before the show started, she decided it would be fun to find Carly and wish her luck. Sneaking backstage would also give her an excuse to see what the rest of the building looked like. She was all set to say "Break a leg" until she reminded herself that that might not be the most appropriate expression in a ski town.

She draped her jacket over the back of her chair to save her seat and then went back into the hallway. She wandered around until she found a door marked Dressing Room, tucked behind the stage.

Mallory was about to knock when she heard voices on the other side of the door. Loud voices. So loud, in fact, that she knew immediately that while only an hour ago Carly and Brett had practically thrown off their clothes right at the table to express their undying love for both lobster and each other, at the moment they were engaged in a heated argument.

"How can you even *think* that?" she heard Carly screech. "For heaven's sake, Brett. I thought you understood!"

"You're not listening to a word I say," Brett countered, his deep voice booming through the closed door. "As usual. You think you know the answer to everything, Carly. Why can't we ever discuss things the way other couples do?"

Mallory slunk away, embarrassed. While she hadn't set eyes on Carly Cassidy for years, in the last three hours she'd learned more about her than she ever wanted to know.

She sank into her seat, relieved that she'd scuttled away without being discovered. Almost immediately the house lights dimmed, enabling her to focus on Carly as she wanted to be seen.

But it wasn't Carly who stepped onto the stage. It was her husband.

"Good evening, ladies and gentlemen, and thank you all for coming," Brett began. He stood next to the lectern, rather than behind it, with one hand in his pocket. He appeared as comfortable onstage as if he were still standing in his own living room. In fact, he looked as if he were about to deliver the opening monologue on his own television talk show. There was certainly no indication of his altercation with Carly just a few minutes before.

"It is with the greatest pleasure that I introduce our speaker for this evening," Brett continued, his powerful voice resonating through the theater. "She is an amazing woman who not only is a dynamic speaker, but also happens to be my wife." He paused to let the audience's polite laughter die down. "But in addition, Carly Cassidy Berman is living proof that the nutritional supplement she's about to tell you about, Rejuva-Juice, really works."

For a moment, Mallory felt as if she was listening to P.T. Barnum introduce his latest find, doing a great job of convincing everyone that what they were about to see truly was a "Feejee Mermaid" when the grotesque creature on display was actually the upper part of a monkey stitched to the bottom half of a fish.

But P. T. Barnum's bizarre attraction was a far cry from the beautiful, confident woman who strode onto the stage, instantly mesmerizing her audience. Carly looked even more radiant than before. Her eyes were bright and her lips, refreshed with darker, shinier lipstick, twitched eagerly as if she couldn't wait to tell the rapt crowd all about the wonders of Rejuva-Juice. Even though she floated across the stage with all the grace of a ballerina—or at least a former cheerleader—at the same time she managed to emanate an amazing amount of energy.

Being in the spotlight certainly agrees with her, Mallory thought with a twinge of jealousy. She fought it off by reminding herself that personally, she'd take hiding in the wings over standing on a stage any day.

"Before I tell you about the wonders of Rejuva-Juice—and believe me, I intend to do exactly that..." Carly paused, a small smile on her lips as she acknowledged the laughter she'd clearly been anticipating. "...I'd like to show you some slides that will demonstrate the lengths I went to in order to bring you this amazing elixir. Lights, please!"

The auditorium grew even darker. As a giant screen descended from the top of the stage, the excitement in the room became palpable. The first slide appeared, featuring the words "The Rejuva-Juice Story" superimposed over a shot of pristine jungle so lush Mallory could practically hear the birds chirping and the insects twittering.

"The story of Rejuva-Juice begins in the Amazon rain forest," Carly went on, "which is where I began my two-year trek. My goal was to discover what primitive people around the world use to maintain good health, high energy, and in many cases, a period of youthfulness that extends far beyond what those of us who live in so-called civilized societies enjoy."

Carly clicked the remote control she clutched in her hand, and another shot of the dense jungle appeared. This time, she was standing in the middle of it. Her khaki shorts and pith helmet might have looked ridiculous on someone else, but with her tall, slender frame and the mane of perfectly coiffed long blond hair flowing around her shoulders, she made safari clothes look even more stylish than the classic little black dress.

"It took me three days to reach this village in Peru," she told the crowd. "In one of the small cities I visited down there, I heard that deep inside the rain forest lived a tribe whose members routinely lived to be one hundred and twenty. The first day I spent twelve hours on a bus that bumped along a dirt road. I spent the two days that followed on a raft, drifting along the Amazon River.

"Eventually, with the help of a native guide, I found the tiny village, if you could even call it that. When I arrived, I was treated like a queen, since no one who looked even remotely like me had ever visited. The people of the tribe had never seen hair my color before. 'The color of the sun,' they called it."

Funny, Mallory thought. And here I thought it was called Number 233—Light Golden Blonde.

"Here in this village," Carly continued, gesturing toward the screen, "I spoke with a shaman for hours—with the help of a translator, of course. Thanks to him, I discovered one of Rejuva-Juice's most important ingredients. It's a nut that grows in only one place in the entire world. That place happens to be located right outside the tiny cluster of huts."

Carly clicked through half a dozen slides of the Amazon rain forest. They included two close-ups of a strange-looking plant and another shot of an equally strange-looking gentleman, his chest elaborately painted in half a dozen colors. He was wearing what appeared to be a dried vine that he had looped around his neck several times. She explained that he was the shaman who knew about the secret nut and its miraculous properties.

"But let's shift gears and travel to an entirely different part of the world," Carly continued. "My next stop—at least, the next one that yielded an important discovery—was in the foothills of the Himalayas. I was staying at a tiny inn in Katmandu when I heard about a remote village where men of ninety-nine still fathered children."

I bet they don't rush to claim the first dance at their daughters' weddings, Mallory thought wryly. Or to referee their soccer games.

"I found another one of Rejuva-Juice's secret ingredients there," Carly told the audience. "It's a powder that local women grind from a root. It's part of a plant that clings to the shallow layer of soil that barely covers the mountainside."

She flashed a few more slides onto the screen. These showed smiling locals dressed in brightly colored clothing. One shot featured Carly standing alongside them, but a few feet away, as if she was embarrassed by the bland colors of her own outfit. Another showed a shriveled-up man holding a baby that Carly claimed was his sixteenth son. It was impossible to tell whether his broad grin was due to the joys of fatherhood or all the fun he'd had getting there.

"The next group of slides takes us to another stop of my journey, a tiny village in New Guinea," Carly continued. The brown barrenness of the Himalayas was gone, replaced once again by greenery so dense that Mallory could almost feel the humidity against her skin. One slide after another flashed on the screen. Once again, they consisted of a couple of close-ups of an odd-looking plant, a few shots of the happy locals, and Carly.

"You'll notice that I'm not wearing a hat in any

of these pictures," she commented. "That's because each of the small villages in New Guinea is ruled by a chief called a *luluai,* and only he is allowed to wear a hat." Chuckling, she added, "Actually, the *luluai* of Mongo-Bongo liked my hat so much that I had no choice but to present it to him as a gift."

Once again, her one-liner was met with laughter.

"Now if you aren't suffering too badly from jet lag, our next stop will be the jungles of Madagascar..."

Mallory glanced around and saw that the crowd was really eating it up. Every pair of eyes in the auditorium was riveted on Carly and her slides. There was no whispered conversation, no fidgeting, not even any gum-chewing.

I have to hand it to her, Mallory thought, once again experiencing a tinge of envy. Carly certainly knows how to give people what they want. And Rejuva-Juice is only part of it. The rest of it is Carly herself.

Frankly, she didn't know whether or not Carly's magic potion worked. But as far as her audience's reaction went, it appeared that the fact that Rejuva-Juice may have been no more authentic than the Feejee Mermaid didn't seem to matter one bit.

At the end of the evening, as Carly fielded questions from her adoring audience, Mallory sneaked out of the auditorium in search of some air, a cold drink, and a ladies' room, not necessarily in that order. She expected to find herself alone in the washroom, since the theatrics hadn't yet ended. But she found she wasn't the only one who had bowed out. So had a short, somewhat stocky woman who stood at one of the sinks, washing her hands.

Mallory nodded hello before disappearing into one of the stalls, glancing at her only long enough to notice that she didn't look as if she belonged in Aspen. Most of the people she'd seen up to this point looked as if they were healthy, rich, and owned more than their share of Gore-Tex. Yet this woman, who was probably in her early thirties, wore a wrinkled white blouse and plaid pleated skirt. Not only did her appearance suggest she might have mugged a Catholic school student; the blouse was untucked, the skirt was pulled too tightly around her thick waist, and the clunky black loafers she wore looked badly stretched out, as if she hadn't yet figured out that she was one of those people who should have been buying wide shoes.

The fact that she was one of the few ordinary-looking people Mallory had spotted since arriving in Aspen made her feel an immediate connection to her.

At last, she thought, someone who doesn't seem obsessed with impressing everyone around her.

When Mallory came out of the stall, the woman was still there, this time peering into the mirror and forcing a comb through a headful of wiry dark brown hair that seemed to have a will of its own.

"She's quite a showman, isn't she?" Mallory commented as she pumped soap out of the metal dispenser.

"She certainly is," the woman agreed. Grinning, she added, "There's nothing Carly loves more than being in the spotlight."

"You sound as if you know her," Mallory observed, talking to the woman's reflection.

"Not only do I know her, I work for her."

"Really? I know Carly, too. She and I went to high school together." Mallory stuck out her hand, even though it was still damp. "I'm Mallory Marlowe. I'm just visiting Aspen for a few days."

"Harriet Vogel." Smiling warmly, the woman shook her hand. "I'm Carly's accountant."

"Nice to meet you, Harriet."

"Same here. Where are you visiting from, Mallory?"

"New York," Mallory replied. "The suburbs, actually. A commuter town called Rivington about half an hour north of the city."

"New York, huh?" Harriet's eyes grew wide. "Gee, I've always wanted to go there. I'd love to see a Broadway play and the Statue of Liberty and the Metropolitan Museum of Art...I don't suppose all those things are close to each other, are they?"

Mallory laughed. "I'm afraid not. New York is huge."

"I have to get there one of these days. Hey, maybe since I was lucky enough to run into you, I should ask you to help me make a list of everything that's worth doing. But what about you? Are you here in Aspen visiting Carly?"

"I'm mainly here for work," Mallory replied. "I'm writing a travel article about Aspen. But this trip is also a chance to catch up with Carly. In fact, I just had dinner with her and Brett at their house."

"It's gorgeous, isn't it? I hope you were there in time for the sunset."

"I was—and I'm practically ready to move in." Sighing, Mallory added, "Carly certainly has it all. Her house, her marriage...and especially her career. And not only is she amazingly successful, she also seems to find her work really fulfilling. She obviously believes in Rejuva-Juice."

"The company is her pride and joy," Harriet agreed, nodding.

"In fact," Mallory continued, "I'm hoping to use her story as the centerpiece for my article. I'm planning to focus on why an entrepreneur like Carly would choose Aspen as the place to open her business."

"Then you'd better hurry up," Harriet said offhandedly.

Mallory frowned. "What do you mean?"

A startled look crossed Harriet's face. Mallory got the feeling she'd just given away more than she'd intended.

"I assumed you knew," she said guardedly. "Since you and Carly go back so many years."

"We're still in the process of catching up," Mallory said, hoping to come across as someone who was an insider, just like Harriet. "We haven't seen each other in a while."

Harriet hesitated for a few seconds before saying, "Let's just say there's a possibility that Carly and Rejuva-Juice will soon be parting ways."

Mallory opened her mouth, but before she had a chance to ask her to explain what she meant, Harriet said, "I should probably get back. Carly is always high as a kite after she gives a presentation like the one she gave tonight. The woman thrives on public attention. She'll expect me to be at her side, offering her a little adoration of my own."

With a little shrug, she added, "It's part of my job description."

Mallory was curious about that comment, too. But before she had a chance to pursue it, Harriet said, "Here, let me give you one of my business cards." She opened her purse and pulled one out. "If you have any questions about Aspen, I'd be happy to answer them."

As she handed it to Mallory, she added, "It has my direct line at Tavaci Springs on it. It'll ring in my office, so you won't have to waste time going through the receptionist."

"Thanks," Mallory said sincerely. "I'll let you know if I need any help."

"Great!" Harriet smiled warmly, then said, "And now I'd better get back." Rolling her eyes, she said, "This is one of those jobs that doesn't end when I leave the office."

"Nice meeting you!" Mallory called after her as she sailed out the door.

She decided it was time for her to make her departure, as well. While she was tempted to go backstage and congratulate Carly at the end of her lecture, she knew she'd be surrounded by fans. Besides, she was suddenly exhausted. Given the two-hour time difference, it felt close to midnight, and it had been an unusually long day.

I'll tell her what a great job she did when I see her on Thursday, she thought.

As soon as she stepped outside, Mallory was struck by the cool freshness of the mountain air. She inhaled deeply, meanwhile noticing how pretty the manicured, red brick town looked at night, with the streetlights and the glowing store windows casting a magical glow.

She'd only taken a few steps when she spotted Gordon striding toward the opera house, his hands stuck deep in his pants pockets.

"Good timing," Mallory commented as he drew near. "The show should be over any minute now."

"Did I miss anything?" he asked, grinning. "A heckler, an unusual question . . . anything that might reveal my disloyalty?"

Mallory laughed. "As far as I can tell the evening went exactly as planned. Although I have to admit that I didn't hang around for the Q and A."

"Shucks," Gordon said, snapping his fingers. "If I'd known you were sneaking out, too, I'd have gladly traded watching the game for an after-dinner drink with you." Teasingly, he added, "And you know what a huge sports fan I am."

"I'm afraid I wouldn't have been very good company," Mallory replied. "I'm still on East Coast time, which means to me it feels two hours later. In about three minutes, my eyes are going to close—and stay that way for the next several hours."

"I could at least walk you back to your hotel."

"Thanks, but I'll be fine."

"Ouch!" Gordon cried. "Rejected again!"

Laughing, Mallory insisted, "Don't take it personally. You just caught me at the end of an extremely long day."

"Aspen's a pretty small place," Gordon assured her. "You may not have seen the last of me yet. And you can consider that a threat."

"I think it's a threat I can live with," she replied, still laughing. "But for now, I've got a date with a pillow."

After they said good night, she turned and strode along the brick walkway, leaving the Wheeler Opera House behind. She was surprised at how much she'd enjoyed herself this evening. It had been fun reconnecting with Carly. Meeting her husband and her friend Gordon, too. She was looking forward to Thursday's interview more than ever.

But at the moment all she wanted to do was get back to her hotel room, climb into bed, and let her long day segue into a relaxing and restful night.

Still, when she reached the Hotel Jerome, before stepping inside she couldn't resist glancing up at the dark blue sky. Studying the stars was something she liked to do when she traveled. Even though she didn't know the first thing about astronomy, she knew the configurations up above were different from the ones at home. Somehow, reminding herself of that simple fact always drove home the fact that she was someplace new, far away from all that was familiar.

Tonight, she noticed that the stars twinkling

above looked exceptionally peaceful. The sight of them was reassuring, as if nothing could possibly go wrong in the world tonight.

Certainly not in Aspen, where history had merged gracefully with the present, designer duds could be purchased at an altitude of eight thousand feet, and visitors could have anything they wanted—even the chance to be young again.

Early the next morning, as Mallory surveyed the breakfast she'd had delivered to her room, she marveled over the fact that although she'd been in Aspen for less than sixteen hours, elk sausage already struck her as commonplace.

The ease with which she'd come to consider wild game one of the Four Basic Food Groups was causing her to realize how much at home she already felt here. She wondered if what made this press trip different from the others she'd been on was that this was the first time she'd come to a destination in which she actually knew someone.

But she wouldn't be seeing Carly again for several days, and as she took her first sip of coffee, she decided that right after breakfast she would get going on what she had come to Aspen to do: explore it with the eager eyes of a tourist.

With that thought in mind, she grabbed the remote and switched on the TV, hoping to get the day's weather report and maybe some news. She liked tuning into local stations whenever she traveled, since the reports generally gave her an idea of the area's character. Here, for example, she expected stories along the lines of "Polarfleece shortage creates panic at Aspen area ski shops" or "Skyrocketing truffle prices send executive chefs back to the drawing board."

First, however, she had to decide whether to smear butter or orange marmalade on the warm, flaky croissant on her plate. She was so engrossed in making her first major decision of the day as she savored another sip of coffee that she was only half listening when she heard the handsome young anchorman somberly deliver a line that included the words "local woman," "entrepreneur," and "murder."

A local entrepreneur, *murdered?* she thought with alarm.

Mallory immediately turned her attention to the television screen—and then felt her entire body go rigid as she saw the familiar face of Carly Cassidy Berman staring back at her.

Chapter 5

"The most important trip you may take in life
is meeting people halfway."
—Henry Boye

No!" Mallory cried, her hand jerking so hard that coffee sloshed out of her cup.

With trembling hands she set it down, then leaned forward to get a better look at the TV screen.

"According to police, early this morning an employee discovered Berman's body at the spa she founded, Tavaci Springs," the newscaster continued. "Berman is the creator of Rejuva-Juice, a beverage she claimed had the power to restore youth and vitality.

"The police are asking anyone who has any information about the murder of Carly Cassidy Berman to contact the TIPS hotline at one-eight hundred..."

Mallory was finding it difficult to take in any more of what the newscaster said. Blood rushed through her temples with such ferocity that she could hardly hear, much less think straight.

Carly Berman...*murdered?*

It just didn't make sense.

I saw her last night! she thought, desperately struggling to make sense of the words the newscaster had just thrown at her. She can't be dead!

Certainly not murdered!

But slowly the meaning of what she had just learned began to sink in. Carly *was* dead. She really *had* been murdered. And the fact that Mallory had seen her only hours before was totally irrelevant.

A feeling of the rug being pulled out from under her made Mallory dizzy. The feeling was familiar. It was the same one she'd experienced when her husband had died. The idea that the entire would could change in a split second, that her sense of order and normalcy could so quickly and dramatically be turned around...

Desperate to know more, Mallory grabbed the remote and began clicking through the channels. But she couldn't find even a mention of the story on any of the other morning news programs. She decided it was probably because they'd all opened their broadcasts with the same story and by now had already moved on to other news.

She slumped against the back of the chair, feeling as if all the wind had been knocked out of her. She'd barely had a chance to form the question, What should I do next? before she came up with the answer.

I have to go back to the Bermans' house, she thought.

Not only was making another visit a way of paying her respects to Carly. It was the best way of following through on her natural instinct, which was to find out whatever she could about this shocking tragedy.

Instantly energized, she catapulted out of her seat and began pulling on clothes.

As Astrid had promised, the hotel concierge was only too happy to arrange for a rental car. In a surprisingly short time, a white Ford Escort was delivered to the hotel. Not exactly a Rolls, but it fulfilled Mallory's primary criterion: It would get her wherever she wanted to go.

As she drove along the same bumpy dirt road she'd traveled on the night before, she was glad she'd paid enough attention that she could retrace her driver's route. As she neared the house—Cass-Ber, as Carly had apparently insisted on calling it—she saw that at least a dozen other cars were parked on the property, most with bigger price tags than her house in Westchester.

Once again, Juanita answered the door, this time with Bijou at her side. Mallory could hear the voices of the others inside. In fact, the buzz was so loud and the atmosphere so charged that she felt as if she'd just arrived at a cocktail party.

"I'm Mallory Marlowe," she introduced herself. "I was here for dinner last night, and—"

"I remember you, Mees Marlowe," Juanita interrupted, sounding indignant at Mallory's assumption that she couldn't remember someone she'd met only the night before. "You are the travel writer who writes about the things most people don't come to a place to do. Come inside weeth all the others."

"Thank you." She couldn't help noticing that Juanita had mastered her employer's gift for slipping veiled insults into the most innocent conversations.

As the Bermans' housekeeper stepped aside to let her in and the friendly, love-starved poodle leaped forward to nuzzle her hand, Juanita let out a deep sigh. Whether it was from grief or the annoyance of having to deal with so many uninvited guests, Mallory couldn't tell. Yet she forgot all about the woman's attitude issues as she marveled over all the people who had converged on the Bermans' house at this terrible time.

Still petting Bijou, she exclaimed, "Goodness, who are all these people?"

While Mallory had meant her comment to be rhetorical, Juanita took her literally.

"That's Meester Swig, the director. You met him last night, remember?" Juanita wasn't shy about pointing. "And that's the Coopers, who live down the road. Their house, eet don't have a name."

"I see," Mallory said politely, hoping she could extract herself from Juanita's overview.

"That man, I don't know heem. That lady, either," Juanita went on. "I can't know who everybody ees. Besides, ees not my job. Ees my job to mind my own business, not to pay attention to who comes and goes."

Aside from the fact that she remembered *me* perfectly well, Mallory thought. Not to mention a few of the other people who dropped by today to pay their respects.

"I am just the housekeeper," Juanita went on, waving her hands in the air as she spoke. "I cook, I clean . . . but I don't say nothing."

"Of course," Mallory said. "The only reason I said that was that I was surprised that so many people—"

"When I overhear Mees Berm and Meester Berm fighting, I don't say nothing," Juanita continued. "I don't tell nobody, I don't say nothing. Even when they throw things at each other, I don't say a word."

Mallory's eyebrows shot up. From the way Juanita spoke, it sounded as if the type of argument she'd accidentally overheard in the dressing room was commonplace. So much for her assumptions about the happy couple—Mr. and Mrs. Huggy-Poo, as it were.

"And when Meester Berm goes out and Mees Berm calls Meester Dusty and tells him ees safe to come over, I don't say a word," Juanita added with a toss of her head.

This time, Mallory's eyebrows were jet-propelled.

"Mister Dusty?" she asked. "Who's that?" A cleaning service with a clever marketing department?

"Eef Mees Berm wants to have friends come over, ees not my business," Juanita went on, waving her hands in the air dismissively. "Even eef they are much too handsome for their own good. Eef there's one thing I learned, eet's that you can not trust a good-looking man. Especially when they know how good-looking they are. But ees not my business. When Mees Berm and Meester Dusty go into the bedroom and close the door, I just go downstairs and watch the TV. I turn up the sound very loud."

Aha, thought Mallory, finally reigning in her overly reactive eyebrows. So this Mister Dusty had nothing to do with eliminating dust bunnies. The service he provided was apparently something completely different.

When the doorbell rang once again and Juanita toddled off to embrace another visitor with her warm, welcoming style, Mallory didn't know whether she was relieved or disappointed. For better or for worse, in the past three minutes she'd learned quite a bit more about the dearly departed than she'd expected.

She was disappointed that Bijou had also headed for the front door, skittering excitedly right behind the housekeeper. Now that she no longer had the dog to distract her, she was painfully aware that she had no one to talk to. The only person here that she recognized was Gordon Swig. And at the moment, he was completely engrossed in conversation with an attractive young woman who looked way too young to remember either Burt Reynolds or Jill Clayburgh, at least in the days before nostalgia and Botox brought both actors back into the public eye.

She glanced around the room, desperately searching for something to do. She was relieved when she spotted another familiar face, the one that belonged to Carly's accountant, Harriet Vogel. But at the moment, Harriet was engrossed in conversation with Brett. While Mallory intended to go over and offer her condolences, they were speaking to each other too earnestly for her to feel comfortable interrupting.

So Mallory headed toward the most obvious distraction: The embarrassingly abundant spread on the dining room table. The food was so attractively arranged that she wondered if a caterer had been called in. Sprawling across the gigantic dining room table were giant platters of artisan cheeses, each one with a small, hand-lettered card that identified not only the variety but also the name of the Colorado cheese-maker that had produced it. Interspersed were bowls of nuts, crackers, and dried fruits, no doubt designed to complement the various cheeses. And for those mourners who had a sweet tooth— even at this hour—the display included a big plate of cookies, tiny cupcakes, and petits fours so carefully decorated that they looked as if they belonged in an art museum.

Mallory wasn't the only one surveying the food. A young man with scraggly blond hair sidled up beside her and studied the spread as intently as if he expected to be tested on it. She couldn't see his face, since his unruly locks kept falling forward so that they half-covered his face. She wondered if he simply couldn't afford a haircut, given the fact that his tight, washed-out jeans looked about to disintegrate and his tweedy brown sports jacket fit him so poorly that he had to have borrowed it for the occasion.

But as he reached across the table for a cupcake, the glob of blue icing on top molded to look like a giant flower, she noticed he was also wearing a large gold watch. From where she stood, it looked an awful lot like a Rolex.

Interesting study in contradictions, Mallory thought, trying not to stare.

He finally brushed back his hair, using the hand that displayed the watch that had cost as much as Mallory's car. As he did, she was surprised to see that he was actually quite good-looking. Cute, even, to use one of Amanda's favorite words, with nicely proportioned features that were highlighted by a pair of very blue eyes.

At the moment, however, his expression said he'd rather be anywhere else. Of course, paying a visit to someone who had just lost a loved one wasn't exactly Mallory's idea of a good time, either.

"It's really sad, isn't it?" she remarked. She helped herself to a cracker, not the least bit hungry but anxious for something to keep her hands busy.

"Yeah, but she was pretty old," the young man commented. "Wasn't she like forty?"

Given the gravity of the occasion, Mallory decided to let that one pass.

"How did you know Carly?" she asked, curious about what could possibly have brought this unlikely visitor to the Berman house.

The young man stopped examining the food long enough to cast her what she thought was an odd smile. "Aspen's a small town," he replied with a little shrug. "People get to know each other."

Before she had a chance to come up with another question that might actually engage him in a meaningful conversation, he turned away, his broad shoulders forming a barrier between them. After glancing around the room surreptitiously, he leaned over the table. Then, holding one of his jacket pockets open with one hand, with the other he smoothly slid a good portion of the cheese into it. Before you could say "stolen Stilton," he clamped the same hand over the plate of cookies and other sweet treats. Almost instantly an impressive number of those disappeared, as well.

When he realized Mallory had been watching him, his cheeks reddened. "For my roommates," he said sheepishly. "It's my turn to cook tonight. It's easier than stopping at the store on my way home."

Ri-i-ight, Mallory thought. Especially since acquiring food from stores, rather than people's homes, generally requires money.

She was beginning to think he was simply a gatecrasher, someone who had sneaked in for the sole purpose of acquiring the ingredients for a meal of lint-covered cheese and broken madeleines. Wanting to escape, she mumbled a few words she hoped would pass for polite and stepped away from the table. She surveyed the room once again, determined to spot someone who could save her from having to stand awkwardly by herself.

She immediately identified a likely candidate. A well-groomed woman who looked as if she was a few years younger than Mallory stood alone in front of the indoor waterfall. There was a natural elegance to her posture, and she wore a tailored beige suit and black low-heeled pumps that made her the most conservatively dressed person Mallory had seen so far in the entire state of Colorado. She wasted no time in sauntering over.

"It's reassuring to see how many people rushed over to the Bermans' house as soon as they got the terrible news," she commented.

The woman nodded. "In a small town like this one, bad news seems to travel fast."

Mallory noticed then how attractive she was, with large eyes that were the same dark brown as a strong cup of espresso and velvet-smooth skin that was almost as deep. Her coarse black hair was pulled back into a severe bun. Given how straight and how shiny it was, Mallory got the impression that this woman had worked long and hard to force it into such a severe style when it would undoubtedly have preferred to fly out freely, rejoicing in its natural waviness.

"Were you and Carly close?" Mallory asked.

"Actually, I barely knew her," the woman replied. "We had more of a . . . business relationship."

Mallory was still trying to come up with a diplomatic way of asking this woman why she was bothering to pay her respects to someone she barely knew when Brett came bustling out of the kitchen.

"Sylvie, there's a call for you on the house phone," he informed her. "Apparently they couldn't get through on your cell, so they tried here. Why don't you pick up in the TV room?"

Sylvie. A lightbulb immediately went on in Mallory's head. That was the name of the woman who had called during dinner the night before, the one Carly had characterized as one of the "have-nots." With her Kate Spade purse and her black suede Joan and David pumps, she certainly didn't fit Carly's description of her as a "have-not."

But what mattered even more was that as Sylvie rushed off to take her phone call and Brett hurried away to talk to one of the other guests, Mallory found herself standing alone once again. She was wondering whether she should chase after him or wait for a more opportune time to offer her condolences when she heard someone say, "I see I'm not the only one who couldn't keep away."

She turned and saw Gordon Swig smiling at her.

"Hello, Gordon," she replied, surprised by how pleased she was to see him again. "As soon as I heard the news, I rushed right over. I think I'm still in shock."

He nodded. "The whole thing is pretty unbelievable, isn't it? It's hard to comprehend the fact that last night, you and I were in this very room, enjoying a pleasant dinner with Carly and Brett. And now . . ."

He let his voice trail off, and the two of them stood in silence for what seemed like a long time.

"I had a chance to talk to Brett," Gordon finally commented. "He's beside himself, of course."

"I haven't been able to get near him," Mallory admitted. "And I'm really anxious to tell him how sorry I am."

"I'm sure you'll have other chances to express your condolences. After things calm down, I mean."

"Do you know any details?" Mallory asked anxiously. "All I found out from watching the news was that Carly was found at the spa."

"That's right," Gordon said somberly. "In one of the treatment rooms. A separate building, actually. The one that's used for mud baths."

Killed at her own spa, a place she'd conceived of and designed. "How did she die?" Mallory asked, her voice wavering.

"Apparently she was drowned in one of the mud baths. Someone held her under until she asphyxiated."

"Oh, my God!" Mallory cried. "How awful!"

"The scenario the cops constructed is that Carly went up to the spa late last night, after her gig at the opera house. No one seems to know why she would have gone up there.

"Very early this morning," he continued, "Harriet discovered her. She went in first thing, apparently to check on some paperwork. She happened to notice that the door to the Mud Hut was ajar, so she went inside to see what was going on. That was when she found Carly."

"Poor Harriet!" Mallory exclaimed. "What a shock!"

"I'm sure it wasn't a pretty sight," Gordon commented grimly. "Not only finding Carly dead, but also finding her submerged in mud. Those in-ground tubs are three feet deep, filled nearly to the top with the stuff."

Mallory shuddered. While she felt bad for Harriet, imagining what Carly had gone through positively made her heart break. The idea of being drowned—in mud, no less, mud that ironically was supposed to have a rejuvenating effect—was almost too horrific to contemplate.

"What will happen now?" she asked. "With the spa and Rejuva-Juice...?"

"All that should be pretty straightforward," Gordon replied. With a little shrug, he added, "I'm sure Brett will inherit all of it."

"And what about you? Will you be heading back to L.A. earlier than you planned?"

"I'm not sure what I'm going to do," he said. "I suddenly have some major rethinking to do."

Mallory was about to ask him what he meant when she heard loud voices from the kitchen.

"Impossible!" Brett yelled, his voice easily penetrating the thick wood of the door. "I'm telling you, you've got it all wrong!"

Who's he fighting with now? she wondered.

Mallory quickly realized she wasn't the only one who was listening. An uncomfortable hush had fallen over the room. Friends who had come to pay their respects now stood frozen, their eyes fixed on their coffee mugs or their shoes.

"I loved Carly!" they all heard Brett exclaim. "Why on earth would I have wanted anything bad to happen to her?"

"I'm sorry, Mr. Berman," another male voice replied, "but we'd like you to come down to the station with us so we can ask you a few questions."

Mallory's stomach lurched. Even though she felt as if she was listening to a radio play, she realized that what was happening in the kitchen wasn't just a figment of some writer's imagination.

Suddenly the kitchen door swung open. Brett stood just beyond the doorway, his expression one of extreme anguish. Behind him was a uniformed police officer, along with a craggy-faced man in a wrinkled suit. Given his fashion sense, or more accurately his lack of it, he had to be a detective.

"We only want to talk to you," insisted the man, who was no stranger to polyester. "We won't take much of your time."

"I demand to speak with a lawyer," Brett insisted.

He turned, his distressed expression immediately morphing into one of surprise. It was as if he'd completely forgotten that his house was full of well-wishers. Either that or he suddenly realized that the people he was closest to, the ones who had rushed to his house to offer him their support, were instead witnessing what was undoubtedly one of the most horrifying moments of his life.

"This is crazy!" he exclaimed. "Juanita, get my attorney on the phone—pronto!"

Good luck with *that*, Mallory thought grimly.

"What's going on?" A high-pitched female voice cut through the chaos. From its distinctive accent, Mallory immediately knew who it belonged to.

"Who are you?" the detective asked Astrid Norland brusquely as she pushed her way through the crowd.

"I happen to be an extremely close friend of the

Bermans," she replied haughtily. "I also work for the city of Aspen. May I ask what is happening here?"

"Nothing you need to be concerned with, miss," the detective assured her. "We're just bringing Mr. Berman down to the station for questioning."

"But I can assure you he had nothing to do with his wife's murder!" Astrid insisted.

"That's what we intend to find out."

"But—but—"

The detective had clearly lost interest in explaining himself to Astrid. He took hold of Brett's arm and began escorting him through the crowd. The uniformed police officer followed closely behind.

"Wait!" Astrid called after them. "It's impossible that Brett had anything to do with Carly's murder!"

The police detective ignored her. In fact, he and his captive were just a few feet away from the front door when Astrid added, "Brett couldn't have killed Carly! He spent the entire night with me!"

Chapter 6

"A passport, as I'm sure you know, is a document
that one shows to government officials whenever one
reaches a border between countries, so the officials can
learn who you are, where you were born,
and how you look when photographed unflatteringly."
—Lemony Snicket

Silence fell over the room as abruptly as if someone had just pressed the mute button on the
remote. Mallory looked around and saw she
wasn't the only person whose mouth had dropped
open.

With one important exception: the police detective. He simply looked skeptical.

"I can prove it!" Astrid insisted. "Brett and I
had...relations. I can even show you my bedroom.
For goodness sake, the bed is still unmade! And there
are other...things that would serve as evidence that
we..."

Too much information! Mallory thought, wishing
she wasn't holding a pocketbook so she could cover
her ears.

"Perhaps we'd better discuss this in private," the

detective suggested to Brett and Astrid in a low, even voice. "Why don't we find a quiet room where we can talk?"

The three of them shuffled off to another part of the house, accompanied by the uniformed officer. By this point, he looked as if he couldn't wait to get home to tell his wife about this.

Almost immediately, the room erupted into excited chatter. And from the level of the buzz, Mallory suspected it wasn't the dearly departed that the crowd was discussing.

As she was wondering whether it was time to slip out the back, she noticed Harriet Vogel standing just a few feet away. The horrified look on her face told Mallory that Carly's loyal employee was just as surprised by this revelation as everyone else in the room.

Mallory sidled over, anxious to get Harriet's take on what had happened. While their interaction the night before hadn't been long, she felt drawn to someone who managed to remain so unassuming and so centered—even in a place like Aspen.

"It seems there were some secrets in your employer's house," Mallory commented in a low voice.

"I can't say I didn't have my suspicions," Harriet replied gravely.

"So you think it's true?" Mallory asked, surprised. "That Brett really was with Astrid all last night?"

Harriet cast her a look of shock. "Are you saying that Astrid might have been *lying*?"

"People lie all the time, Harriet. Especially when a murder has been committed."

"In other words, you think she could just be trying

to protect him." From the dazed look on Harriet's face, Mallory wondered if this new development had elicited feelings other than surprise. Perhaps even some along the lines of jealousy.

"It's a possibility." In Mallory's eyes, it was much more than just a possibility. As far as she was concerned, Astrid was simply doing what PR people did as a matter of course: putting a positive spin on anything and everything. Even if doing so required telling tall tales to the police.

Deciding she may have been wading into waters that were much too deep, she quickly added, "But of course I barely know Brett. Or Astrid. Or even Carly, for that matter. It's really not my place to speculate about any of this."

Harriet suddenly shook her head hard. "I don't know about you," she said, "but I think I've had enough. I've got to get out of here."

"My thoughts exactly," Mallory agreed.

"Actually," Harriet said thoughtfully, "I should get over to Tavaci Springs to make sure the place hasn't disintegrated into total chaos. I contacted the manager, Daisy, and told her to cancel all appointments for the rest of the day and to call the staff to tell them not to come in. But I'd like to go over myself to make sure everything is okay."

"That's probably not a bad idea," Mallory said. Sighing, she added, "I suppose that when it comes to running a business, the responsibility never ends. And from what I've heard about Tavaci Springs, it caters to a pretty high-maintenance crowd, which means it probably requires some pretty high maintenance itself."

"*Oh,* yeah," Harriet agreed. Suddenly she brightened. "Mallory, would you do me a huge favor and come with me? The idea of confronting the place now that Carly—now that this has happened—is a little overwhelming. It's just too strange. I'd really appreciate the company. That is, if you're not too busy.

"Besides," she added, "this might be your only chance to see it, now that Carly's gone."

That's funny, Mallory thought. I was just thinking the exact same thing.

Given the caliber of the vehicles she'd come into contact with so far, Mallory was surprised that Harriet drove a dark blue Ford Escort, the same model as the car she'd rented. Only Harriet's was at least six years old and had a large dent in the door.

As she backed it out of the Bermans' driveway, Harriet was strangely quiet. She continued to remain silent as she maneuvered along a winding mountain road for what seemed like a very long time.

But Mallory's concern over her new friend's apparent distress paled beside her increasing nervousness as the road got steeper, the drops more dramatic, and the curves more and more treacherous. When she finally mustered up the courage to take a good look out the window, she saw that right outside the car, only inches away from the tires, was a sheer drop of hundreds of feet.

"Tavaci Springs is all the way up here?" she asked, her voice cracking.

Harriet nodded. "Its remote location reflects Carly's philosophy. The idea is that being isolated enables the guests to focus only on themselves."

Mallory suspected that people who were in the habit of spending fifteen hundred dollars a day to drink magical youth-inducing potions were pretty much in the habit of doing that anyway.

"In fact," Harriet went on, "Tavaci Springs has very strict rules. Carly dubbed them Lifestyle Policies. No television or radios, no newspapers, no computers, *definitely* no cell phones."

"I bet there's one modern convenience that's more than welcome," Mallory commented wryly. "Credit cards."

Harriet laughed. "You got me there."

She rounded a curve in the road that was so terrifying that Mallory closed her eyes. She figured there was no point in witnessing what the director of *Thelma and Louise* had so tastefully omitted.

"Everyone at Tavaci Springs follows the same schedule," Harriet continued. "Guests are awakened every morning at six with a soft knock at the door. They get a half hour to shower and dress before breakfast. Like all the meals, it's announced by a tinkling bell. In fact, bells are used throughout the day to move guests from one event to the next. Carly feels they're much more gentle than buzzers or even announcements made by the staff."

Mallory noticed that Harriet continued to speak about her former boss as if she were still alive.

I guess it just hasn't sunk in yet, she thought sadly.

"Carly feels there are four aspects to keeping young: physical, mental, spiritual, and occupational," Harriet went on. "She calls them The Elements, and each day at Tavaci Springs is specially planned to balance all four. The physical element is mainly addressed in the morning. Guests are led through a series of activities like mountain hikes, yoga classes, and Tai Chi. The mental element is rooted in meditation and lectures. Carly gives some of the lectures herself, but she also brings in experts in everything from meditation to colonics."

Silently Mallory thanked Astrid for putting her up at the Jerome, rather than Tavaci Springs. Cleansing the mind was one thing. Doing the same for any of her other body parts was something else entirely.

"The spiritual element is primarily developed through the appreciation of nature." The almost robotic way in which Harriet spoke made it clear that she'd given this little spiel once or twice before. "To take advantage of Tavaci Springs's surroundings— the spectacular mountains and forests, of course, but also the gorgeous sunsets and, at night, the moon and the sky filled with stars—a lot of the lectures and classes are held outside on the patio. We call it The Ledge."

"What about the occupational element?" Mallory asked, wondering if basket weaving was part of the Tavaci Springs regimen.

"Carly believes that rewarding work is vital for staying young," Harriet replied. "So guests at Tavaci Springs help maintain the facility."

"You mean like doing dishes?"

Harriet chuckled. "Not quite, but you're not that far off, either. Gathering wood in the forest for the fireplace is big. So is food preparation, but I'm talking about really basic stuff like shucking oysters and shelling peas. Basically, we engage guests in activities that bring them closer to the natural foods they'll be eating and the processes involved in preparing them."

Keeps down the overhead, too, Mallory thought. That Carly was one crafty lady.

She thought she was being punished for thinking ill of the dead when her shoulder suddenly rammed against the car door. But she saw that Harriet had merely made a sharp turn onto a poorly maintained dirt road.

They drove only a few hundred yards before lurching to a halt.

"Is there a problem with the car?" Mallory asked, alarmed. She pictured herself hiking down the horrendously steep mountain road that had almost proved too much for Harriet's aging vehicle. And going down was guaranteed to be even more terrifying than going up.

"We're here," Harriet replied with a shrug.

Sure enough, after trudging behind Harriet a short distance, Mallory spotted a series of low wooden buildings nestled against the mountainside. The largest one, closest to the path, looked more like a hunting lodge than a luxury resort. In fact, she decided it was a classic example of the "Let's go shoot something furry and four-legged" architectural style.

When Harriet tried the door and found it locked, she pulled a tremendous set of keys out of her purse. She switched on a light as the two of them walked inside, the echo of their footsteps an indication that they had the place to themselves.

Given the rugged exterior, Mallory wasn't surprised that the interior also looked like something Teddy Roosevelt had designed. The walls were rough-hewn knotty pine and the lighting fixtures were made from the horns of some large, macho, elk- or mooselike animal. A huge stone fireplace dominated one wall. The seating was also made of crude-looking wood, big chairs and wide-legged tables with surfaces so rough she wondered if the Tavaci Springs guests suffered from chronic splinters.

"This is the reception area," Harriet informed her. "There's no front desk, since when guests first come in, they don't wait in line or fill out forms. In fact, they don't have to check in at all, since they've all made reservations in advance.

"Instead, when they arrive, they sit down and make themselves comfortable while a staff member comes over to them with a mug filled with a steaming hot beverage made with Rejuva-Juice. The staff member, called a Nurturer, explains the Lifestyle Policies and tells them about the daily schedule. Each guest is also given a big box that's wrapped up like a present. Inside they find a few gift items designed to make their stay more enjoyable and more productive. Things like a fluffy bathrobe, rubber flip-flops, scented candles, and small bottles of special oils and lotions containing some of the same ingredients as Rejuva-Juice."

"Carly was certainly a wizard when it came to making guests feel important," Mallory commented.

"Definitely," Harriet agreed. "No matter what her personal failings may have been, no one can deny that when it came to running a business, Carly was a genius."

Mallory was suddenly overcome with a tremendous wave of sadness, perhaps because she was seeing firsthand what a wonderful place Carly had built.

Harriet must have felt it, too, because all of a sudden she gripped Mallory's arm and cried, "Oh, my God! I can't believe she's gone!"

"I know, I know," Mallory said, awkwardly patting her on the back. "It's such a tragedy. We're all in shock."

"I'm sorry," Harriet said, pulling herself away. "It's just that this is all so sudden. So unexpected! I never thought Carly would just disappear like this!"

Disappear? Mallory thought. Harriet makes it sound as if she suddenly decided to fly off to Gordon's house in L.A. for dessert and coffee.

"Do you think the police will find her killer?" Harriet's voice sounded soft and high-pitched, like a little girl's. "I mean, they will find the person who murdered her, won't they?"

"I'm sure they will," Mallory assured her. "I know how hard the police work on a case like this. In fact, I ran into something similar just a few months ago."

Harriet blinked. "You did?"

Mallory instantly regretted having brought up her past experiences with homicide. But now that she had, she had no choice but to fill her new friend in on the details. At least, a select few of them.

"I was on a press trip in Orlando, Florida, back in January and someone was murdered," she told her. "I ended up—well, let's just say that while the police worked on the case day and night, I did a little investigating of my own."

"Did you find the killer?" Harriet asked breathlessly. "I mean you *personally?*"

Mallory thought for a few seconds, trying to come up with a diplomatic answer. "I suppose I played a small role in seeing that justice was served."

"Wow." Harriet was silent for a long time. "I had no idea you'd ever done anything like that. You don't exactly seem like the type—"

"Why don't you show me the rest of Tavaci Springs?" Mallory interrupted. "Since we came all this way. Besides, you said yourself that it might be my only chance to see the place. And to see what all the fuss was about."

"Okay," Harriet said, sniffing. She swiped at her nose with the back of her hand, a gesture that immediately made Mallory think of Jordan. It also reminded her that like her son, this woman didn't yet have a lot of living under her belt.

Harriet squared her shoulders as she led the way through a doorway off to one side of the reception area. "This is the dining room," she announced.

With a wan smile, she added, "Carly insisted that we refer to it as the Digestorium. I still haven't decided whether that one was a bit over the top."

"Definitely over the top," Mallory said, laughing. "Still, you can't help being impressed by Carly's creativity."

Peeking inside, she saw a cavernous room with windows on three sides. Like the furniture in the lobby, the tables and chairs were crafted from crude pieces of wood. Yet she spotted at least a few nods to the traditional definition of luxury. White linen tablecloths graced the tables, each of which was decorated with white candles and a clear glass vase filled with fresh white blossoms. She was relieved that staying young didn't require a *completely* Spartan lifestyle.

"Beautiful," she commented.

"Now I'll show you the spa," Harriet said, leading the way toward the French doors at the far end of the lobby. "Tavaci Springs offers two types of treatments: tranquilizing and energizing. Tranquilizing treatments are geared toward making guests look young, while energizing treatments make them *feel* young. The spa offers the usual treatments, too. You know, like facials and massages and body wraps. But they all use Rejuva-Juice's rejuvenating ingredients."

By that point, they had left the main building. They headed toward the back of the property, walking along a path made of uneven-edged squares of slate and bordered with beds of colorful wildflowers. Mallory stretched her neck to get a better look at the mountains. As she did, the sun warmed her face. All around her, the only sound was the cheerful chirping of the birds flitting through the trees. The place was so appealing, in fact, that she was beginning to think a stay here was worth the hefty price tag.

But her mood shifted as soon as they crossed a small wooden bridge that arched over a soothing reflecting pool. To her left, Mallory spotted a small, rustic building, more of a hut than anything else.

She knew immediately that it had to be the Mud Hut. If the building didn't look exactly the way she would have expected one called "the Mud Hut" to look, bright yellow plastic strips that cordoned it off from the rest of the property emblazoned with the words "Crime Scene. Do Not Cross" took away any lingering doubts.

Mallory stopped dead in her tracks. In a choked voice, she asked, "Is this where—"

"That's right," Harriet answered quickly.

"Oh, Harriet, it must have been so awful for you!" Mallory cried. "I know how fond you were of Carly. And to be the one who found her—"

"Mallory, I know you mean well," Harriet said, her tone strained. "But if you don't mind, I'd rather not talk about it."

"Of course," Mallory said quickly. "We should probably go see the rest of the spa facilities."

As they walked past the Mud Hut, Mallory tried not to look at it. She noticed that that was what Harriet was doing. But she couldn't keep her eyes off it. It was the same experience she had whenever she drove by a car accident. There was something about a place in which something terrible had happened that made it impossible to ignore.

She was relieved when they reached the much larger wooden building at the end of the walkway.

"This is the spa," Harriet announced as she punched a code into a keypad. Since Mallory was standing right next to her, she couldn't help noticing how simple it was: 5–5–2–2.

"Wow!" Mallory exclaimed the moment she stepped inside. While the building's exterior reflected the same rustic architectural style as the rest of the place, the interior was an elegant mélange of wood, glass, and iridescent tile. The facility was outfitted with every possible indulgence: steam rooms, saunas, showers, and small, private rooms where those rejuvenating treatments Mallory had read about were undoubtedly performed. The entire back wall was made of glass, bringing the jaw-dropping mountain views inside. In fact, a large hot tub, sunken into the floor and surrounded by tiles in earth tones, was positioned in just the right spot for a nearly three-hundred-sixty-degree panorama.

"Well, it looks as if everything is fine," Harriet concluded with a little shrug. "I'll call Daisy later. But since we're here, if you don't mind, I need to stop into my office for a minute."

"No problem."

As they walked down another hallway, entering a part of the building Mallory hadn't noticed before, she casually asked, "What about you, Harriet? How did you get interested in the health field?" Once again, Mallory was at a loss as to how to refer to the rejuvenation biz. But using the word "health" struck her as close enough. "After all, you're an accountant. You could probably work in any industry you wanted."

"That's true," Harriet agreed. "My background with numbers does give me a lot of flexibility. But I guess I was attracted to Carly's business because of my childhood experiences with bad health. When I was little, I contracted polio."

Mallory frowned. "I thought polio had been wiped out, thanks to the vaccine."

"Actually, the last case of polio that wasn't caused by someone reacting to the vaccine occurred in 1979," Harriet explained patiently.

"But you don't show any signs of having had the illness," Mallory observed.

"I was one of the lucky ones," Harriet said with a little shrug. "I pretty much had a complete return to normal function. The only negative effect it's had in the long run is fatigue. I get tired a lot more easily than most people. In fact, there have been studies linking the kind of damage to the brain stem that polio causes with the kind that causes chronic fatigue syndrome.

"But I had a taste of what it means to be debilitated—and I had to confront the possibility of living with paralysis the rest of my life," she continued, her voice strained. "Anyway, I think that's the root of my interest in the health field. Staying young is part of staying healthy, which is why I find the whole concept of Rejuva-Juice so intriguing."

Mallory nodded. So Harriet's interest in Carly's business was about more than dollars and cents. She also had a strong emotional investment in what Rejuva-Juice could do for people.

Which undoubtedly made the loss she had just experienced even more devastating.

They had reached the back hallway of the spa, the area in which the offices were tucked away. As they walked through, Mallory couldn't help peering through the open doors into the various offices. The first one was undoubtedly Carly's. It was tastefully decorated in beige and soft shades of pink, with large windows on two of the walls that afforded fabulous views. A colorful bouquet of flowers, still fresh, sat on a low table behind the imposing wooden desk.

The next office had views that were just as spectacular, but it was slightly smaller. Because it was decorated in masculine browns, Mallory suspected that it belonged to Brett. The fact that it had no file cabinets, no papers, not even a paper clip, led her to wonder if he ever used it for anything besides ordering Colorado wines and snatching one-of-a-kind lobsters away from the French.

The office that was Harriet's last stop was way in back. The view from its single window was of the rock garden. Still pleasant, but not even close to being in the same league as the view enjoyed by her employers. It was also decorated like any ordinary office, with nondescript metal furniture, an ancient-looking computer, and more than its share of both papers and paper clips strewn about.

Mallory waited in the hallway politely while Harriet bustled around inside for a few minutes. When she had finished whatever she'd come in for, she closed the door behind her.

As they walked back to the car, Mallory commented, "Harriet, I'm curious about something you mentioned at the Wheeler Opera House last night. What you said about Carly and Rejuva-Juice being on the verge of parting ways, I mean."

Harriet sighed. "It was supposed to be top secret. But I guess that doesn't matter anymore, now that she's gone." She hesitated before explaining, "Carly was on the verge of selling both Tavaci Springs and the rights to Rejuva-Juice to a big corporation. HoliHealth, Inc., based outside of San Francisco."

"I've never heard of it," Mallory said, as if to assure Harriet she wasn't about to run out and buy up all their stock. "Then again, I'm not exactly what you'd call savvy when it comes to the business world."

"An entrepreneur started it decades ago," Harriet explained. "He started out selling vitamins, but his little company grew tremendously. Today HoliHealth sells all kinds of holistic treatments, mostly in health food stores but in big chains like Wal-Mart and Kmart, too. The company expanded into things like protein powders for body builders, herbal treatments for every ailment you can think of, skin care products, yoga mats, gel packs for muscle aches, you name it. They basically sell anything and everything that's dedicated to helping people look good and feel good. But lately they've been facing increasing competition, especially over the past few years. Somehow they decided that getting hold of Rejuva-Juice would give them what they needed to dominate the market."

Her mouth twisting into a sneer, she added, "In fact, that's why that vile Sylvie Snowdon is in town. She came to try to convince Carly to sell. It was something Carly could never make up her mind about." She sighed deeply. "But one thing's for sure: Selling would undoubtedly mean that I'd be collecting unemployment soon."

"But even if the sale went through, wouldn't HoliHealth want to keep you on staff?" Mallory asked, surprised. "After all, you probably know more about Carly's company than anybody. You probably know more about Rejuva-Juice, too."

"That's not how corporations work," Harriet replied bitterly. "If they buy Rejuva-Juice, they'll want their own people to run it. And even in the unlikely event that they did offer me a job, I wouldn't want it. I've never been very good when it comes to big, impersonal organizations. What's even worse is that I'm sure I'd be unhappy with what they did with Rejuva-Juice. Even if I gave it my best shot, I know I wouldn't last for long."

"Even though Carly is gone," Mallory said thoughtfully, "won't Brett want to keep running it by himself?"

Harriet's expression hardened. "Brett Berman is probably the biggest phony in Aspen. And believe me, that's saying a lot. If you ask me, the only reason he latched onto Carly in the first place is that he was looking for a female version of a sugar daddy. He's been living off her since day one. I can't imagine him running a lemonade stand, much less the Rejuva-Juice empire. I'd bet anything that he can't wait to unload the company and collect a huge check."

"Harriet, I don't think you have anything to worry about, no matter what happens," Mallory assured her. "I haven't known you for long, but you impress me as an extremely intelligent and capable young woman."

Mallory hated sounding like an ancient wise woman, but the truth was that Harriet reminded Mallory of her daughter, Amanda. "Even if Rejuva-Juice does get sold," she continued, "you'll still land on your feet."

"Thanks," Harriet said, sounding sincerely grateful. "That's something it feels really good to hear. Especially at a time like this."

With a sigh, she added, "You're a good listener, Mallory. Thanks for putting up with me."

"Not at all," Mallory insisted.

"You'd make a great friend," Harriet said. "It's too bad you live so far away."

Mallory had just been thinking the exact same thing. "I have your business card, but I never gave you mine." She pulled one out of her purse. "It has my cell phone number on it, and this is my home phone."

"Thanks." Harriet smiled shyly. "Who knows? Maybe I'll actually make it to New York one of these days."

Her smile faded as she added, "Especially since my entire life is suddenly up for grabs. Now that Carly is gone, I don't know what the future holds for me."

Mallory found it a great relief to be back in downtown Aspen, where the relative hustle-bustle served as a reminder that even in the face of death, life went on. Glancing at her watch, she was surprised to see it was still early. So much had happened since she'd gotten out of bed that she was practically ready for lunch. Or at least a coffee break.

She decided to spend the rest of the morning doing the next best thing after imbibing caffeine: shopping.

Doing research, she corrected herself. From what I've seen of Aspen so far, if there's one way a non-skier can keep busy in this town, it's by hitting the stores.

After checking to make sure her notebook was tucked away inside her purse, she wandered around town. She began her trek by passing a few real estate offices with their bargains posted in the window: "Country Living on Alps Road. Mountain Views, In-Ground Pool, 7 Bedrooms, 3+ Fireplaces, Media Center/Home Theater, In-Home Fitness Center, Fireplaces. $29 million. Must See!"

But before long, the establishments lining the quaint streets turned to those that sold more affordable merchandise—or at least merchandise with prices that didn't require so many zeros they had to be written out in words. She wandered around streets that could have been in any small town in America, except for the fact that instead of hardware stores and dry cleaners, the signs in front read Fendi, Gucci, Prada, and Polo Ralph Lauren. Jewelry stores were tucked in among art galleries, and there were a few shops that catered to young ski bums of both sexes, albeit young ski bums with hefty credit lines.

Mallory was delighted by the section of town that had been turned into a pedestrian walkway. Shops lined both sides of what had been dubbed Hyman Avenue Mall, some geared toward tourists who were addicted to T-shirts with cute sayings and others with more diverse wares. But what interested her even more than the specifics of the shops was how pleasant the area was. A row of evergreens and deciduous trees several stories high ran up the middle of the red brick walkway, and crude benches were placed every few feet. Her favorite part was the pleasant-looking life-size bear carved out of wood, standing erect as if he was just waiting for his picture to be taken. She hoped he wasn't offended by the fact that just a few steps away was a store that sold fur coats.

She plopped down on one of the benches to scribble some notes. "The fact that downtown Aspen still retains its Wild West feeling, rather than an ambience of glitz and glamour, makes browsing through shops that sell cashmere sweaters and Gucci purses a wonderfully incongruous experience..."

She jotted down the names of some of the shops, then took up her wandering once again. She turned a corner and found herself in front of an inviting-looking establishment called Amen Wardy. The name didn't give much of a clue as to what kind of store it was, so she peered inside.

The shelves of the good-sized shop were packed with items for the home, all of them wonderful, luxurious, and basically things it would be easy to live without. And most had price tags that would make the average Joe inclined to do just that.

Then again, this was Aspen, a town that wasn't exactly populated by average Joes. Visited by them, either. So it made sense that the shop's inventory included items such as a doll named Vernon who was made of fake Vidalia onions for one hundred fifty bucks, and an attractive but moderate-sized box of caramels for forty-five.

Talk about a wealthy and sophisticated clientele, she thought with amazement, remembering her initial pitch to Trevor. I can't wait to tell him about these price tags.

Still, Mallory prided herself on being a good shopper, and given the store's commitment to all things cute and clever, she figured that this might be a good place to pick up an interesting souvenir for Amanda. She reached for a pair of rubber gloves, the kind used for washing dishes, that was decorated with ruffles, fake flowers, and a rhinestone "diamond ring" glued on one finger. She thought the gloves might be just the thing until she checked the price tag. Forty smackers. Yet even that didn't look bad when she noticed a shower cap on a shelf nearby that was the same price.

The T-shirts are starting to look a lot better, she thought, putting back the gloves.

And then, just for a moment, she stepped out of herself and noticed how much she was enjoying her expedition.

This is fun, Mallory thought, as surprised as she was pleased. Puttering around in a new place, finding out what it's all about, is why I like this job.

She realized that wandering around Aspen without a schedule to follow or anyone to tell her what to do or where to go was also the perfect antidote to what had been an extremely traumatic morning.

Turning her attention back to shopping for her daughter, Mallory picked up a brightly colored hair dryer decorated with flowers and a whimsical fairy. After a brief debate, she decided the cheery design wasn't enough to justify its seventy-five-dollar price tag.

She was actually relieved when she found an organic room spray made with green oolong tea and orchids. It struck her as exactly the kind of thing Amanda would enjoy.

Maybe it'll even help her relax, Mallory thought with a wry smile.

She was standing at the cash register, tucking her credit card back into her wallet, when her cell phone began to warble.

Speak of the devil, she thought, assuming her daughter was calling. Instead, as she tossed her purchase into her purse, she checked the caller ID screen and spotted a number with an Aspen area code.

"Hello?" she answered, sounding as puzzled as she felt.

"Mallory?" a soft, wavering voice asked.

She was fairly certain the voice belonged to Harriet Vogel. But while it sounded like her, this version didn't sound at all like the strong, independent accountant she'd barely gotten to know.

"Harriet, is that you?" she asked, still not sure she was right about her caller's identity.

"Yes, it's me," Harriet replied, her voice now close to a sob. "Mallory, I don't know what to do. Something terrible has happened!"

"What is it?" Mallory demanded. She could already feel the adrenaline coursing through her veins. "Where are you?"

"I'm at the police station." In a voice so choked that Mallory could hardly make out the words, Harriet added, "The police brought me here. They—they think I killed Carly!"

Chapter 7

"If God had really intended men to fly,
he'd make it easier to get to the airport."
—George Winters

B ut that's impossible!" Mallory insisted. "Why on earth would the police think you had anything to do with Carly's murder?"

"Because of something stupid they found!" Harriet replied, her voice unusually shrill. "But I promise you, Mallory, it's all a hideous mistake! I'll explain everything when I see you."

"Harriet, I'm so sorry," Mallory said, her breathlessness reflecting her frustration. "What a nightmare! But why are you calling me, of all people?"

"Because I need your help," Harriet said.

"Me?" Mallory asked, surprised. "But what can I do?"

"First of all, you can find me a good lawyer. I've lived in Aspen for three years, but I've never needed any legal assistance before."

"Okay," Mallory agreed, her mind already racing as she tried to come up with a good method for finding the best defense attorney in town. "I can do that. But what's the second thing?"

"The second thing..." Harriet took a deep breath. "Mallory, would you be willing to come down to the police station? There's something I need to talk to you about in person."

"Of course," Mallory agreed, already rushing out of the store.

It took her less than ten minutes to reach the Pitkin County Courthouse, which was located on the edge of town on the same street as the Hotel Jerome. While the three-story red brick building had a dignified look, it also had a historical feeling to it. That, Mallory knew from her research, was because it had been commissioned in the late 1880s; it still looked perfectly preserved.

She also remembered reading that the Pitkin County Courthouse was the oldest courthouse in Colorado that was still used for its original purpose. When she'd come across that information, she'd filed it away as an interesting fact, but one she probably wouldn't be able to weave into her article.

At the time, it had never even occurred to her that she might be visiting it during her short stay. Especially under circumstances like these.

Parked outside the building was a gray SUV emblazoned with the words *Aspen Police*. In addition to a red-and-gold seven-pointed star that appeared to be the department's logo, its side doors were decorated with tremendous leaves that looked as if they'd been painted in gold.

Only in Aspen, Mallory thought wryly, picturing the stodgy sedans that the cops used in just about every other place she could think of.

She would have been amused if it wasn't for the sick feeling lodged in her stomach that was the result of the horrible injustice that had been imposed upon her new friend.

As she grew closer to the courthouse, she noticed another low structure right behind it. It, too, was made of red brick, but this one looked considerably older. From where she stood, she could barely make out the words on the front: Pitkin County Jail.

Spotting it made the sick feeling even worse.

Inside the courthouse were walls and carpets the same subdued grays that one would expect to find in any public building. What was different, however, was this one's creaky floors, slightly musty smell, and the general feeling that she'd just stepped into a place that was replete with history. Two wooden staircases with ornate wooden banisters flanked the entryway, and graceful archways led to the two hallways that extended outward on both sides.

Mallory checked the directory just inside the entry, which was framed in the same type of wood as the staircases. The D.A. and probation office were on the first floor, and the courts and the reporting area for jury duty were on the top floor.

The police and sheriff's offices were in the basement. Of course, this being Aspen, the basement was referred to as the Garden Level.

Mallory took a deep breath, then went downstairs to the lower level. Instead of the dungeon she expected, she found herself at the end of a corridor that was surprisingly pleasant. One of its long walls was made entirely of red brick, while a large section of the other was made of craggy gray stone. The floor was tiled in red terra-cotta. A water cooler dispensed water to anyone who wanted it, a considerate touch.

She stopped in front of the door marked Investigations. Through the glass window, she could see Harriet, sitting slumped in an uncomfortable-looking metal chair with her floppy oversized purse on the floor beside her. Her clothes were wrinkled and her wavy hair hung in her face. But even through the disheveled strands, Mallory could see that her eyes were rimmed in red.

As soon as Mallory turned the doorknob, Harriet jumped up.

"Thank you so much for coming!" Harriet cried, rushing over to give her a quick hug. "Did you have any luck getting hold of a lawyer?"

"I've got good news," Mallory reported. "I called the Colorado Bar Association right after we spoke. They gave me the name and number of someone they swore was the best defense attorney in the area. He should be here any minute."

"*Thank* you!" Harriet exclaimed.

Mallory glanced around the stark, unfriendly room. "What happens now?" she asked.

Harriet sighed, then sank back into her chair. "I guess I wait until the lawyer gets here. The police want to question me, but I knew enough not to say anything until I had a lawyer present."

"That's very smart," Mallory said, nodding. "Harriet, you still haven't told me why the police sus—why they even wanted to question you in the first place."

"I'm telling you, Mallory, it's all nothing but a silly misunderstanding! It seems the police found some stupid note I wrote in Carly's purse."

"A note?" Mallory repeated, frowning. "What did it say?"

"I don't remember, exactly," Harriet replied morosely. "Something like 'It's urgent that we meet. We really have to clear this up once and for all.'"

Mallory was silent for a few seconds as she digested the message Harriet had written. She could certainly understand why it could raise some questions—questions important enough that the police would be curious about exactly what it was that needed clearing up.

Mallory, too.

"I see," she said. Gently, she added, "And what was all that about?"

"To tell you the truth, I have no idea." Harriet bit her lip. "I can't even remember when I wrote it. It could have been months ago. And it could have referred to anything from what color the labels should be on Rejuva-Juice's new Mountain Berry flavor to whether the spa was going to start offering manicures!"

"In that case," Mallory said, "if you just explain to the police that it didn't mean anything at all, maybe that will make them realize that you had nothing to do with—with what happened."

"I think I'll leave that up to my lawyer," Harriet said. "Mallory, I can't tell you how grateful I am that you found someone for me."

"I was happy to do whatever I could to help," Mallory replied. "Speaking of which, you mentioned on the phone that there was something else you needed me to do."

Mallory expected Harriet to ask for her help with some other logistical concern that had cropped up when Harriet suddenly and unexpectedly found herself in police custody. Something along the lines of feeding her cat, locking her house, or canceling some appointments.

So she nearly fell over when Harriet calmly said, "Mallory, I want you to find out who really killed Carly."

"*Me?*" Mallory squawked.

"That's right," Harriet replied, still sounding matter-of-fact. "You told me yourself you had experience with that kind of thing. When you were in Orlando. You said somebody there was murdered and you solved the crime."

"But—but that's not what I said, Harriet!"

She certainly hadn't intended to give Harriet the impression that she was Nancy Drew with laugh lines. The last thing she wanted was for her new friend to hand her the responsibility of getting her off the hook by finding a murderer—especially in a town she'd been in for less than twenty-four hours.

As well as a town she expected to leave in just a few days.

"Harriet," Mallory said firmly, "I don't see how *I*, of all people, could possibly—"

"You've got to help me!" Harriet insisted. "The fact that Carly was rich and successful and—and famous means there's a ton of pressure on the police to solve this crime—and to solve it fast. At first, they focused on Brett, probably because as her husband, he was the most obvious suspect. But now that he has an alibi, they're in a hurry to find someone else to pin it on. They need somebody who was close to Carly—as I was—and they need a piece of evidence that ties that person to the crime. That also points to me. At least it does now that they found that stupid note! According to them, that makes me the next most likely suspect. And now that they've set their sights on me, they don't have much of a reason to look too hard for the real murderer."

"I understand all that," Mallory said, sounding as frustrated as she felt. "But honestly, Harriet, if you're counting on me to get you out of this mess, I really think you're making a mistake."

"Don't you get it, Mallory?" Harriet cried, choking on her words. "I don't *have* anyone else!"

Mallory's head was buzzing as, five minutes later, she slowly climbed down the front steps of the courthouse. All kinds of reasons for her not to get involved in Carly Berman's murder were careening around inside her brain like a swarm of angry bees.

But it was too late.

Somehow, the sight of Carly's former employee, sitting alone in a police station with her red eyes, scraggly hair, and stained pocketbook, had brought up visions of her own children. And how terrified they would feel if they ever had the bad luck to find themselves in a similar situation.

I've been there myself, she thought, remembering her horrifying experience on the last press trip in which someone had ended up dead.

So despite the gnawing in the pit of her stomach, and despite the feeling she already had that she might come to regret this moment, Mallory had found herself saying, "All right, Harriet. I'll do whatever I can to help prove that you're innocent."

What have I done? Mallory wondered as she walked back toward town. How can I possibly be of help to poor Harriet?

But she was already committed. She'd told her she would help, and now she had no choice but to make good on her promise.

Yet despite the low level feeling of panic that still engulfed her, one part of her brain was already clicking away.

Even though she'd only gotten to Aspen the day before, she'd already learned a little about the place—and a lot about the murder victim. One of the most intriguing things was her housekeeper's claim that she'd been having an affair with someone named Mr. Dusty—or, more likely, Dusty.

If Mallory was going to investigate Carly's murder, talking to the man who had been the deceased's paramour struck her as a very good place to start.

Of course, she had very little to go on. She didn't even know the gentleman's full name.

Still, she figured there couldn't be many people in a small town like this one who were named Dusty.

Even if that town happened to be Aspen.

Chapter 8

"There are only two emotions in a plane:
boredom and terror."
—Orson Welles

The best way to track down a local, Mallory reasoned, was through another local.

With that plan in mind, as soon as she left the courthouse she headed straight to a small bookshop that was on the same block as her hotel. She had noticed the sign reading EXPLORE BOOKSELLERS AND BISTRO during all her comings and goings and wondered if she'd find time to stop in.

Now, it struck her as more than a place to track down something interesting to read. She hoped it would help her track down the man who according to the Bermans' nosy housekeeper had been Carly's lover.

As soon as she stepped inside the chocolate brown Victorian, she was enveloped with the warm, inviting feeling she usually got in bookstores. The countless volumes lined up on the shelves packed into the compact space seemed to beckon to her, crying, "Read me!"

She zeroed in on a display in front that featured books with an Aspen theme. She'd just picked up a large picture book chock-full of awe-inspiring photographs of the Rockies when a clerk wearing jeans and a black turtleneck sauntered over.

"Anything I can help you with?" he asked cheerfully.

"I'm just browsing," she told him. "I'm from out of town, but I ran into someone who mentioned that this was a great bookstore." She paused. "I think he said his name was Dusty."

"Dusty Raines?" the clerk said, sounding surprised. "The guy who works over at the Rogue River Ski Shop? The place on Durant, over by the mountain?"

A skier, Mallory thought. Good muscle tone, great hand-eye coordination... That could well be the Dusty in question.

"Unless you know anybody else in town with that name," she said casually.

"He's the only one I know of," the clerk replied.

"Then it must be him."

"Funny," he mused. "I wouldn't have pegged him as much of a reader."

Mallory spent a few more minutes perusing the shelves, wanting to give the impression that she'd come into the store to shop rather than to do some undercover work. She even found a guidebook written by a local and published by a small press in

Colorado that she hoped might give her some extra information for her article.

Once she was back on the sidewalk, she pulled out her map of Aspen to look for a street named Durant. But she quickly put it back. The clerk had mentioned that the shop was over by the mountain, and here in Aspen, where it was impossible to lose sight of the beautiful giant looming over the town, a map wasn't necessary.

Sure enough, she found a small ski and snowboard shop a few paces away from the lift ticket booth. Hanging in the window was a huge sign advertising an end of the season blowout sale.

As she went in, she realized she'd never actually been inside a store that sold ski equipment before. Even though this one was small, it was packed with merchandise. Skis of all sizes were lined up along one wall, some stretching nearly to the ceiling, some not much longer than yardsticks that were no doubt for the pint-sized crowd. Lined up alongside them were snowboards, which were much more colorful and in most cases imprinted with some sort of weird design like orange and black op-art swirls or tree branches or zany cartoon faces. She decided that based on design alone, if she ever ventured onto a mountain, it would be on a snowboard, not boring old skis.

The display of serious-looking helmets pushed that fantasy out of her mind almost as fast as it had entered. And while she loved to shop, even she was overwhelmed by all the accessories that were apparently required simply to slide down a mountain slope. She surveyed a display of hats of all kinds, ranging from head-hugging caps made of every color of Polarfleece imaginable to a considerably less practical model that was shaped like a giant beer mug. Next to them was a shelf piled high with long underwear with the ironic name Hot Chillys.

But basic clothing was just the beginning. The small shop was overflowing with tinted goggles, waterproof pants that she suspected would make anyone look ten pounds heavier, foot warmers, hand warmers, padded gloves to put over the hand warmers, silk gloves to put under the gloves but over the hand warmers...

If it's that cold and that wet out there, Mallory thought, *why not just stay inside by the fire?*

She reminded herself she wasn't here to consider whether skiing was the sport for her. Instead of focusing on the doodads and geegaws designed to keep skiers and snowboarders safe, warm, and dry, she zeroed in on the shop's sole employee.

She had to admit that the man standing at the cash register, animatedly discussing the pros and cons of something called corn snow with a customer, was one of the more attractive representatives of the male gender she'd ever laid eyes on. He was probably about fifty, but like so many Aspenites, he boasted an exceptionally lean, muscular frame. He also had carefully styled hair that didn't have a single gray strand in it, along with the year-round tan that she was learning was an essential requirement around here. In short, he had the rugged good looks that Mallory was beginning to think were as common in this town as ski jackets.

As his customer headed out of the store, he turned to Mallory.

"Can I help you?" he asked. As he smiled, the skin around his eyes crinkled in a most attractive way. It was a look that always reminded Mallory of the cowboys in the movies she'd watched growing up.

"I'm looking for Dusty Raines," she told him.

But instead of saying, "You've found your man" or something else befitting a Colorado mountain man, he replied, "He's in back. I'll get him."

Turning toward the back of the shop, he yelled, "Dusty? Somebody wants to talk to you."

Mallory expected someone with the same demographic profile as this gentleman to emerge from the back. Instead, a young man carrying a brand-new snowboard that was still wrapped in clear plastic sauntered toward her.

Her mouth dropped open as she found herself face-to-face with the cheese thief from Carly's house.

"*You're* Dusty?" she cried.

"Ye-e-ah," he replied, looking confused by her confusion.

And then a look of recognition crossed his face.

"Hey, I know you!" he announced, his head bobbing up and down. "You were at Carly's house this morning, right?"

Mallory couldn't stop staring. She knew she was being rude, but she couldn't help herself. She was too blown away by the fact that this ski dude was Dusty

Raines—the man who had been Carly's paramour, at least if Juanita had been correct in her assessment of the soap opera going on around her.

Frankly, she didn't know whether to be impressed or horrified that Carly had had a lover who was literally young enough to be her son.

"So what can I do for a fine lady like you?" Dusty asked breezily. "Skis or snowboard?"

As if, Mallory thought, glancing at the treacherous-looking equipment hanging menacingly on the wall.

"Neither, thanks," she said quickly. "Actually, I wanted to talk to you about Carly."

"Yeah, what a bummer," he said, once again bobbing his head up and down so that his blond hair flopped against his forehead. "What about her?"

Realizing she needed to come up with a good reason for interrogating him, Mallory did some fast thinking. "Carly and I knew each other in high school. We were pretty good friends back then."

She hoped her nose wasn't growing longer and longer with each word that came out of her mouth. Every time she referred to Carly as a friend, she couldn't help thinking that somewhere on the planet, the former members of her popular school-mate's entourage were rolling their eyes and having a good laugh over such a far-fetched version of their shared adolescence.

"But we didn't exactly stay in close touch over the years," Mallory went on. "She ended up here in Aspen, while I stayed in New York . . ."

"New York, huh?" Dusty's mouth stretched into an appealing grin. "I always wanted to go there. I don't mean to sound full of myself or anything, but a couple of people I've met here in Aspen told me that they thought if I moved to New York, I might be able to make it as a model."

Mallory could easily picture him on a building-size billboard on Times Square. Especially if he was clad in nothing but a pair of Calvins.

She reminded herself that Dusty was also young enough to be *her* son.

"Yeah, they tell me there's a lot of money to be made that way," Dusty went on. "Not that it's about the money, of course. It's about the freedom. You know, having the resources to do the stuff you want."

"Like traveling?" Mallory asked, curious about this young man's secret dreams and desires.

"Definitely traveling," he agreed. "There are totally cool mountains all over the world. Switzerland, New Zealand, Chile...Hey, I hear there's even good skiing in South America."

Ri-i-ight, Mallory thought dryly. The next best thing to flying all the way to Chile.

"Not that I don't love Aspen," he continued, "but it sure is an expensive town. I live in an apartment over on Waters Avenue with, like, four other guys. We hardly have any furniture." Flashing her a million-dollar grin, he added, "And you already know that our food budget isn't exactly humongous."

Mallory's eyes automatically traveled down to the Rolex on his wrist. Maybe it's a fake, she told herself.

She wondered what else about Dusty Raines was fake.

But this wasn't the best time or place for finding out. Not with other people wandering in and out of the store, perusing merchandise that was guaranteed to make it hard for them to get life insurance.

On impulse, she blurted out, "Dusty, would you have lunch with me?"

A startled look crossed his face. "You mean like a date?"

"I mean like two people who are mourning the loss of someone they knew, spending some time together, just...remembering." When he still looked uncertain, she added, "Lunch would be on me, of course."

From the way his face lit up, she knew she'd said the magic words.

"Cool!" Thoughtfully, he added, "But not today. Gotta work late. I usually get off at one, but with the sale and everything, we're extra busy."

"How about tomorrow?" Mallory suggested.

"Tomorrow would be awesome," he said, nodding enthusiastically. "I should be outta here at the usual time."

As they decided on a meeting place, Mallory wondered if Dusty thought he'd just found himself a new sugar mommy. She certainly didn't come close to Carly in the looks department. But if this young man's true agenda was acquiring some additional accessories to go with his Rolex, he probably wouldn't care much about what his Good Fairy looked like.

Besides, she reminded herself as she left the store,

what Dusty thinks doesn't really matter. What's important is that the dude is too young to have learned that there's no such thing as a free lunch.

As she walked back to the Hotel Jerome, Mallory glanced at her watch. When she saw it wasn't even noon, she stared at it for a few seconds to make sure the second hand was moving.

It was hard to believe how much had happened in the few hours since she'd gotten out of bed that morning. She'd started the day by getting the shocking news that Carly had been murdered. She'd immediately rushed over to Cass-Ber to offer Brett whatever support she could. Next she toured Tavaci Springs, where she'd actually spotted the scene of the crime, at least from the outside. As if all that hadn't been draining enough, she'd then learned that the police now considered Harriet a suspect in Carly's murder.

Thanks to that new wrinkle, Mallory now found herself smack in the middle of the murder investigation. She'd even set up a meeting with one of her top suspects: Carly's lover-boy.

With the emphasis on "boy," she thought wryly.

She was looking forward to retreating to her hotel room while she tried to figure out exactly how she was going to help clear Harriet of suspicion at the same time she did all the research she needed to do in order to write her magazine article. Ordering lunch from room service—and eating it with her shoes off and her feet up—sounded like a really good way to plan her strategy.

As she strode inside the Hotel Jerome, she contemplated what she felt like eating while she took that relaxing in-room lunch break. But before she had a chance to decide whether she was in the mood for a local delicacy like mountain lion stew or something more conventional, she noticed that someone familiar was standing at the front desk, even though her back was to Mallory.

Sylvie Snowdon. The woman Harriet had spoken of so bitterly, mainly because her ruthless determination to acquire the Rejuva-Juice empire for HoliHealth would most likely cost her her job.

Mallory hung back, ducking behind a cart piled high with luggage. That particular location put her far away enough from Sylvie not to be noticed but close enough to overhear. She only hoped one of the bellmen wouldn't think she was trying to filch somebody's carry-on and sic security on her.

Peering over the hot pink molded plastic suitcase balanced precariously on top of the cart, Mallory struggled to hear what Sylvie was saying.

"It's getting close to lunchtime," Sylvie told the man at the front desk, "and I wondered if you could suggest a good restaurant."

"Aspen is full of great restaurants," the clerk replied politely. "May I ask what kind of place you're looking for?"

"Someplace quiet," Sylvie answered quickly. "Someplace private."

The clerk thought for a few seconds. "If you have a little time, I'd suggest the Pine Creek Cookhouse.

It's a bit out of the way, about a half-hour drive outside of town. And once you get there, you have to be transported up the side of a mountain. But getting there is half the fun. Of course, if you'd rather stay in town—"

"No, it sounds perfect," Sylvie assured him.

"In that case, I'll be happy to make you a reservation." As the clerk picked up the phone, he asked, "Will that be for one person?"

Sylvie hesitated before saying, "No, make it for two. And make it for one-fifteen. I'll head over as soon as I can."

Mallory was curious about who Sylvie knew in Aspen—well enough to plan a lunch date, no less. Here she'd just assumed she come into town alone.

It could be anyone, she told herself. She could have friends or even family in Aspen. Just because she works for a company that's based outside of San Francisco doesn't mean she doesn't know people in other parts in the country.

But she was suddenly extremely interested in finding out.

The Pine Creek Cookhouse, Mallory repeated to herself. One-fifteen. That means there's plenty of time for me to get there, too.

As she rode up the elevator, mourning the loss of her shoeless, stressless lunch even though she recognized that it was for a good cause, her cell phone trilled. When she glanced at caller ID, she saw her home number flashing on the screen.

She would bet anything it was Amanda. Jordan only called in case of emergencies—for example, to ask where she was hiding the plastic garbage bags or to get the name of the Chinese restaurant that made that great shrimp fried rice.

"Hello, Amanda," she answered.

Bingo.

"Mother, are you all right?" her daughter demanded anxiously.

"I'm fine," Mallory told her. "Why wouldn't I be?"

"Don't they have newspapers in Colorado?"

"Not yet," Mallory replied cheerfully. "The sheriff simply posts the latest Wanted poster outside the jail, which is located next door to the saloon—"

"This is nothing to joke about!" Amanda cried. "Mother, Carly Berman was murdered!"

"Yes, I know." Mallory was suddenly as serious as Amanda. "I didn't realize the story had made the news back east."

"Of course it has! Everyone in my dorm has been glued to the TV. And since it happened right in Aspen, I've been worried sick about you."

"What on earth for? It's not likely that whoever had it in for poor Carly made me number two on his hit list."

"You don't seem to be taking this very seriously," Amanda accused.

"Believe me, I'm taking it very seriously," Mallory assured her.

She held her cell phone in one hand and with the other used her key card to open the door of her room. As soon as she walked inside, she let out a gasp.

"Oh, my goodness!" she cried.

"What's wrong?" Amanda exclaimed.

"Nothing's wrong. I just walked into my room here at the hotel and there's a bouquet of flowers on the dresser. Roses, in fact. Red ones. Beautiful, long-stemmed red roses."

And they were probably flown into Aspen on a flight that took even longer than the one those poor lobsters endured, she thought.

"Who do you know in Aspen who's sending you flowers?" Amanda demanded.

"They must be a gift from the Jerome," Mallory replied.

"Jerome?" Amanda asked anxiously. "Who's Jerome?"

"Relax, Amanda." Mallory sighed. "The Hotel Jerome is where I'm staying. The management must have sent up the flowers. Hotels often go out of their way to make travel writers feel welcome."

She noticed a small white envelope nestled among the stems. Exhibiting impressive manual dexterity, she managed to rip it open with one hand.

Yet she nearly dropped the phone when she saw what was written on it.

"I'd love to take you to dinner tonight," the card read. "Call me. Gordon Swig."

Underneath was a phone number.

"Amanda, I have to go," she told her daughter.

"Don't you think you should come home, Mother?" Amanda wheedled.

"Come home?" Mallory sputtered. "That's—

that's preposterous! I'm working, for goodness sake!"

"But—but Aspen sounds so *dangerous!*"

Mallory had to keep herself from laughing. Aside from Carly's murder, the only crime she could imagine being committed in this town was wearing last year's styles.

"I'll be sure to keep my wits about me whenever I walk through a dark alley," she assured her daughter. "Thanks for your concern, Amanda, but I'll be fine. In fact, I'll call you later."

The main reason she hung up was that she wanted to call Gordon to tell him she'd love to have dinner with him. But she hadn't even had a chance to punch in the number printed on his business card before her cell phone buzzed a second time.

Goodness, that girl won't take no for an answer, she thought crossly.

But this time, caller ID told her it wasn't her daughter who was calling. It was her boss.

"Mallory?" Trevor Pierce said brusquely. "Goodness, are you all right?"

The East Coast media is obviously doing a fabulous job of portraying Aspen as the Wild West, she thought. *Either that or Trevor and Amanda should be competing in America's Top Worrywart.*

She wasn't sure whether to be amused by their shared Mother Hen complex or upset that neither of them seemed to think she was capable of taking care of herself.

"I'm fine, Trevor," she told him in the same even

voice in which she'd just assured her daughter the exact same thing.

"But the headlines are full of Carly Berman's murder!" Trevor exclaimed. "What's going on out there? Did you see her? Have you two talked?"

"I was scheduled to interview her on Thursday, but I called her as soon as I got in and she invited me to dinner at her house last night." Mallory hoped her admission wasn't fueling his concerns. "Then I went to a presentation she gave in town, pushing the youth serum she invented. But I went back to the hotel right afterward. That was the last I heard of her until I turned on the news this morning."

"Just promise me you'll be okay." He hesitated before adding, "After all, the whole reason you're out there in Colorado is that you're working on an assignment for the magazine. That means I feel responsible, both personally and professionally."

"I'm fine," she told him one more time. "But I'm afraid I really have to get off the phone. There's something I have to do right now."

"Nothing dangerous, right?" Trevor asked anxiously.

She laughed, hoping he wouldn't notice how fake her merriment was. "I promise, it's nothing more terrifying than going out for lunch."

Mallory didn't see any reason to mention that there was something a bit out of the ordinary on the menu: a side order of espionage.

Chapter 9

*"Most travel is best of all in the anticipation
or the remembering; the reality has more
to do with losing your luggage."*
—Regina Nadelson

What does one wear when playing Mata Hari?
Mallory wondered as she stared at the sparse
contents of her hotel room closet.

A large hat, she decided. Not that she'd thought
to pack anything along those lines. Still, the one cer-
tainty about Aspen was that it offered just about
anything money could buy. Especially a *lot* of money.

So after she surreptitiously sidled up to the
front desk to ask the clerk to make her a lunch
reservation—same time, same place as Sylvie's—
Mallory's next stop was the drugstore next door
to the Hotel Jerome. Just from walking by Carl's
Pharmacy a few times, she had ascertained that it
was one of those magical emporia that sold everything from sunblock to Aspen T-shirts to wine.

Sure enough, she'd barely stepped inside and

cased the joint before she spotted a display of hats, right at the edge of the art supplies aisle. While the assortment wasn't huge, what it lacked in numbers it more than made up for in diversity. She considered a red Polarfleece stocking cap with a whimsical tassel, a woolen ski hat that looked as if it had been knitted by someone who knew how to yodel, and a straw hat suitable for members of a barbershop quartet.

But it was the floppy purple felt hat with a brim wide enough to dip fetchingly over the wearer's eyes that she grabbed. It was perfect for her mission, a *chapeau* that might have stuck out anywhere else but somehow suited Aspen. It was so perfect, in fact, that she carried it over to the cash register without bothering to glance at the price tag—and then didn't even bat an eyelash when it came time to hand over her MasterCard.

Her next challenge was getting to the Pine Creek Cookhouse before Sylvie and her mysterious lunch date arrived. Mallory hurried to her rental car, spread out the map on the seat beside her, and headed for the hills—literally.

She began her trip by winding along the same mountain road that she knew led to both Cass-Ber and Tavaci Springs. She bit her lip as she passed the barely noticeable dirt road that meandered toward the Bermans' house.

This is the reason I'm doing this in the first place, she reminded herself. To find out who *really* killed poor Carly.

Her determination stronger than ever, she continued on for a few more miles, too fixated on trying to make good time to appreciate the scenery. She finally spotted a parking lot up ahead, right where the road ended. In case there was any question as to whether she'd arrived at her destination, a big white sign reading Pine Creek Cookhouse stood at the side of the road.

Mallory pulled into a parking space and turned off the ignition.

"Here goes," she muttered.

With the help of the rear view mirror, she pulled the purple felt hat down over her ears and tucked her hair underneath it. Then she trudged up a small hill to the wooden shack that appeared to be the rendezvous point.

Inside, half a dozen people sat on the built-in wooden benches lining the walls. She presumed that, like her, they were waiting to take a ridiculously outdated mode of transportation up into the mountains to enjoy trendy, up-to-date foods.

Anxiously she checked each face, hoping none of them would turn out to be Sylvie Snowdon's. She was relieved to see that, instead, she was sharing the small space inside the ramshackle building with what appeared to be a honeymoon couple who couldn't keep their hands off each other and a family consisting of a mother, a father, a surly teenage girl seeking refuge from her parents with an iPod, and an equally surly teenage boy trying to achieve the same goal with a Game Boy.

For a fleeting moment, Mallory wished that Amanda and Jordan were with her. Then she remembered that her children were busy with their own lives.

Besides, she thought with amusement, Amanda is probably thinking about me right now, agonizing over how her poor helpless mother is faring in this cold, cruel world.

Just as well she doesn't know that at the moment, said mother is attempting to conceal her identity with a drugstore hat as she throws herself into investigating a murder as if someone's life depended on it.

Which, of course, it did.

"Hi, everybody," a young man who could have been Dusty Raines's little brother greeted the group as he sashayed into the wooden hut. "All set to take a ride up to Pine Creek?"

He checked out the teenage girl, who emerged from her musical haze long enough to reciprocate. When no sparks flew, the dude instructed, "Then follow me."

The seven of them dutifully tromped after their mountain guide, their feet crunching against the thin layer of half-melted snow that still covered the ground. A few hundred feet away stood a boxy wooden sleigh with two horses hitched in front.

Mallory stayed behind to take some photos. But it turned out she wasn't alone in wanting to capture the moment. In fact, so many cameras were flashing as the honeymooners and the family of four took pictures that it looked as if Michael Jackson had just put in a surprise appearance.

"Howdy, folks." The driver, a Burl Ives look-alike, greeted them after the group members had stepped up into the sleigh one by one. "Welcome to the Pine Creek Cookhouse. Before we git on our way, lemme tell you about the three rules we got here. Number one, keep your hands inside the sleigh. Number two, enjoy the scenery. And number three, if you feel like tipping, give it to me, not the horses."

The group laughed politely. At least those members who weren't too absorbed by technology to tune into what was actually going on around them.

As the horses began chugging up the hill, Mallory sat back in her seat and decided to do her best to follow Rule Number Two.

Might as well enjoy the ride, she thought.

Not that she wasn't as concerned about Harriet as she'd been since she'd gotten her frantic phone call. It was just that she wasn't about to forget that the main reason she was here was to write a travel article. The last thing she wanted to do was let down her editor.

Especially since she'd been hoping to find time to come to the Pine Creek Cookhouse ever since she'd first read about it. It had sounded like a great spot to include in her article, since even people who didn't ski were likely to enjoy a ride up a snow-covered mountain in a horse-drawn sleigh.

She'd also checked out the menu on the restaurant's Web site. The offerings sounded like suitably Colorado-style fare, especially the Jack Daniel's–marinated caribou and the wild game kebab.

But for the moment, she concentrated on breathing in the exhilaratingly fresh mountain air as she was hauled uphill by two of the strongest horses she'd ever encountered. The sun smiled down from high in the sky, its golden rays glistening on the snow.

The air was scented by the smell of pine, and the bells around the horses' necks jingled merrily.

Once again, Mallory found herself missing her children. She was overcome with a yearning to bring them here, at least until she reminded herself that they weren't kids anymore. Like the two teenagers she'd just been observing, they were at that awkward age when their main concern was acting grown up. It would be another decade or two before they could go back to savoring the same simple pleasures that children were so good at appreciating.

The ride wasn't long, and they reached their destination before she'd had enough of taking in the pristine countryside and listening to the crunch of horses' hooves against ice-covered snow. Like so many other buildings in Aspen, the restaurant was made of wood. Only this time, the façade went whole hog in recapturing the spirit of Colorado, since the building was actually a log cabin.

But this being Aspen, it wasn't the type of log cabin the early settlers had *really* lived in. This was an architect's fantasy of what a log cabin could be, given unlimited resources and modern-day building equipment. A series of peaked roofs jutted up, echoing the silhouette of the mountains behind them. Below each were large windows, some overlooking a deck area that allowed for al fresco dining.

The same decorating theme—wood as far as the eye could see—was incorporated into the interior as well. In fact, if knotty pine was capable of causing an allergic reaction, Mallory figured, she'd be having a mighty hard time breathing right about now. Everything inside the Pine Creek Cookhouse was made of knot-covered wood that looked like an illustration in a book of Grimms fairy tales: the walls, ceiling, beams, columns, and even the tables and chairs. While the two rows of chandeliers that illuminated the dining room weren't made of wood, they had been fashioned from the next best thing: antlers.

I sure hope there aren't any termites in Aspen, Mallory thought as she smiled at the hostess heading in her direction.

"One?" the hostess asked pleasantly.

"That's right," Mallory said, noticing that the other two groups who had come up the mountain with her had already been seated.

"Anyplace in particular you'd like to sit?"

The most discreet seat in the house, Mallory thought.

She did a quick survey of the restaurant and spotted a table in the corner. Not only was it out of the way, it also happened to be shielded by one of the thick wooden columns.

"How about that one?" she asked.

"Right this way," the hostess said.

As soon as she sat down, Mallory checked her watch. According to her calculations, Sylvie would be coming up the mountain on the very next commuter sleigh. That meant she still had a few minutes to jot down some notes.

"Pine Creek Cookhouse," she wrote at the top of a clean page in her notebook. "Horse-drawn sleigh. Mountain views. Friendly staff. KNOTTY PINE!!!"

The sound of animated voices and raucous laughter caused her to glance up. A new group was filing in through the front door, their pink cheeks and bright eyes a sure sign that they had just had the total sleigh experience.

One of the first people she spotted in the crowd was Sylvie, dressed in a blindingly white ski jacket and fur boots that made her look as if she'd mugged Sasquatch.

But it wasn't the woman's fashion statement she was interested in. It was her lunch date.

Mallory's heartbeat quickened as she peered out from under the brim of her hat, anxious to see who Sylvie had brought to the most secluded restaurant she could find.

When her eyes zeroed in on another familiar face in the crowd, she clamped her hand over her mouth to keep from gasping.

Harriet!

Mallory was so startled that it took a few seconds for cogent thoughts to begin forming in her head. Once they did, they swirled around so fast and furious she could barely reign them in.

What on earth is Harriet doing here—with Sylvie, no less? Is it possible that the police let her go and she didn't even bother to *tell* me? Even though I'm the one person she claimed she trusted enough to call upon for help in her darkest hour, the person she begged to get her off the hook by finding the real killer . . . the person she'd insisted was the only one she knew in Aspen who could help her?

But instead of calling *her*, it appeared that Harriet

had decided to go out for lunch with someone else. Sylvie, no less, a woman she had spoken about so bitterly that frogs and spiders had practically leaped out of her mouth. Mallory could still hear the venom in Harriet's voice as she referred to Silvie as "vile."

Yet with her very own eyes Mallory could see that the two of them were not only meeting at the most private, tucked-away eatery in town, they were laughing together as if they were the best of friends.

The whole situation was so preposterous, in fact, that Mallory wondered if she was completely misreading it.

Harriet *can't* be Sylvie's secret lunch date! She thought. Maybe it's just a coincidence that they both decided to have lunch here today . . .

By that point, Sylvie and Harriet had sauntered up to the hostess.

"Table for two?" she asked them pleasantly.

"That's right," Sylvie replied. "I made a reservation. Actually, my hotel did. The name is Snowdon."

So they *are* having lunch together! Mallory thought, watching as Sylvie followed the hostess to a table with Harriet trailing after her. And is it my imagination, or is Sylvie looking from side to side nervously as if she wished she, too, had thought to wear a gigantic Mata Hari hat?

Mallory felt as if the entire room was swirling around her. While Harriet had looked like the victim of a police investigation gone awry as she sat in the basement of the courthouse, she'd changed her clothes, brushed her hair, and was now laughing and chattering and acting as if she didn't have a care in the world. With Sylvie, no less!

Mallory had been totally supportive of Harriet up to this point—and completely convinced by her claim that she was innocent. But she suddenly didn't know *what* to believe.

At the moment, however, Mallory knew her first priority was hightailing it out of there. The Pine Creek Cookhouse was big, but it wasn't that big. Even the floppiest hat could only do so much, and she was desperate to sneak out of the restaurant before either one of them spotted her.

So while Sylvie and Harriet were absorbed in the waiter's recitation of the day's specials, Mallory pulled her hat down even farther over her head, stood up, and headed toward the front door. She took care to hide behind every column she passed.

"I—I won't be staying for lunch after all," she told the hostess as she neared the front door. "Something came up." She pulled out her cell phone and pointed at it, meanwhile putting on the most apologetic look she could manage. "Family emergency."

"I'm so sorry!" the hostess said. "Would you like me to call—"

But Mallory was already out of there.

She found a spot near the corner of the building that shielded her from view. As she waited for the next sleigh, she sucked in as much cool, clean mountain air as she could, hoping it would help her think straight.

Was Harriet really the hapless victim of an over-zealous police force, someone who was being unjustly accused of a horrendous crime she was incapable of committing? she wondered. Or was her plea for help simply a ruse—a way of diverting attention away from the fact that she was, indeed, the killer?

At this point, Mallory simply didn't know. But there was one thing she *did* know: Now that Harriet had dragged her into this, she had every intention of following through until she found out for herself who the actual killer was.

Returning to downtown Aspen was a relief.

The first thing Mallory did was grab lunch at a deli called the Butcher's Block. While she waited for her sandwich to be constructed, she noted that the menu included caviar. Not exactly standard deli fare, at least where she came from. Then she contemplated what to do for the next few hours before dinner at Montagne. While part of her wanted nothing more than to retreat to her hotel room, stretching out on the bed with a good book, Mallory's more practical side urged her to use her free afternoon to do some sightseeing for her article.

As she sat in her car in a parking garage at the edge of downtown Aspen, she consulted her guidebook, which was chock-full of Post-its marking places that sounded worth a visit. She was debating between going to the Aspen Art Museum and checking out bus tours of celebrity homes when her cell phone rang.

She glanced at the caller ID screen and saw a number she didn't recognize.

A local number.

"Mallory?" a familiar voice replied when she said hello. "It's me, Harriet."

"Harriet!" she cried, her surprise sincere. "Where are you?"

"I'm out! The police let me go."

"That's great! When?"

"About a half hour ago."

A bold-faced lie, Mallory thought angrily. But she'd already decided that the best way to proceed was by going along with whatever Harriet told her.

"It turns out the police weren't actually going to arrest me," Harriet continued. "They just wanted to bring me in for questioning. But they still consider me a suspect. The fact that they found that silly letter has made me what they're referring to as 'a person of interest.'"

Frankly, I'm finding you kind of interesting, too, Mallory thought wryly.

Aloud, she said, "I hope the lawyer was helpful."

"Very. Thanks for finding him for me, Mallory. As soon as he got there, he gave the cops a dozen reasons why they couldn't hold me. They gave me this little speech about how I shouldn't leave town, of course—as if I have anyplace to go!"

Maybe you do and maybe you don't, Mallory thought, still not sure what to believe.

"That's great news," she said evenly. "So what time did you actually get out of the police station?"

"I'm not sure," Harriet replied. With a nervous laugh, she added, "To tell you the truth, I was so glad to get out of there that I didn't even look at my watch."

The truth. Mallory was beginning to wonder if Harriet even knew the meaning of the word.

"I was so scared, Mallory. I still am. As soon as they let me out, I decided that the first thing I was going to do was run home and take a long, hot shower. All I want to do right now is hide, you know?"

At this point, I don't know *what* I know, Mallory thought.

But she simply replied, "Of course. Who could blame you?"

"Anyway, I was wondering if I could take you out for lunch or something," Harriet went on breathlessly. "To thank you for helping me out—and to pick your brain. I'm still hoping you'll do the thing we talked about you doing. Just because the police let me go after my lawyer showed up doesn't mean they're convinced that I'm innocent. And they won't be until the real killer has been caught!"

"Yes, let's get together," Mallory agreed. "How about coffee tomorrow afternoon? I may know more by then."

But sharing information with Harriet wasn't her real reason for wanting to get together. She was actually hoping to *get* information.

And she hoped that getting together the following afternoon would help her accomplish exactly that. Without ever letting on, of course, that she'd noticed that even though Harriet was an accountant, things didn't always add up.

Chapter 10

"Too often travel, instead of broadening the mind,
merely lengthens the conversation."
—Elizabeth Drew

It's not a real date, Mallory told herself firmly a few hours later as she leaned closer to the bathroom mirror and flicked a mascara wand over her lashes. After all, *having dinner at fancy restaurants is part of my job. It makes sense to bring someone else with me. That way, I have an excuse to taste twice as much of the food.*

When that line of reasoning didn't banish the butterflies from her stomach, she tried a different argument.

Gordon Swig is just a nice guy who recognized that I'm all alone in this town, the same way he is. He probably doesn't have anyone else to have dinner with, either. Besides, we've both suffered a terrible shock, so a little companionship will be comforting.

It's not as if he's interested in me, she reasoned. Not *that* way. And I'm not interested in him, either.

Besides, a mischievous little voice piped up, even if you were interested, the two of you live on opposite coasts of what happens to be an extremely large country.

Mallory was fully aware that this wasn't the first time since David's death that she'd been forced to face her ambivalence about being with a new man. The butterflies that went with it, either. On her very first press trip, back in January, she had met another man who, like Gordon, was charming, fun to be with, and, much to her amazement, interested in her. Yet just like Gordon, Wade McKay lived far away, in Toronto. While they'd kept in touch via e-mail ever since those few days they'd spent in Orlando, the same sense of uncertainty had kept her from allowing that relationship to go any further.

With a sigh, Mallory took a step back from the mirror and scrutinized her outfit: a loose-fitting, tomato red jacket splashed with gigantic Chinese characters, a black silk T-shirt, and tailored black pants. She wondered if she should dress up, dress down, or just accept the fact that whatever she wore, she would never convince herself that she'd made a good choice.

Good thing this isn't a real date, she thought wryly, objective enough to be amused by her own behavior. Lord knows what state I'd be in if it were.

She relaxed a bit when she rode down to the main floor and found Gordon standing awkwardly in the lobby, his eyes glued to the elevators. She remembered that what she had first noticed about him was that he was on the short side, on the bald side, and not even close to being a contender for Best Dressed. Yet this evening she found his unpretentious appearance refreshing. Like Harriet, he struck her as someone who had more important things to think about than whether every hair was in place or whether he was wearing the most expensive suit in the room.

As for the anxious expression on his face, it reminded her of the way dogs look when they're tied to parking meters outside stores, waiting for their masters.

Okay, so maybe this *is* a date, she thought. And that's not necessarily a bad thing.

Her reassessment of the evening ahead was reinforced by the way Gordon brightened the moment he spotted her. If he had a tail, Mallory suspected he'd be wagging it.

"Aren't you a sight for sore eyes!" he greeted her, flashing that same warm smile that had grabbed her attention the night before. Maybe Gordon Swig didn't have the ego of a typical Hollywood director, but he certainly had the charisma. She bet that Jill Clayburgh and Burt Reynolds had pulled every string they needed to in order to get the chance to work with him.

"You're not so bad yourself," she returned, giving him the sunniest smile in her repertoire.

Whoa! Mallory thought. Where did *that* come from?

She could feel herself blushing, horrified by how

shamelessly she was flirting. Calm down, girl! she warned herself. You and Gordon haven't even made it to the restaurant, and you're already looking so far into the future that you're going to end up with eye strain.

"I've heard great things about this restaurant," she commented as they headed across the Hotel Jerome's ornate lobby, deciding to stick to business, at least for now. She even resisted the urge to take his arm as they stepped outside and were suddenly enveloped by the refreshingly cool mountain air that descended upon the town at dusk. The entire town spread out before them like a red carpet, inviting them to stroll along the charming red brick walkways. All around them, lights were coming on, twinkling like the stars strewn across the darkening cobalt blue sky.

"Montagna is excellent," Gordon agreed. "One of my favorite restaurants in Aspen, in fact."

"I didn't know you'd eaten there before." Mallory sometimes forgot that not everyone was seeing the places she was visiting on assignment for the first time, the way she usually was.

"I've been there two or three times," he said. "But never with a charming travel writer who's undoubtedly going to give me an entirely new perspective on the experience."

Mallory laughed. "If by that you mean that I'm going to insist on sampling everything on your plate, you've got that right."

Montagna was located inside one of Aspen's

other top hotels, the Little Nell, which had the distinction of being the only ski-in, ski-out resort in town—meaning guests could literally put their skis on at the hotel and then ski right up to the lift. Thanks to both Astrid and her guidebooks, Mallory knew all about its ski concierge, who not only stored hotel guests' skis overnight in a small building just a few feet away from the lift, but also waxed their skis, warmed their ski boots, and plied them with hot coffee.

The hotel lobby had a modern feeling that stood in sharp contrast to the Hotel Jerome's old-fashioned, almost kitsch Wild West feeling. The first floor of the Little Nell was all straight lines and neutral colors. Yet comfortable couches faced an inviting fireplace and the view from the seating areas was delightfully serene: a courtyard with a small swimming pool, viewed through wall-size windows. Mallory found herself taking mental notes, constructing phrases like, "cozy without being prissy" and "coolly elegant but at the same time inviting."

Montagna, nestled in a back corner, was considerably more ornate. The restaurant was on two levels separated by a railing supported by wine-barrel-shaped columns. Both the railing and the columns were made of the same dark, heavy wood. While the walls were pale yellow, the room had a dark, romantic look, thanks to the deep red Oriental carpeting and the banquettes with upholstered cushions in the same shade. The dim lighting, the result of the opaque parchment colored shades on the lamps, added to the romantic ambience, as did the colorful bouquets of flowers on each table.

"The décor looks kind of like Early Brothel," Gordon commented after they had been seated and presented with a wine list. "But not necessarily in a bad way."

Mallory picked up the impressively thick wine list that their waiter had presented to them with pride. "Wow, this is heavy," she exclaimed. "I understand the wine cellar is stocked with fifteen thousand bottles. No wonder this thing is sixty-nine pages long!"

"The last thing I read that was that long was a Dostoevsky novel I was thinking of making into a movie," Gordon said.

"It even has its own table of contents," Mallory observed, leafing through the tome. She handed it to Gordon. "I think I'll leave this up to you."

"I have a better idea. Let's ask the sommelier to choose something."

After a deep discussion with an earnest young man who clearly knew his way around a wine cellar, they decided on a cabernet. The sommelier delivered it with the usual fanfare, showing both of them the label, uncorking the bottle, and pouring a sample for Gordon's approval before filling their wineglasses.

"Nice," Mallory commented after taking her first sip. "Asking the pro to choose for us was a terrific strategy."

"One of the most important things I learned as a director is the value of delegating," Gordon said. "Especially when decisions need to be made in an area I know nothing about."

"And here I would have pegged you as one of those people who can quote the best year for every wine imaginable," she teased.

"Not at all. My feelings about wine are similar to those about art: I don't know much about it, but I get pretty excited when I stumble upon something I like." Staring at her intently, he added, "I guess that's true in a lot of different areas."

Was that a compliment? Mallory thought, alarm bells going off in her head. Maybe I'm not as good at this flirting business as I thought.

"Speaking of wine," she said lightly, trying to move the conversation back to a more comfortable topic, "I'm hoping to learn something about it tomorrow. I'm scheduled to take a workshop at the Cooking School of Aspen. The participants prepare an entire five-course dinner, and then they're instructed in which wines to pair with each course. The best part is at the end, when the class gets to sit down and eat what they made."

"That sounds like fun," Gordon said. "Want some company?"

So much for safer territory! Mallory thought. "I— I don't know. Astrid made a reservation for me a few days in advance, so I'm not sure if there's any room."

"I'll give them a call first thing tomorrow," Gordon insisted. "I bet they can fit in one more person."

"Great," she said simply after they picked a place to meet right before the class was scheduled to start.

"It sounds as if you're really keeping busy while you're here," Gordon observed.

"I have to," Mallory replied with a shrug. "My job entails becoming an expert on a place in a very short time. That means squeezing in as many activities as I can."

"I hope you appreciate what a great job you have!" he said heartily.

"I do." She swirled the wine in her glass, watching its movement and admiring its deep red color. "But this time is different. I actually feel bad having such a nice time after what happened." Sighing, she added, "I'm still reeling. Aspen seems like such an idyllic place that it's hard to believe that something as horrible as murder could actually take place here."

"It's not the first time, either." Gordon paused to sip his wine. "You're probably too young to remember this, but in 1976, an Olympic skier named Spider Sabich—his first name was actually Vladimir—was murdered by a former showgirl. She was French and spoke with a very strong accent. At the time the incident occurred, she had a mildly successful career as a singer and an actress. She'd also been married to a famous crooner, Andy Williams, which did wonders for her visibility."

"I remember all that," Mallory said. "Her name was Claudine Longet, wasn't it? I was barely a teenager back then, but the case was all over the news. It was a really big story."

Gordon nodded. "Huge. If I recall the details correctly, Spider had recently told Claudine that their relationship was cramping his lifestyle. The fact that she had a few kids—three, I believe, all of them still pretty young—no doubt had something to do with it. Anyway, the next thing you know, the two of them are in a room together right after he delivered the news and the gun she's holding goes off and kills him. At the trial, she claimed it was an accident. Her story was that Spider was showing her how the gun worked when it accidentally fired."

"Was she found guilty?" Mallory asked. "I remember the sensational headlines, but not the outcome."

"The jury found her guilty of criminally negligent homicide after not much deliberation. She could have gotten two years. Instead, she convinced the judge that her doing time would be bad for her kids. In the end, she spent something like thirty days in jail."

Gordon took another sip of his wine. "Legend has it that she had her cell at the Pitkin County courthouse here in Aspen redecorated. I've heard that she had the walls painted pink. But one thing I know *is* true is that before she showed up to serve her sentence, she was allowed time to take a month-long vacation in Mexico. With her defense attorney. Who happened to be married at the time. Of course, he didn't stay that way for long. He got divorced and married her."

"You'd think a defense attorney would know better than to marry a woman who'd already bumped off one of her lovers," Mallory observed.

Gordon chuckled. "I guess some people never learn."

"Still, this relationship must be going better, since I haven't seen her name mentioned in conjunction with any other murders." Mallory thought for a few seconds. "I seem to remember something about the Rolling Stones writing a song about the incident."

"That's right. It was called 'Claudine.' They actually recorded it, but they never released it because they were so afraid of lawsuits."

With a shudder, Mallory commented, "It all sounds like something you'd see in a movie."

"It *was* a movie," Gordon replied. "A TV movie. And it had an absolutely awful title: *Murder On the Slopes.*"

"How dreadful!" Mallory exclaimed.

"The title or the murder?"

She couldn't help laughing. "Both, actually. Still, even though it was a terrible thing to have happened, I can see that it made for a good film."

"Ah. So you're one of those people who has an eye for a story," Gordon observed. "Maybe I should hire you. To help me fulfill my fantasy of finding a good script, I mean."

"Don't tell me that's the best fantasy you can come up with." Mallory had barely gotten the words out before she set her nearly empty wineglass down firmly on the table. She suddenly had the frightening feeling that she was overdoing it in the flirting department—and that the wine was at least partly to blame.

"Actually, my fantasy isn't to find a good script. It's to find a *great* script." He poured more wine into Mallory's glass, then refilled his own. "In fact, that's why I came to Aspen in the first place."

Aha, she thought. So it wasn't the excellent cuisine at the Bermans' after all. "Let me guess—in addition to all the movie stars who supposedly live here there are also a few screenwriters."

"There may be. But it wasn't writers who brought me here." Now it was his turn to swirl the wine in his glass and stare at it as if he was enthralled. "I wasn't kidding last night when I joked about having an ulterior motive for being in Aspen. I was hoping to talk Carly into selling me the rights to her life story."

"For a movie?" Mallory asked, surprised.

"That's right," Gordon replied. "You've got to admit that she had a pretty fascinating life. Since you two grew up together, I'm sure you know that she started out on what looked like a clear trajectory. She was the star of her high school class, wasn't she? Pretty, popular, athletic, the whole kit and caboodle."

Miss Red Delicious, too, she thought generously. *Don't forget that.*

"But it all faded fast," he continued, "with not one but two disastrous marriages."

Mallory was instantly jerked out of the delightful haze the wine had lured her into. "I didn't realize they were that bad," she said. "She mentioned something about having been married twice before at dinner last night, but I wasn't even sure she was serious."

"She was serious, all right," Gordon assured her. "Her first husband abused her. Physically, I mean. It was actually a relief when he ended up in prison. It gave her an excuse to divorce him that even her parents couldn't argue with."

"I had no idea." A wave of sympathy swept over Mallory as she realized that Carly had not only met up with a tragic end, she had also withstood more than her share of misfortune while she was still alive. "What was the story with her second husband?"

"He died," Gordon said simply. "Once again, I'm pretty sure that having him out of the picture was actually a great relief for her."

"Oh, my," Mallory said breathlessly.

The dinner conversation was taking such a dramatic downward turn that Mallory was relieved when the waiter chose this moment to return for their order. An animated discussion of the pros and cons of the small plates on the menu versus the large plates was much more pleasant.

"Are you willing to order several small plates and share them with me?" Mallory asked Gordon. "I'm supposed to be evaluating the food for my article, so the more different entrees I get to try, the better."

"So you weren't kidding when you threatened to eat the food off my plate."

"I never joke about food."

"I'm certainly not one to stand in the way of someone doing their job," Gordon said seriously. "Order away. In fact, I'll leave the whole thing up to you."

"Delegating again, huh?" she said with a grin.

"You got it."

Mallory took a few moments to study the menu, earnestly considering each item and trying to come up with a combination that would give her the best idea of the chef's talents. But as she sat in silence, she wasn't only weighing the pros and cons of the farm green salad with homemade goat cheese versus the Tuscan-style tomato soup.

Spending time with Gordon was giving her the chance to discover how clever he was. How intelligent. And how appealing he looked when he spoke about something he cared about and his eyes lit up. In fact, she had already reversed her initial impression of him as someone she didn't find physically attractive.

After she ordered four small plates for them to share, she turned to her dinner companion and said, "My friends back in Westchester are going to be very impressed when they find out I had dinner with a real live Hollywood director."

His response was a grimace. "Frankly, I don't think they'll be all that impressed, since as you probably know I haven't made a picture in nearly two decades." With a wry smile, he added, "If you hadn't known that already, Brett certainly made a point of pointing it out to you."

"Given everything I've ever heard about Hollywood, it's hardly surprising," Mallory said quickly, doing her best to be diplomatic. "From what I understand, talent means nothing. Instead, it's all about money."

"Some people might argue that talent and making money go hand in hand," he commented lightly. "Or that the ability to make money is a talent in itself."

"At any rate, I'm sure Carly's life story would make a wonderful movie," Mallory went on. "Especially the part about traveling all over the world to create a potion that people have been seeking for... well, probably forever."

"You're right. It would have made a terrific film," Gordon said somberly. "In fact, I was convinced that her story would provide me with the opportunity to make my comeback."

"But you're talking about it in the past tense," Mallory protested. "You can still make a movie about her, even though this horrible thing has happened."

He shook his head. "I'm afraid not. It's extremely unlikely, now that she's gone. Brett was never crazy about the idea. Now that she's gone, there's no way he'll ever let me get my hands on the rights."

"Why not? Isn't he proud of everything his wife accomplished?"

Gordon just smiled. "Let's just say that while I like Brett personally, he puts a lot of effort into convincing people he's the way he wants them to see him. That doesn't necessarily mean it's the way he really is."

Interesting, Mallory thought. Exactly Harriet's take on the man.

Of course, the word she had used—*phony*—wasn't quite as kind.

"But we didn't come here to this lovely restaurant to talk about movies that will never get made," Gordon said jovially. "We came to get to know each other better. And to sample some of this renowned chef's cuisine. I suppose we could classify it as 'nouvelle.' Or perhaps we should call it 'nouv-elk'...?"

Even though he made a face at his own bad pun, Mallory laughed. "I like that turn of phrase," she said. "Do you mind if I use it in my article?"

"Not at all. But I bet you anything your editor takes it right out."

"I'm going to take the risk." As she pulled out her notepad to jot it down, she added, "Promise that if I borrow your idea you won't think I'm doing something unethical?"

"I'm from Hollywood, where doing unethical things is as commonplace as plastic surgery," he said seriously. "Or guzzling Rejuva-Juice in the hopes that it will take off enough years to land a coveted role."

When they'd finished their meal and their waiter brought the dessert menu, Mallory couldn't resist poring over it.

"Fortunately, I'm not in the movie business," she told Gordon, "so I don't have to worry about looking young enough *or* thin enough."

But as soon as she glanced at it, she gasped.

"Are the desserts that outstanding?" Gordon asked, looking amused.

"It's more like I've never encountered an eighteen-dollar dessert before."

"Are you joking?" Gordon picked up the other menu and studied it. "Wow! And here I thought L.A. was out of control!"

"Fortunately, this entire meal is on the magazine," Mallory replied. "Which means we can't say no to the El Rey Chocolate Tasting." Reading aloud, she said, "'Venezuelan artisan chocolates that include a milk chocolate almond tartlet with Earl Grey gelato, chocolate cake with peppermint crème, orange pudding cake, and a malted chocolate milkshake' . . . How can one person possibly eat all those desserts?"

"Trust me. You're going to need a magnifying glass to find them."

When the waiter came by, she ordered one chocolate tasting and two forks.

"Microscopic or not, I'm counting on you to help me out with this," she told Gordon.

"How could I live with myself if I refused to come to the aid of a damsel in distress?" he replied.

Mallory laughed. "Or at least one who was at a terrible risk of not being able to fit in her clothes anymore."

When dessert arrived, Mallory saw he was right.

"No wonder no one in Aspen is overweight," she joked, peering at the narrow rectangular plate dotted with three dollop-size blobs of chocolate and a chocolate milkshake in a shot glass.

"Are you sure you still want me to split that with you?" Gordon teased.

"A deal is a deal."

As he picked up his fork, he commented, "I hope you're not just being nice because you're planning on having your way with me later. It just so happens that chocolate is my weakness. One of them, anyway."

Once again, Mallory could feel her cheeks burning. "No! I—I wouldn't . . . I mean—"

He smiled. "You're not very good at this, are you?"

"It depends on what you mean," she replied, still flustered. "Do you mean eating in restaurants, handling alcohol, dating—"

"That last one," he said earnestly, gesturing with his fork.

By this point, her cheeks were burning. She would have bet the entire dessert that her face was as red as the wine in their glasses.

"I guess I owe you an explanation," she said. "I recently lost my husband—"

"I was only joking," he insisted. "And seriously, Mallory, you don't owe me anything. The last thing I want to do is embarrass you." He reached over and took her hand. "It sounds as if you just need a little practice."

"You're right," she admitted.

"In that case," Gordon said, digging into the chocolate cake, "you can consider me a willing rehearsal partner."

Walking on air was such a tired old expression, yet as Mallory stood outside the Hotel Jerome, watching Gordon walk away, she had to admit that it perfectly described the way she felt.

She wanted to savor the moment, to luxuriate in the feeling of having just experienced such a marvelous evening. In fact, as she turned and floated into the hotel lobby, it was all she could do to keep from breaking into "I Could Have Danced All Night."

She was picturing herself sliding between the silky sheets and reliving every moment of the evening when the concierge interrupted her reverie.

"Ms. Marlowe?" he asked as she passed the front desk. "There's someone here to see you. He's waiting in the lobby."

She stopped in her tracks. "Someone to see *me?*" she asked, frowning.

"He specifically said Mallory Marlowe." Pointing toward the sitting area just beyond where they stood, he added, "He's right over there."

Mallory was still convinced that the concierge had to be mistaken. That is, until she stepped onto the thick Oriental carpet in front of the black marble fireplace and spotted the silhouette of a man. She recognized him immediately, even though he was sitting in one of the upholstered chairs with his back to her.

"*Trevor?*" she cried in astonishment, for a moment wondering if she was hallucinating or if her boss, the managing editor of *The Good Life,* had really materialized here in Aspen. "What are *you* doing here?"

He jumped to his feet and whirled around. "Good God, Mallory. I've come to see what's going on with the story I assigned you, now that Carly Berman has been murdered! I also wanted to make sure you're all right!"

Trevor ran the fingers of one hand through his dark, silver-flecked hair. While he always wore it on the long side, at the moment it was so disheveled that it perfectly matched his wrinkled dark brown pants. He also wore a puffy blue coat that struck Mallory as the kind of jacket Manhattanites assumed people wore in ski towns like Aspen. The bags under his hazel eyes were almost as puffy. In short, he looked like someone who had just spent too many hours on a cramped plane, suffered from jet lag, and badly needed to down a few quarts of water before serious dehydration set in.

"But . . . but there was no reason to come all this way!" she cried. "I told you on the phone that everything was fine. I'm perfectly all right!"

"But you didn't *sound* all right." Trevor sighed deeply. Holding out both hands helplessly, he said, "Look, Mallory. I was worried. Can I help that? It's not that I don't think you can take care of yourself. Of course I do! Otherwise, I never would have hired you. Not for a job that requires infinite flexibility and plenty of common sense and the ability to think on one's feet . . ."

He stopped long enough to take a deep breath. "For heaven's sake, since I came all this way, aren't you at least going to invite me to join you for a drink so we can talk about what's been going on out here?"

Mallory's indignation over her boss's surprise appearance had already melted. "Trevor, I appreciate your concern," she said, reaching over and lightly touching his shoulder. "But right now I happen to be exhausted. As you can imagine, I had a very long day. One that began with some pretty devastating news."

She decided not to mention that the day in question also happened to have ended with a dinner date that left her feeling like a sixteen-year-old girl, one whose hormones were just beginning to demonstrate the kinds of tricks they were capable of playing.

"But I thought you'd find it helpful to have some-one to talk to," he protested.

"Absolutely," she agreed. "But right now, the only thing I want to do is get some rest." Peering at him more closely, she gently added, "You look as if you could use some rest, too. But drink a lot of water be-fore you get into bed. It's one of the best ways of combating jet lag. And the word around here is that it's a good idea to avoid alcohol until your body's had a chance to get used to the altitude."

"All good advice." Trevor's shoulders slumped. "It *is* one A.M. my time, after all."

"Why don't we meet for breakfast tomorrow morning after we've both had a good night's sleep?" Mallory suggested.

"Fine," he replied. "How about right here in the hotel? I managed to get a room."

Mallory nodded. "Just tell me when and where."

She was willing to agree to anything, since at the moment, tomorrow seemed a long way off. Besides, now that she'd recovered from her astonishment over finding her boss in the lobby of her hotel, she was ea-ger to get back to her original plan: drifting upstairs to her room to enjoy what she expected would be a night filled with sweet dreams.

Chapter 11

"Travelers never think that *they* are the foreigners."
—Mason Cooley

Trevor looked considerably better over breakfast.
In fact, as Mallory appraised the man sitting opposite her at the hotel's restaurant, she realized that even though she'd sat in a room with him three or four times since he'd hired her, she'd never really taken a good look at him before. That is, one in which she viewed him as a man, rather than merely her boss.

Yet in the dawn's early light—or at least seven o'clock, since they were both enjoying the ease of rising early thanks to still being on East Coast time—she noticed that he was actually quite handsome.

Of course, she'd noticed before that he had a nice face with a thin-lipped mouth that easily broke into a slightly lopsided smile, a straight, unobtrusive nose, and hazel eyes edged by those crinkled laugh lines she found so attractive. But she'd never quite responded to his good looks this way before.

She was as surprised by how good he looked to her as she was by her strong reaction to him.

Get a grip, girlfriend, she scolded herself. Just because you're in the Wild West doesn't mean you have to turn into a wild woman.

Mallory figured her sudden compulsion to assess every member of the male gender in terms of his physical attributes was merely a spillover effect from having been wined and dined by Gordon the night before—even if she had technically been the one doing both the wining and the dining. Either that or it was merely the fact that the two of them were huddled together over coffee in a cozy hotel dining room instead of discussing the magazine's circulation and demographics in a sterile, impersonal office setting.

"So what is it about you," Trevor drawled, wrapping his fingers around his coffee mug, "that leads to someone being murdered practically every time you travel to a new destination?"

Mallory opened her mouth to protest even before she'd decided whether to be amused or offended. But she quickly snapped it shut. Even she had to admit that he had a point.

Still, this was no joking matter. Carly Berman's murder had hit her hard. Not only did the two of them share a history. She had also spent the evening before Carly was killed in her company.

"You really don't have to worry about me, Trevor," she insisted. "I know I've had a few bad experiences since I started this job. But that doesn't mean I can't handle it."

"I know you can handle it, Mallory." Trevor pushed his coffee mug away, folded his hands on the table, and gazed at her intently. "But I have a magazine to put out. If your story about Aspen falls apart, I don't have a lot of time to find a way to fill those pages."

"I'll just have to shift gears," Mallory said thoughtfully. "Instead of focusing on what attracts entrepreneurs like Carly to Aspen, I'll stick to your original concept: activities for nonskiers."

"Sounds like a plan." His voice softening, he added, "Actually, there's another reason why I came. I thought you might need someone to talk to. About how the murder of an old friend of yours is affecting you, I mean."

"I feel terrible about it, Trevor," she told him sincerely. "True, I hadn't seen Carly in decades. And we were never close. We were never more than acquaintances, in fact, if you could even call it that. We just happened to know each other because we were in the same grade at school."

She picked up a packet of sugar and began to fiddle with it. "But the idea that someone you know can just disappear like that, someone you've just spoken to and laughed with—even if it's just because you had the same gym teacher thirty years ago . . . Well, it brought up all kinds of feelings that remind me of how I felt—how I still feel, in fact—about losing my husband."

"And how is that?" Trevor asked, his tone gentle.

"As if going through life is like living in an earthquake zone," she replied, methodically folding over each corner of the sugar packet. "At any moment, the ground beneath you can just fall away, swallowing up things you just assumed would be there forever. But I finally realized that if you're left behind to deal with the rubble, you owe it to those who are gone to pick up the pieces and set things right again."

She paused, then thoughtfully added, "You owe it to yourself, too, since the whole point of life is to keep living."

"I know exactly what you mean," Trevor said softly. "I felt the same way when I got divorced. The thing about the earthquakes, I mean."

Mallory hesitated for a few seconds before saying, "You've never told me anything about your divorce."

With a sad smile, "I've never had a chance. Unfortunately, it's taken something this extreme for the two of us to sit down together and have a real conversation."

"I'd like to listen," she said softly, "if you'd like to tell me."

Staring into the depths of his coffee mug, Trevor said, "Admitting that our marriage wasn't working, and that it hadn't been for some time, was one of the most difficult things I'd ever done. Making the decision to end it was at least as difficult. And even though losing a connection by getting divorced is different from losing a spouse through death, it was still incredibly painful.

"I thought I had it all under control," he continued. "For the first couple of months, I acted as if nothing in my life had changed. I got up, went to work, spent a couple of hours at the gym, kept myself busy with errands on weekends...I was the picture of efficiency. No one at work could believe how well I was handling things.

"But then I crashed. I went into a deep depression. Nothing seemed right. I walked around like a zombie. I even felt uncomfortable living in my own body." He spoke as if he was in a daze, his voice so soft Mallory could barely hear him. "I slept too much. Hardly ate anything. Didn't exercise at all. It was as if all the normal human feelings, even the basic ones like hunger, were beyond me. It was at that point that somebody at work suggested that it might not be a bad idea for me to get some help."

Trevor sighed. "It was the best advice I ever got in my life. I found myself a shrink and started talking about everything. My marriage, its failure...I even dredged up stuff from a long, long time ago. After a few months, I started to feel like my old self again. I realized that my life wasn't over; it had just started a new phase. And that deep down I had the strength to adjust to my new circumstances. I began to look forward to what was ahead instead of simply mourning what I'd lost."

He stopped abruptly, glancing up at her shyly. "End of sob story," he said with forced joviality. "I'll shut up now."

They were both silent for a long time, each of them acting as if the simple act of sipping coffee was such an intense experience that it required all their concentration.

"I really appreciate your being so open with me," Mallory finally said. "And if for some reason you ever regret it, I'm willing to pretend this conversation never happened."

Trevor didn't respond, so she had no way of knowing if he was already sorry. But she knew that from her own perspective, she had no remorse over having been honest with him.

"So what happens now?" she asked lightly. "I mean, are you planning to stay in Aspen or go back to New York . . . ?"

"I think I'll stay for another day or two," he replied, without looking at her. "Maybe I didn't come to Aspen under the best of circumstances. But now that I'm here, I'm thinking it wouldn't be such a bad idea for me to spend a couple of days away from the office. It's been too long since I've taken a trip of my own. I could probably benefit from a break."

"Are you sure you're not just checking up on me?" Mallory teased. "Making sure I'm doing my job?"

"Maybe I am," he replied. Without looking at her directly, he added, "Or maybe I just want to make sure nothing bad happens to you."

Given how worried Trevor seemed to be, Mallory decided not to mention that she was doing more here in Aspen than writing a magazine article. When he announced after breakfast that he was going to take a walk around town to get his bearings, leaving

Mallory to get some work done, she decided it was a good time to pay Sylvie a visit.

She had thought the HoliHealth executive was worth looking at from the beginning. But the fact that it was Sylvie, and not Mallory, that Harriet had chosen to rendezvous with immediately after the police had released her had catapulted Sylvie to a top spot on Mallory's list of suspects.

She rifled through her suitcase until she found a silk scarf she'd tossed in at the last minute. It was one she'd never been all that attached to anyway, so she figured that if she lost it while she was traveling, leaving it behind in a restaurant or failing to notice that it had slipped off her shoulders, she wouldn't care.

Clutching it in her hand, she went back down to the lobby. She stood half hidden by a large potted plant, scoping out the area until she spotted the youngest, most gullible-looking bellman around. The sandy blond stubble that covered his head and his round rosy cheeks made him look as if not long before, he'd been driving a tractor instead of pushing a luggage cart.

"Excuse me," she said after making a beeline in his direction, "I'm Mallory Marlowe. I'm a guest at the hotel. A friend of mine left this in my car last night. She's staying here, too, but I don't know her room number. Do you think you could deliver it to her?"

His eyes traveled nervously between Mallory and the scarf she was waving in front of him. "I'm on luggage duty today. We've got a big crowd coming in.

But you could call the front desk and I'm sure they'd put you through to her room."

Mallory did her best to look like a damsel in distress. "I would, but I know for a fact that she's not in her room right now. She's, uh, out somewhere having breakfast."

"In that case, you could still call her room and leave her a message—"

"Please," she interrupted, wondering when farm boys had gotten so feisty, "I'm on my way out to an important meeting and I really don't have much time. Do you think you could just find out what room she's in and drop this off?"

When he still hesitated, she decided to try the New York way of doing things. She reached into her wallet and pulled out a ten-dollar bill.

"Thank you so much," she said, shoving it at him as if it was clear she wasn't about to take no for an answer. "I really appreciate your doing this."

"I'll get on it right away," he assured her, his eyes widening and his rosy cheeks growing even rosier as he stared at the bill in his hand.

Glad to know ten bucks still buys *something* in this town, Mallory thought wryly as she told him Sylvie's name, then watched him walk away.

After he got Sylvie's room number from the clerk at the front desk, he headed toward the pair of elevators that served the front section of the hotel. Mallory was relieved that Sylvie's room was in the original building. It was only three stories high, which would make it easier to track him.

As soon as the elevator doors had closed, she

rushed toward the fire stairs and raced up them. When she reached the second floor, she opened the door and peered down the hallway. No one was there, and there was no pinging sound to tell her that the elevator was stopping there. She ducked back into the stairwell and emerged on the third floor, where she stuck her head out the door even more carefully than before. Sure enough, she could see the bellman standing in the hallway a few doors down.

"I'm really sorry about the mistake," he was saying to whoever was standing opposite him as he tucked the scarf into his pocket. "She told me this belonged to you, but I guess she was confused."

Confused . . . like a fox, Mallory thought.

She retreated back into the stairwell one more time, closing the fire door and waiting until she heard the pings that told her the elevator was whisking her emissary away. Once she knew she was safe, she ventured out again, checked to make sure the coast was clear, and then headed straight for the same door at which she'd seen him standing.

She rapped on the door loudly, doing her best to sound authoritative.

"Goodness, what is it *now*?" a female voice muttered from inside room 312.

When the woman flung open the door, she looked surprised, as if she'd just assumed she'd find the same bellman standing there. Mallory took advantage of having caught her off guard by sticking her foot in the doorway just far enough that Sylvie couldn't close it and leave her out in the hallway.

"Do I know you?" Sylvie asked curtly. Almost

immediately, her expression softened. "I do, don't I? You and I spoke at the Bermans' house yesterday morning."

"That's right." Mallory shook her head. "Isn't it the saddest thing? I've been so upset ever since I heard the news . . ." Rubbing her forehead, she added, "Do you think I could sit down? I keep getting light-headed. I don't know if it's the altitude or just being so freaked out about poor Carly . . ."

The threat of having the limp body of someone who had just fainted cluttering up her doorway was clearly too much for the woman. Sylvie quickly moved aside. "Of course. Come in. Can I get you anything? A glass of water?"

"Water would be great."

Mallory plopped into the nearest chair while Sylvie disappeared into the bathroom. As she listened to the water running, she glanced around, surprised by what she saw.

A large open suitcase sat on one end of the king-sized bed, piled high with neatly folded clothes. A large leather tote bag, its mouth gaping open, sat on the floor nearby. From where Mallory sat, she could see that stuffed into it was a laptop computer and a stack of manila file folders.

"Thanks," she said when Sylvie came out of the bathroom with a glass of water, wearing a concerned expression.

After taking a few gulps and doing her best to look perkier, Mallory observed, "I see you're on the way out. I don't mean to keep you."

"That's okay. My flight isn't until two o'clock. I

wanted to leave earlier, but when I called to change my flight, this was the first one I could get."

Aha, Mallory thought. So Sylvie's decided to get out of Dodge.

Still, it was possible that the only reason she was suddenly in such a hurry to get out was that her business here in Aspen was done. With no Carly to negotiate with, what would be the point of staying?

The point, she quickly realized, could be trying to work out a deal with the husband of the deceased. Especially since a good businesswoman would know that negotiating with someone who was under great stress could well yield an even better deal than usual.

Of course, it was possible that Brett Berman simply refused to deal with her right now. Whatever the explanation for Sylvie's hurried departure may have been, Mallory intended to do her best to find out precisely what it was.

"I understand you and Carly had a business relationship," she said, "which means you two weren't friends, the way she and I were." Once again, she was nearly certain that her cavalier use of the word *friends* was making her nose grow longer. "The two of you *were* just business associates, weren't you?"

"Not yet," Sylvie replied, her voice tinged with bitterness. "What I mean is, that's what I was hoping for. But I wasn't able to make that happen before she got—before all this happened."

From her tone, it sounded as if she was annoyed that Carly's murder had gotten in the way of her business plan.

"I've been working on this deal for nearly two

years," Sylvie went on resentfully. "And I have nothing to show for it. Nothing! I can just imagine the laugh they're having back at headquarters."

"Even these days, it must be tough, being a woman executive," Mallory commented, trying to sound sympathetic.

"Hah!" Sylvie snapped. "Try being an African-American woman in a company full of white men! It's the pits."

"And you'd think a company that specializes in health-related products would be a bit more progressive," Mallory added, trying to fuel the fire that was obviously lurking not far below the surface, even though it was covered up by a button-down shirt and a tailored jacket.

If Sylvie wondered how Mallory came to know so much about her business, she didn't show it. Like most people, she probably just assumed that everyone she came across traveled in the same sphere she did and that they all shared the same outlook, not to mention similar experiences.

"You would think that," Sylvie said, "except for the fact that the company I work for is run by the founder's two grandsons. Even though it's the twenty-first century, somehow they manage to maintain the same world view that their granddaddy probably held."

"I didn't realize HoliHealth was that old," Mallory said.

Sylvie nodded. "The company started back in the early 1950s, right after World War Two. It was called Henderson Health and Healing back then. The old guy, Cliff Henderson, was a real health food nut. A big follower of exercise gurus like Jack LaLanne and advocates of vitamin therapy like Adelle Davis. He was from Iowa, but he was attracted to California because he was convinced it was going to become the health food capital of the world."

"Good move," Mallory observed.

"Definitely," Sylvie agreed. "He started selling vitamins to health food stores—at least the few that were already in business back in those days. Cliff Henderson just muddled along for a decade or so. But then the sixties came along, and all of a sudden HH and H took off. In addition to vitamins, the company started selling protein powder, exercise equipment, books—you name it. By the 1970s, Cliff Henderson's son, Cliff Junior, was old enough to come into the business. The third generation took over in the late eighties. They hired some marketing firm to update the company. Flax and Bulgar, the grandsons, are also the ones who came up with the new name, HoliHealth."

"Flax and Bulgar?" Mallory repeated. "You're kidding!"

"Nope. I'm afraid not."

"I guess it's better than naming your kids Bran and Wheat Germ," Mallory mused. "But it sounds as if despite their names, Flax and Bulgar aren't exactly the most open-minded people in the world," she prompted.

Sylvie snorted. "Hardly. The two of them must be the most conservative guys in the entire state. They actually wear suits and ties and wingtip shoes to work every day." Glancing down at her own conservative outfit, she added, "That's the only reason I dress like this. I have to, since it's part of our corporate culture.

"And speaking of corporate culture, Flax and Bulgar treat their products as if they were widgets," she went on, her tone growing even more bitter. "I mean, it doesn't matter that they're selling health and vitality. For them, it's all about the bottom line. They could be selling socks or cars or ... or machine guns. I swear that the only reason they hired me is because they thought having an African-American woman in a high-powered position would make them look good."

With a tired sigh, Sylvie added, "I tell you, working with these guys day in and day out is a real strain. I feel as if I'm constantly beating my head against a wall, trying to get them to accept my ideas."

"Then why not just move on?" Mallory asked, sincerely curious about a woman like Sylvie, one who was clearly quite capable, would stay in a job that caused her so much resentment.

"Because I'm not a quitter." Sylvie stood up straighter, her dark brown eyes narrowing. "Four years at Princeton and another two at Harvard getting my MBA taught me to work hard and to face any challenge I meet head-on."

Even if all that head-banging leads to a chronic headache? Mallory wondered.

"I really believed this deal was going to make the difference," Sylvie continued, sounding as if she was talking more to herself than to Mallory. "I thought that this time, I'd show them."

"Then you must be terribly disappointed that it's not likely to go through after all. Now that Carly's gone, I imagine that things will be in a state of chaos for some time."

Sylvie looked startled by Mallory's observation. She opened her mouth to speak, then quickly snapped it shut. "That's exactly right," she said simply.

Before Mallory had a chance to explore Sylvie's feelings about the possible acquisition of Rejuva-Juice any further, their conversation was interrupted by the sound of knuckles rapping loudly on the door.

"What now?" Sylvie muttered.

As soon as Sylvie opened the door and Mallory spotted the two men standing in the hallway, she knew the answer to that question.

"Ms. Snowdon? I'm Detective Lieutenant Derbas. Homicide."

"Is something wrong?" Sylvie asked, her voice thick.

"We'd like to ask you a few questions." The detective glanced around the hotel room, his eyes lighting on the suitcase on the bed. "In fact, if you're thinking of leaving town, you'd better think again. I'm afraid we'll need you to stick around until we get this whole thing sorted out."

Chapter 12

"To travel is to discover that everyone is wrong
about other countries."
—Aldous Huxley

So I'm not the only one who thinks Sylvie had reason to kill Carly, Mallory thought with satisfaction after the cops hustled her out of Sylvie's
hotel room.

But rather than hurrying away, she positioned herself outside the door, wishing she had somehow been
blessed with the ears of an Irish wolfhound.

The more she thought about it, the more plausible
it seemed that Sylvie was the murderer. Sylvie could
easily have flown into a rage if Carly had finally announced she was never going to agree to sell the
Rejuva-Juice empire to HoliHealth. Not only was
it a deal Sylvie'd been working on for two years;
pulling off the acquisition of Carly's company
would have also been the coup Sylvie needed to show
Flax and Bulgar the stuff she was made of.

Even though Mallory was dying to find out what was going on in Sylvie's hotel room, she quickly ascertained that the doors at the Jerome were thick enough to make that impossible. Besides, when she glanced at her watch, she remembered there was someplace she was supposed to be. She'd been so distracted by Trevor's arrival and her determination to squeeze her own personal investigation of Carly's murder into her work schedule that she'd nearly forgotten she had a late morning appointment for a massage at the St. Regis Hotel.

She raced back to her room to grab her jacket. Lying on the bed was the scarf she'd used to find out which room was Sylvie's. Tucked underneath was a handwritten note: "Sorry. Ms. Snowdon said this wasn't hers."

One of the nice things about Aspen, Mallory thought as she turned onto Dean Street and the hotel came into view, was that everything was packed into just a few compact blocks. That meant that most of the sights, shops, and restaurants were within walking distance, a real plus for nonskiers who might not want to get into a car in order to enjoy the city. And visitors who wanted to venture farther away, especially to the area's other three ski mountains, could avail themselves of the free shuttle buses the town had thoughtfully provided. On Mallory's first day in town, Astrid had pointed out the red brick bus station in the center of town, the Rubey Park Transit Center, overlooking the town's public ice skating rink. Not only did it provide comfortable and convenient transportation, it even had free wi-fi Internet access.

She was making mental notes about Aspen's convenient layout, wondering if it was worth mentioning in her article, when a flash of silver caught her eye. She instinctively turned her head in time to see a Rolls-Royce that looked exactly like the Bermans' whizzing by.

Brett?

Mallory's heartbeat immediately accelerated to a speed almost as fast as that of the high-priced car zooming off. Without hesitation, she picked up her pace and half walked, half jogged in the same direction as the car.

It made a right turn, and she did the same. Even though she couldn't come close to keeping up, she glued her eyes to it. When the vehicle made another right turn, she noted exactly where it did so she could continue her chase.

But when she turned onto that street, there was no sign of it.

Not quite ready to give up, she walked another block. She reached the next intersection and glanced to the right, then the left.

"Yes!" she cried aloud when she spotted the silver Rolls parked in front of a row of shops.

Mallory adopted a pace that she thought of as ambling in the hopes that her breathing would return to normal. She also patted her hair in place, hoping she didn't look as if she'd just run the four-hundred-meter.

When she reached the first shop in the strip, she

stopped and peered into it through the display window.

No one was inside, aside from two young women behind the counter who obviously worked there. Still, she concluded that the boutique wasn't a likely destination for Brett, since it sold women's shoes.

Frowning, she scanned the row of stores in front of her, deciding to use common sense to figure out where he'd gone.

She immediately zeroed in on a likely candidate: a shop devoted exclusively to men's clothing made by a well-known Italian designer.

Maintaining her casual gait, Mallory strolled over to the shop and glanced into the window. Sure enough: Inside, beyond the well-tailored wool jackets featured in the display, she spotted a familiar-looking head of thick silver hair, each strand neatly combed and gelled into place.

Even from where she stood, she could see how earnestly Brett was studying the beige suit the impeccably dressed salesman held out for his approval.

Here goes, Mallory thought, pulling open the door and stepping inside.

"Definitely quality stuff," Brett was saying to the salesman. "The question is, is it really *me*?"

"Brett?" Mallory asked, doing her best to sound surprised.

He jerked his head up abruptly. "Mallory!"

A shocked look crossed his face. But the tension in his expression quickly dissipated. In place of the frown was an easy, relaxed smile that revealed his gleaming white teeth. To Mallory, it looked like a smile he'd spent hours practicing in the mirror.

"What brings you here?" he asked, sounding as warm and welcoming if he were receiving her at his home.

"I thought I'd try to find a souvenir for my teenage son," she answered. She hoped he wouldn't notice how improbable her explanation was. An Aspen T-shirt, maybe. But a silk tie from an Italian designer who had shops all around the world?

"They have some great stuff," Brett said, nodding approvingly.

The tension suddenly came back into his face, as if he'd just remembered his situation. "I, uh, realized I had to come into town because I didn't have anything appropriate to wear. To the funeral, I mean. And, well, there's bound to be a lot of press buzzing around over the next few days. I figured looking good is a show of respect for Carly."

"Of course." Mallory did her best to sound sympathetic, even though she was cynically thinking, What better time to worry about one's appearance than when one's spouse has just been murdered?

Brett seemed to have read her mind. "It's the last thing I want to be thinking about right now, as you can imagine—"

"Sometimes doing something mindless can be the best distraction." Realizing she might be judging him too quickly, she added, "I know what you must be going through, Brett. I lost my husband not long ago."

"Perhaps I should leave you two alone," the salesman said in a thick Italian accent, his dark brown eyes clouding over. "I can see this is a terrible time for you both."

The two of them were silent as he quickly walked into the back room.

"It was a good idea to close Tavaci Springs for a while," she commented once they were alone. "It's probably a relief that you don't have to think about the business for a while."

"I can't let things go for too long," Brett replied sharply.

A look of surprise crossed his face, as if he hadn't expected to sound so prickly. In a gentler tone, he added, "What I mean is, a lot of people depend on us. Our employees, mainly, but our customers, too. It wouldn't be right to let them down."

"Still, it's going to be difficult," Mallory noted. "Without Carly at your side, I mean."

Nodding, Brett said, "It will be quite a challenge to run the business on a day-to-day basis. Carly always took care of most of that. I tried to get more involved, but it was her baby. She was the one who made most of the decisions—not that I blame her."

He stopped abruptly. "Besides," he added with a casual shrug, "I'm hoping that throwing myself into my work will help me get over my grief."

"It sounds as if you've decided to run the company yourself," Mallory commented.

"Why wouldn't I?" Brett asked. "After all, I've been involved in it right from the get-go."

"It's just that I've been hearing...rumors."

"What kind of rumors?"

Mallory took a deep breath. "I understand that Sylvie Snowdon is interested in buying the company."

"You're right about that," Brett said with a scowl. "That obnoxious woman's been working on Carly for months, trying to get her to sell. In fact, she started getting pretty aggressive about it in the past weeks."

"Really?" Mallory didn't try to hide her surprise. "But she seems so even-tempered. So…professional."

Brett snorted. "Giving that impression is part of her job. But trust me: beneath that cool, calm, and collected surface lurks a barracuda. And she was determined to acquire Rejuva-Juice. I can't tell you how many times she flew to Aspen to try to talk Carly into selling. And the longer she worked on her, the more persistent she got. Ever hear of the Concorde fallacy?"

"I don't think I have."

"Remember that airplane, the Concorde? It went twice the speed of sound, meaning it could fly from New York to Europe in under four hours. But tickets cost a fortune, as much as ten thousand bucks." Snickering, he added, "That's a lot even for me.

"But the thing was that the French and British governments kept pouring tons of money into it even after it became clear it didn't make sense economically," he continued. "The reason was that they'd put so much cash into it already that they couldn't bring themselves to walk away from their investment."

With a shrug, he added, "That's how I think it was with Sylvie. She kept banging her head against the wall, trying to get Carly to sell but not making any progress. And the harder she pushed, the more desperate she became."

Desperate enough to fly into a rage and kill her? Mallory wondered.

It was true that Sylvie appeared to be a woman of great self-control. But she had to agree with Brett that someone's outer appearance didn't mean a thing. Besides, even the police considered her a suspect.

Which meant Mallory had no choice but to look past the well-tailored suits and the icy façade and keep Sylvie Snowdon high on her list of suspects as well.

Mallory was still ruminating about her brief interaction with Brett Berman as she hurried off to her spa appointment.

He certainly sounds as if he has no intention of selling the company, she thought. That's bad news for Sylvie, of course. But it's good news for Harriet, who won't have to worry about keeping her job. That is, assuming he'll keep her on. Still, even he must realize what an asset she is.

When she turned a corner and caught sight of the St. Regis Hotel, Mallory saw that it looked like a castle. The sprawling red brick building was huge by Aspen standards. Not only did it stand four stories high; its edges flanked two long streets almost as far as the eye could see. At the point at which the two sides of the building met was a corner entrance so regal it looked as if should have a moat in front to separate it from the place where the commonfolk lived.

The lobby was just as grand. While it was furnished in the same style as so much of Aspen—lots of wood, fireplaces, and a few rustic touches such as walls made entirely of rough-hewn stones—the floors were covered in thick Oriental carpets. Mallory could only imagine what a couple of ski poles gone awry could do to those.

The Remède Spa was located downstairs. Mallory knew from her research that it was on as tremendous a scale as the rest of the hotel, with fifteen treatment rooms. In addition to steam rooms, saunas, and an oxygen lounge, it also had something called vapor caves. To her, that sounded like a place where Victorian ladies who had misbehaved would have been sent.

"You're the writer, aren't you?" the woman working in the reception area asked when she gave her name.

"That's right," Mallory replied.

"We have a gift bag for you with some of the products we use here," the clerk said. "I'll hold it until you're ready to leave."

Such a tough job, Mallory thought.

"And you still have a bit of time before your hematite and basalt stone massage," the woman added. "In the meantime, you're welcome to help yourself to champagne and truffles in the relaxation room."

A *really* tough job.

"You can also use any of the facilities. I suggest you check out the confluence room."

More punishment for naughty Victorians? Mallory thought. "What's that?"

"It's an area made of natural stone, with several waterfalls that were inspired by Colorado's mineral springs. It also has a hot whirlpool tub and a cold plunge pool. It's pretty amazing."

While Mallory didn't know what to expect, she had to agree that this part of the spa really was nothing short of amazing. The most spectacular part was the pool set amidst a grotto, with three waterfalls cascading down the stone walls. After luxuriating in the swirling waters for a few minutes, Mallory moved on to the section just beyond, which consisted of a huge round tub surrounded by more stone. Most of it was a hot tub, but a small round section, separated by a below-the-surface wall, was the cold plunge pool. As far as she was concerned, immersing her entire body in icy water was not something she needed to do. Certainly not in the name of research.

She was half sitting, half lying in the hot tub with her eyes closed, feeling the tension in her muscles start to drain away, when she heard a rustling sound that meant someone else had come in. She opened her eyes and found Astrid Norland standing at the edge of the plunge pool.

"Hello, Mallory," Astrid said in her lilting voice. "I thought you might like some company. Do you mind if I join you?"

"Not at all," Mallory replied, hiding her surprise.

"Great." As Astrid slid off her fluffy white terrycloth robe, Mallory did her best not to stare. But it was difficult not to, since the woman was not only completely naked; she had the kind of body that was usually associated with Victoria's Secret models. In fact, as she stood perched at the edge of the hot tub, Astrid looked like a twenty-first century version of the Venus de Milo—after she'd given up carbs and started lifting weights.

Her statuesque form included breasts of the variety that were frequently described as "perky." Mallory wished the lighting was brighter so she could see if there were any scars indicating that at least some of her perfection was the result of a skilled surgeon's knife. Still, Mallory's conclusion was that like so much of Colorado, Astrid Norland was one hundred percent natural.

"I'm actually using you as an excuse," Astrid said with a conspiratorial smile. "I knew you had an appointment here at the spa, so I told everyone in the office that I had to act as your tour guide this morning. But the truth is, I just needed to relax." As she lowered herself into the icy water in the plunge pool without even flinching, she let out a deep sigh. "This has been such a trying week."

It's been trying for a lot of us, Mallory thought ruefully. Especially Carly Berman.

"The police actually made me go down to the station to answer questions," Astrid went on, her tone as cold as the water she was immersed in. "I have never been more humiliated in my life."

"That must have been awful," Mallory said, trying to sound sympathetic.

"You can't imagine." Astrid shook her head, which by this point was the only part of her that wasn't underwater. "The police acted as if they didn't believe that Brett and I had a perfectly sound alibi for the entire night before Carly's murder. As if we would lie about being together, when admitting it was bound to cause a scandal!"

As if putting up with a little gossip isn't a whole lot better than being charged with murder, Mallory thought. While she was pretty much convinced that Astrid's perfect breasts were genuine, she couldn't say the same for the alibi the PR pro had concocted on the spot.

"And as if that wasn't bad enough," Astrid went on, "I've been playing nursemaid to Brett. As you can imagine, he's extremely traumatized."

"I've been wondering how poor Brett was doing," Mallory said, deciding not to mention their recent conversation. "Is he holding up okay?"

"The man is strong beyond belief," Astrid replied firmly. "Even in the face of something this shocking."

Strong enough to make critical decisions about linen versus worsted wool, Mallory thought dryly.

"But Carly and Brett's marriage must have been troubled," Mallory commented, trying to sound casual. "For him to look elsewhere for . . . emotional fulfillment."

"Their marriage has been a total disaster for years!" Astrid exclaimed. "That woman was driven.

She gave new meaning to the term workaholic. She was also a control freak. Everything had to be her way. And once she hit the big time, she made the mistake of believing what she read about herself.

"But on top of all that, she was an absolute shrew. The way she treated poor Brett was deplorable. And he's such a wonderful person. He deserves so much more!"

Funny, Mallory thought. From what I observed, Carly seemed to adore him. Then again, Aspen is famous for its actors.

"How did you and Brett meet?" Mallory asked.

Ordinarily, she wouldn't have had the nerve to ask a woman who was having an affair with a married man—a woman she barely knew, no less—how the whole sordid relationship had started. But there was something about two people both being immersed in water, half naked—or in Astrid's case, completely naked—that created an air of instant intimacy.

"A couple of years ago, Carly decided to hire a public relations firm," Astrid replied. "At that time, I was working for a small PR company here in Aspen. I went over to the spa with a couple of other people from the firm to make our pitch. Carly and Brett were both there.

"It was like a scene in a movie," she continued. A faraway look had come into her eyes. "Brett and I just looked at each other across the conference table, and it was like a lightning bolt shot through both of us. I can't tell you what a hard time I had getting through that business meeting. When I handed my business card to them both at the end, Brett looked me in the eyes and said, 'No matter what we decide, I'll definitely be in touch.' "

"Did your firm get the account?" Mallory was almost sorry to interrupt Astrid's dreamy mood.

"No." Astrid laughed. "But I got something so much better: Brett."

Debatable, Mallory thought. But she just nodded.

"It's not really any of my business," she commented, "but if Brett wasn't in love with his wife anymore, why didn't he just leave her?"

"Because he's too nice," Astrid replied bitterly.

Or maybe because he liked being Mr. Carly Berman too much, Mallory thought. Especially since his wife was so willing to pay the bills. A lot of people would put up with a little crankiness if it meant having their favorite lobster flown in from the Caribbean every week.

Besides, if Brett was getting both the physical and emotional love he needed from a tall, adoring blonde with legs as long as the cable for the Silver Queen Gondola ski lift, why not keep a good thing going?

But while Mallory could understand Brett's reasons for staying in an unsatisfying marriage, her waterlogged conversation with Astrid was also helping her see things from the perspective of the Other Woman. Which was also giving her a very good idea of why Astrid would have wanted Carly out of the picture.

In fact, the scenario was so classic it had become a cliché. It was a love triangle, one in which the wife would have wanted the mistress out of the picture and the mistress would have wanted the wife to disappear.

Of course, the third person in the triangle, Brett, could also have wanted to simplify the situation. Not only did taking Carly out of the picture free him up to be with Astrid—it also gave him full control of the Rejuva-Juice empire.

Mallory was trying to come up with a way of asking Astrid for her take on Brett's potential as a businessman when the woman who had greeted her poked her head in.

"Ms. Marlowe?" she said in a soft, gentle voice. "It's time for your massage."

Just what the doctor ordered, Mallory thought as she reluctantly dragged herself out of the hot tub. But given the tangle of relationships and emotions that I'm determined to unravel, this massage therapist is going to have to have magic hands if she's ever going to get *these* muscles to relax.

Even though the massage therapist actually managed to loosen up every one of Mallory's muscles, as soon as she left the spa they returned to the same rigid state that as of late had become the norm. Then she checked her watch and realized that if she didn't tense up her leg muscles even more, she was going to be late for her rendezvous with Dusty Raines.

As she hurried along Durant Avenue toward their meeting place, she fretted over the possibility that he would have forgotten all about their lunch date. Somehow, Dusty impressed her as someone who was much better at maneuvering his way around a ski slope than through life—even if he did own a Rolex to help him keep track of the time.

But as she neared their meeting point, she spotted him standing near the ticket booth at the base of Aspen Mountain, just as they'd planned. He was wearing the same jeans he'd had on the day before. Either that, or he owned more than one pair with shredded knees. He also wore a dark ski jacket and a pair of sneakers that was an even brighter shade of yellow than his hair. As usual, it looked as if combing his wild mane hadn't made it to his To Do list.

"Hey!" he greeted her, his blue eyes lighting up.

"You're right on time," Mallory noted as she caught up with him.

"Nothing like food to get me motivated," he joked. "In fact, that's the only thing that gets me out of bed in the morning."

No doubt getting you out is a lot harder than getting you in, Mallory thought. But she simply said, "I'm glad you could join me."

"So where are we going?" Dusty asked with the eagerness of an eight-year-old boy.

"I thought we'd aim high."

"Huh?"

She smiled. "Let's take the gondola up Aspen Mountain and have lunch at the Sundeck."

"Suh-we-e-et," he replied, somehow managing to squeeze several extra syllables out of what was normally a one-syllable word.

Both the Silver Queen Gondola and the Sundeck Lodge at the top remained open year round. Since ski season was over, the line for the gondola was mercifully short. Mallory could only imagine how crowded it got at the height of the season. Coping with crowds in addition to lugging heavy fiberglass skis while wearing equally heavy plastic boots held absolutely no appeal for her. Especially since hauling all that equipment around simply to get it up the mountain was undoubtedly the easy part.

She and Dusty were silent as they rode up, traveling at an alarmingly brisk pace for the entire two-mile trip. Mallory wondered what the other occupants of the cable car—the size of a Buick—thought of their unlikely pairing. But they seemed too busy to notice as they stared out the windows that encircled the entire car, oohing and aahing as the buildings and trees below shrank before their very eyes.

"I understand this runs all year-round," Mallory commented to Dusty, wanting to break the uncomfortable silence. "It's great that even people who don't ski can go to the top of the mountain. It's not every day someone gets a chance to see the planet from eleven thousand feet above sea level."

"It's totally awesome," he agreed, nodding ferociously.

Mallory wondered how she was ever going to manage to eat an entire meal with this man.

When they reached the top and climbed out of the gondola, they were rewarded with the most spectacular view so far. Simply standing at the top of the mountain was an exhilarating experience.

Okay, so maybe skiers aren't completely nuts, she decided.

Still, she found the sight of the treacherous-looking slope below intimidating enough that she wasn't about to waver on the issue of joining them.

While the view easily made the trip up the mountain worthwhile, she couldn't say the same for the restaurant. The Sundeck Lodge did, indeed, possess a sundeck, one that happened to be crowded with outdoor diners enjoying the sun. But the indoor area was about as appealing as a high school cafeteria, albeit a high school cafeteria located somewhere in the Alps.

"This is actually kind of a disappointment," Mallory commented. She surveyed the large, angular space that consisted of nothing but a short cafeteria line and nondescript tables and chairs packed together.

"It's pretty typical for ski resorts," Dusty replied. "But this one has better food. They have the usual burgers and pizza, but they also have stir-fried veggies and Tandoori chicken."

Mallory hoped he wasn't going to try to slip either of *those* into his pocket.

"Besides," he went on, "for people who are into something fancier, there's a private club right next door." He pointed at a terrace that they could see through the window, one that jutted out from another section of the building. "The Aspen Mountain Club. That place is really sick."

Thanks to her son, Mallory knew that these days, "sick" was a good thing. Perhaps even better than "sweet."

"It costs fifty thousand dollars to join," Dusty added. "But it's totally awesome. The best part is the dining room. There's this ceiling that's, like, a dome, but it's got windows in it, and a big sun painted on it, with this huge chandelier-thing hanging down—"

"You've been inside?" Mallory asked, surprised.

An odd look crossed his face. "Somebody told me about it once. Uh, a friend of mine who belongs."

"Carly?" Quickly she fibbed, "I seem to remember her mentioning that she was a member."

A stricken look immediately crossed Dusty's face.

"Uh, no, not Carly," he said, without looking her in the eye. "It was somebody else I know here in Aspen."

Mallory wondered if that "somebody else" was another one of Dusty's lady friends. Or gentleman friends. Unfortunately, she couldn't think of a diplomatic way to ask.

Once they'd gotten their food—the Tandoori chicken for Mallory, a cheeseburger for Dusty with a pile of fries nearly as high as the mountain they were sitting on—they put their trays down on a table near the window.

"Wow, I can't believe they have the curly fries," Dusty exclaimed as he slid into the seat opposite Mallory's.

He's such a kid, Mallory thought. Granted, a good-looking kid, but one who still acts like he's in high school. I realize the stimulation Carly was seeking wasn't exactly of the intellectual variety. Still, I would have expected her to go for someone more suave.

She wondered if Juanita could have possibly been wrong about the nature of Carly's relationship with

Dusty. Then again, Juanita impressed her as someone who didn't miss much, at least in terms of what went on in the Berman household—even behind closed doors.

Mallory stuck her fork into a chunk of chicken, hoping that the only requirement for becoming a chef at this establishment wasn't the ability to function in a low-oxygen environment. "It's funny," she said conversationally, "I don't remember Carly mentioning anything about you."

Dusty's eyes narrowed, just a fraction of a millimeter. "I thought you said you and Carly hadn't really stayed in touch since high school."

He remembered that? Mallory thought, surprised. Maybe he's smarter than he looks.

Flashing him a smile, she added, "What I meant was that we weren't really that close. At least, not the way we were in high school. But that doesn't mean we didn't send each other Christmas cards, photos, e-mails... We e-mailed each other all the time."

Dusty nodded, which Mallory was beginning to realize was pretty much his response to everything. "I guess I'm not surprised she never mentioned me," he said. "I mean, we were buds too, but it's not like we were that close or anything." He hesitated before adding, "I've got a girlfriend, so don't start thinking it was anything like that."

"I wasn't thinking that at all," Mallory insisted.

Not reacting to that simple statement required a great deal of self-control. To hide her shock, she stabbed another piece of chicken. At least the chef turned out to have more going for him than good lungs. "Tell me about your girlfriend. What's her name?"

"Autumn."

Dusty and Autumn, she thought. Why am I not surprised?

"Does she work in the ski industry, too?"

"No way."

"Really? What does she do?"

He was silent for a few seconds, as if he wasn't sure he wanted to share a detail as intimate as his girlfriend's profession. "Yoga. She teaches it, I mean."

Dusty's reluctance to talk about the woman who had reportedly stolen his heart piqued Mallory's curiosity. But she didn't feel the need to press him for more details. She had a feeling that it wouldn't be that difficult to locate a yoga instructor named Autumn in a town this size.

Beside, it was Carly she'd come here to talk about.

"I'm curious, Dusty," she said casually. "How did someone like you happen to meet Carly Berman?"

"You're sure asking a lot of questions," Dusty replied, studying her warily over his mound of curly fries. "I thought you wanted to talk about her, not me."

"I do want to talk about her," Mallory replied evenly. "I'm really anxious to learn everything I can about what her life her in Aspen was like. And that includes getting to know her friends."

"Then you're taking the wrong dude to lunch," he replied, impatience creeping into his tone. "Like I said, me and Carly weren't close. We just knew each other because Aspen's a pretty small place."

So is Carly's bedroom, Mallory thought. *Which is why I'm trying to find out how you came to spend so much time in there—behind closed doors.*

"If you want to know more about your friend's social life," Dusty added, "I'd talk to her husband."

"Brett?"

"That's right. Carly was crazy about the guy."

"Really." It was true that she'd made the same observation, based on the small amount of time she'd spent with the Bermans. But if that was really the case, what was she doing with Dusty?

She had hoped he'd be able to help her clarify that point. Not that he was likely to come right out and admit that he and Carly were having an affair. Still, he seemed strangely sincere in his insistence that Mr. Huggy-Poo really was the love of her life.

Maybe Dusty was jealous of Carly's feelings for her husband, she thought. He could have insisted that she leave Brett, then flown into a rage when she refused . . .

But if she loved her husband so much, she asked herself again what was she doing with Dusty in the first place?

Instead of clarifying things, Mallory's interrogation in the sky was only confusing her even more.

Still, there was suddenly someone new in the picture, someone who just might be able to cast a little more light on the puzzling subject of Carly Berman's love life.

Besides, adding "take a yoga class" to her list of Aspen's activities for nonskiers struck her as an excellent idea.

Chapter 13

"Like all great travelers, I have seen more than I
remember, and remember more than I have seen."
—Benjamin Disraeli

Rather than attempting to locate Dusty Raines's
yoga instructor girlfriend by asking around town,
Mallory decided to try the high-tech method.
Immediately after saying good-bye to Dusty, she made
a beeline for her hotel room, where she turned on her
laptop and Googled "Autumn Aspen Yoga."

While she got a few links to Web sites that referred
to local yoga studios with programs that changed
with each season, she did stumble upon one that
treated Autumn as a proper noun. Eagerly she
clicked on the link.

"Autumn Drake, Yoga Instructor," the headline
said. Underneath was a photograph of a pretty
young woman who Mallory estimated was about
Amanda's age. She had the same long, straight hair

as her daughter, too, except hers was pale blond. Wispy, too. Its color and texture, combined with her heavy-lidded green eyes, tiny nose, gaunt cheeks, and narrow shoulders that indicated a willowy frame, gave her fragile, slightly spaced-out look.

"We recently welcomed Autumn Drake to our staff," the blurb on the Web site read. "While Autumn brings a special interest in Vinyasa Flow yoga and Iyengar to our studio, she also incorporates the Ashtanga, Bhakti, and Jivamukti traditions into her classes. Her specialty is chakra balancing. A native of Nebraska, Autumn recently came to Aspen by way of southern California."

Sounds like our girl, Mallory thought.

She clicked onto the home page and discovered that the name of the studio that employed Autumn was the Earth, Wind, Fire, and Water Sanctuary for Mind, Body, and Spirit. Its name made for a lengthy Web address—www.EarthWindFireWater.com—but it was the yoga studio's street address that she was interested in.

The studio was located on the outskirts of town, less than half a mile away, according to her calculations. After jotting down the address on a page from the Hotel Jerome notepad, Mallory slipped it into her purse and headed down Main Street, a route she'd learned well thanks to all her auto trips out of town.

Her stroll took her past wonderful old Victorian houses, small parks with thick green lawns, and motels and lodges that looked as if they had been built in the 1970s and gotten stuck in a time warp. This primarily residential section of Aspen looked like Anytown, U.S.A., thanks to its good-size yards, tall trees, and sidewalks running through the grid of houses packed onto quiet streets that veered off the main drag.

The yoga studio reminded her that she wasn't in Anytown, after all. It was located in one of the larger Victorians, which was perched on a corner. The shingles were painted bright blue, with purple shutters and metal wind chimes dangling from the front porch. The sign above the door was hand-painted, with the letters of "earth" made out of vines, "wind" made from white wisps, "fire" yellow flames, and "water" spelled out with blue droplets.

Mallory was growing increasingly nervous. She hoped this part of her investigation wouldn't necessitate twisting her unyielding middle-aged body into pretzel-like shapes. The last thing she wanted was for somebody to decide that her chakras were in serious need of balancing.

But she took a deep breath and swung open the door. Her ears were immediately treated to the gentle tinkling of a bell, and her nostrils tingled with the intoxicating smell of spicy orange incense. She hadn't even said hello and she was already feeling mellower.

"Welcome to the sanctuary," a dark-haired woman about her age greeted her. "How can I work with you to improve your mind, body, and spirit?"

The first two are doing just fine, thank you, Mallory thought. *But I suppose I could use a little help with the third.*

"Actually, I'm interested in speaking with one of your yoga instructors," she said. She stood up straight and looked the woman in the eye. Just being here gave her the distinct feeling that her chakras were way out of line, but she was hoping no one would notice. "I'd like to interview her for a magazine article I'm writing."

The woman brightened. "A magazine article? For *Yoga and You*?"

"Uh, no. Actually, it's not for a yoga magazine. It's a travel article about Aspen I'm writing for a lifestyle magazine."

"Which one?"

"*The Good Life.*"

"Ah." From the way the woman frowned, Mallory wondered if she disapproved. After all, the "good life" her readers were interested in had more to do with sleek sports cars, Sub-Zero freezers, and vacations in glitzy destinations than inner peace.

"And I know that Autumn's background includes all kinds of yoga," Mallory went on, anxious to sell this woman, who was in essence guarding the door, on the idea of giving her a few minutes with Dusty's better half. "That's why I'd like to interview her for my article."

When the woman still looked skeptical, Mallory added, "Of course I'd be able to mention Earth, Wind, and Fire and give you some free publicity."

She had a feeling there was another element in there somewhere, but it had slipped her mind.

The woman didn't bother to correct her. In fact, for whatever reason—perhaps having reached a higher plane—it appeared that she had decided to forgive Mallory for her slip. "Autumn is in back. If you'd like, I'll see if she's free."

As Mallory waited, she checked out the merchandise lined up on the shelves. Apparently even the most spiritual person couldn't live by yoga alone. Also necessary were yoga pants, yoga shirts, yoga jackets, and yoga bags to put it all into. In addition to yoga mats, there were special sprays and wipes to keep them clean. There were also scented candles, sticks of incense, lotions, CDs with yoga-appropriate music, meditation cushions, meditation benches, and silk eye pillows.

So much for giving up one's worldly goods, Mallory thought, fingering a silver pendant with the word *Om* nestled within a swarm of curlicues. Who knew that yoga required almost as much equipment as skiing?

A wave of disappointment swept over Mallory when the same woman returned—alone. But with a serene smile, she said, "Autumn will meet with you in the Crystal Room. It's behind the curtain."

"Thank you."

Mallory didn't know what she'd find back there. But as she pushed aside the long, bead-studded hot pink silk curtain hanging from the ceiling, she discovered a large, modern room with mirrors lining one entire wall. It reminded her of the type of space in which ballet classes are taught.

Autumn was at the other end, twisted not as much like a pretzel as a rubber Gumby doll. Her body faced one way, her head faced the other, and her right arm reached high into the air. Frankly, she didn't look the least bit comfortable. Nevertheless, the expression on her face was one of total bliss.

"Come in," she greeted Mallory without looking in her direction. "I understand you want to learn about yoga."

"Uh, I actually want to learn about yoga classes," Mallory corrected her. She noticed that Autumn was wearing a pair of yoga capris and a yoga tank top that looked a lot like the ones she'd spotted on sale up front. Her blond hair was pulled back into a haphazard knot, with wisps falling out hither, thither, and yon. "I'm writing a magazine article about things to do in Aspen that have nothing to do with skiing. The point is to explore whether it's a good place to travel even for people who have no interest in getting on the mountain."

"I see." Autumn twisted around so that all of her body parts were facing the same direction. But instead of coming over to talk to Mallory, she got down onto the floor, raised her legs up into the air until she was in a headstand position, and then bent her legs. She looked enough like a pretzel that Mallory had to keep from pointing and exclaiming, "Aha! Just as I thought!"

"Which magazine?" Autumn asked.

"Uh, *The Good Life*." Mallory had never realized how difficult it was to talk to someone who was upside down. "It's based in New York."

"New York?" Autumn brightened. "I was there once." Her aura quickly went from positive to negative. "Too many people. Very bad karma."

And you don't even pay taxes there, Mallory thought.

"How did you find *me*?" Autumn asked.

Exactly the segue I've been hoping for. "I met a friend of yours."

"Really? Who?"

"Dusty Raines." As she was still debating whether or not to identify him in the terms he'd supplied, she blurted out the words. "Your boyfriend."

Autumn snapped out of her headstand faster than an Olympic gymnast going for the gold. "Dusty told you he's my boyfriend?"

"That's right," Mallory replied, trying to sound casual.

She could practically see Autumn's chakras becoming dangerously unbalanced.

"As a matter of fact," she continued breezily, "he told me that you'd be a good person to talk to. For my article, I mean. Since you're involved in something other than skiing and all."

"Well, he's certainly not my boyfriend." Autumn spat out the words. "At least not anymore. Not since he started hanging out with that—that old crone!"

Hey, wait a minute! Mallory thought. *I happen to have been in the same algebra class as that old crone. And in a lot of the world—that is, in places that aren't Aspen—forty-five isn't exactly considered the ideal age to be put out to sea on an ice floe.*

But aloud she said, "I'm not sure who you mean."

"Carly Berman. The woman who owns Tavaci Springs. The one who was just murdered." Shaking her head, Autumn added, "Boy, is he gonna miss *her*."

"You almost make it sound as if he was her lover," Mallory said evenly.

"If you can call it that," Autumn shot back. "More like her gigolo. Not only were they having sex. Plenty of it, too, at least if you believe all his bragging. And she was always buying him stuff. I got the feeling it wasn't only her surgically enhanced breasts that turned him on. I think he also found her credit cards pretty alluring."

"You mean she bought him things?"

"Yea-a-ah." Autumn replied, casting her a look of disbelief over her naiveté. "I don't suppose you noticed the watch he wears. It's a Rolex. A real one. Do you have any idea what those things cost?"

"Not really. I'm kind of a Timex girl myself," Mallory replied.

"Well, believe me, they're ridiculously expensive," Autumn exclaimed. "Not exactly the kind of watch you'd expect a ski bum like Dusty to be wearing. Besides, that pretentious watch isn't even his taste. It's got Carly Berman written all over it."

So Carly *was* the source of Dusty's top-of-the-line wristwatch, Mallory thought. Suspicion confirmed.

"In that case, Dusty must be pretty upset about what happened to Carly," Mallory commented, searching Autumn's face.

"*Oh*, yeah. I'm sure he's beside himself. He had a really good thing going, and now it's over." Crossing her arms, she grumbled, "He might even have to get a job. A real one, I mean, instead of just hanging out at the ski shop, chatting up the customers all day."

From the way Autumn described Dusty's situation, it sounded as if the last thing he'd have wanted was for anything to get in the way of his relationship with Carly. Especially something as final as murder. Chances were good that she'd never written him into her will, which meant that all he had to show for his trouble was his fancy wristwatch.

Autumn's expression suddenly changed. "But you didn't come here to talk about Dusty and his sordid love life," she said, somehow calling upon whatever reserves she possessed and quickly bringing herself back to a considerably more tranquil state. "Let me tell you about what we do here at Earth, Wind, Fire, and Water."

"Shoot," Mallory said, pulling out her notebook and pen.

But as Autumn patiently explained the differences between Bhakti and Jivamukti, Mallory couldn't help evaluating what she had told her.

Is it possible I was wrong to consider Dusty a suspect? Mallory wondered. Could he really be one of the few people in this town who actually fits that old saying, what you see is what you get?

After all, if someone wanted to become a full-fledged ski bum, complete with an attractive older woman to help ease the discomforts of low-income living, Aspen was definitely the place to do it.

As soon as she left the yoga studio, Mallory pulled out her cell phone to call Harriet and firm up their afternoon coffee date. She'd just assumed that they'd arrange to meet someplace in town. But Harriet insisted she was too swamped with paperwork to spare much time and suggested that they meet at Tavaci Springs.

Instead of being put off by her suggestion, Mallory was secretly glad. She was anxious to get a closer look at Harriet in the setting in which she had worked—which also happened to be the same place in which Carly had been murdered.

Before heading out of town, she made a quick stop at the Ink Coffee Company even though it was a few blocks out of her way. She'd read that it was known for the high quality of its coffee, since Ink roasted its own beans. It sounded like a place she might be able to include in her article. Wanting to have the full experience, she also picked up something to go with the coffee before getting back into her car and driving into the mountains.

When she reached the spa, she found it just as deserted as it had been the day before. The only car parked out front was Harriet's dark blue Escort, with the huge dent in the door that reminded Mallory of a big, ugly bruise.

Mallory pulled her car into the space beside it, then bypassed the main building and headed directly toward the spa in back. Following that route required passing the Mud Hut, which was still marked off by yellow crime scene tape. The harshness of the bright color superimposed over the place in which something so horrific had recently occurred, combined with the silence that shrouded the entire property, created an eerie feeling that made her quicken her step.

When she found the door of the spa building unlocked, she let herself in, meanwhile struggling to balance two cups of coffee and a white paper bag stuffed with scones.

"Harriet?" she called once she was inside.

"I'm in back," she heard her yell in response. "In my office."

When Mallory retraced the route she and Harriet had followed the day before, she found Harriet sitting at her desk, surrounded by mounds of paper. One more stack sat in her lap, its top few pages looking as if they were about to slide off her navy blue wool skirt.

"See?" Harriet greeted her, grimacing. "I wasn't exaggerating when I said I was drowning in paperwork."

"So I see," Mallory said sympathetically.

"You brought coffee!" Harriet exclaimed. "How thoughtful of you!"

"No problem," Mallory assured her. "I'm glad to help, since I can imagine how busy you must be right now."

She glanced around the tiny office, noticing that a foot-wide area of the credenza that lined one wall was actually bare. Since there didn't appear to be anywhere else to sit, she leaned against it and began snapping the lids off the paper coffee cups.

"I'm overwhelmed by how much I have to do." Harriet sighed. "I'm pretty organized, as a rule. But I also operate under the assumption that I'll have a reasonable amount of time to get things done. Now that Carly is . . . now that this has happened, I have to get all the accounts in order pronto so her estate can be settled.

"But enough about my paperwork nightmare." She scooped up the pile in her lap and plopped it on top of another pile that was sitting on the desk, then reached for her cup of coffee. "Tell me what you've been up to. Have you found out anything that might help identify Carly's killer?"

Mallory shook her head. "I've spoken to a few people who knew Carly, and I'm starting to get a better feel for the world she traveled in. But I haven't learned anything that points to any one person." Or clears anyone, she thought grimly. Including you.

"Aside from that," she went on, "I've been trying to squeeze in as much sightseeing as I can. Even though it's kind of hard to focus, I still have to write the article I was sent here to write. I've checked out a few of the shops in town, and last night I had dinner at Montagna, over at the Little Nell."

"Poor you, having dinner at such a nice restaurant all alone!"

"Actually, I wasn't alone." Mallory hesitated for a few moments before explaining, "I had dinner with Gordon."

Harriet's eyebrows shot up to her hairline. "Gordon Swig?"

"Yes, that's right." Puzzled by her reaction, Mallory added, "Why, is there something wrong with that?"

Harriet shook her head slowly. "Mallory, I had no

idea you were seeing Gordon. If I did, I would have told you about him earlier."

"Told me what?"

"Look," Harriet said with a sigh, "the last thing I want to do is to go around spreading rumors about people. But when murder is involved..."

Mallory just stared. The déjà vu she was suddenly experiencing made her light-headed.

"Are you telling me you think Gordon may have had something to do with Carly's being killed?" she asked breathlessly.

Harriet bit her lip. "Let's just say it's not impossible."

This is exactly what happened in Florida, too, Mallory thought, her stomach tightening like a fist. On that trip, I also met a man I felt a connection with—and then began to suspect that he, too, could have been involved in murder.

"I mean, it's not like I know anything for sure," Harriet continued. "It's just that... well, there's been some tension between them lately."

"Really?" Mallory frowned. "I didn't notice anything out of the ordinary when I had dinner at Carly's house the night before she was killed."

"Maybe Gordon picked up a few pointers from all those actors he's worked with." Harriet had barely gotten the words out before she clamped her hand over her mouth. "Oh, my gosh! That was a terrible thing to say, wasn't it?"

"We're all feeling stressed out," Mallory assured her. Despite her own turmoil, she was trying to sound sympathetic. The last thing she wanted Harriet to do was hold back on the truth. Or at least her perception of the truth.

"Don't get me wrong, Mallory," Harriet said, her cheeks reddening. "I like Gordon. I always have. I think he's the nicest man in the world. It's just that there were such major issues between him and Carly, and the fact that he just happened to be in town when she was murdered . . ."

"What kind of issues?" Mallory asked. She tried to sound offhanded, but her question came out sounding like a demand.

Hesitantly Harriet said, "I don't know if Gordon mentioned anything about this, but he was interested in making a movie about Carly's life story." She looked pained, as if speaking badly of someone was truly difficult for her. Mallory's cynical side couldn't help wondering if Harriet, too, had mastered a few acting techniques along the way.

"He's been thinking about doing the film for a long time," Harriet went on. "From what I understand, at the beginning of their negotiations, Carly led him to believe it was practically a done deal. So Gordon went out on a limb and hyped the idea all over Hollywood. He told everyone he had this fabulous project in the works that was going to enable him to make his big comeback. I heard that he used his own money to hire a well-known screenwriter to write the script, one of those big names who gets over a million dollars for a project. Gordon even went so far as to line up actors. He'd gotten to the point of wining and dining producers when Carly started to waver."

"Why?" Mallory asked, genuinely surprised. "Carly impressed me as someone who would have loved to become super-famous."

"As far as I know, she never gave a definite reason for why she was vacillating," Harriet replied. "At one point, she said something about the timing not being right. On a few other occasions, she said she wasn't sure Gordon was the best person to make the film. It's not that she didn't like him personally. It was just that once he expressed interest and got her thinking about the whole idea, she started throwing around names like Ang Lee and James Cameron."

That I can understand, Mallory thought, since it sounds more like the Carly I knew way back when.

"What about Brett?" she asked. "Was he in favor of Gordon making the movie?"

Harriet glanced from side to side, as if wanting to make sure they were completely alone. She seemed to notice Mallory's surprise at her cautiousness because she added, "Sometimes I wonder if these walls have ears. All I can say is that Brett wasn't averse to anything that was likely to bring in more money. I don't think he cared much about where it came from.

"Anyway," she went on with a sigh, "Carly's unexpected change of heart at the point when she was this close to signing a contract was a real blow for Gordon. It was making him lose credibility in the Hollywood circles that really count. Here he'd been promising such great things, and all of a sudden it was starting to look like he had nothing. It was making him look really bad."

"So Gordon had good reason to be furious with Carly," Mallory mused.

While she sounded as if she was merely making an objective observation, her head was spinning.

Gordon—a killer? she thought. Is that possible?

She struggled to put what Harriet had just told her in perspective. She certainly didn't want to believe that Gordon could be capable of murder. Not when she'd allowed herself to enjoy his company and even feel attracted to him.

Am I really such a poor judge of character? she wondered mournfully.

The whole idea of dating again—of developing an interest in someone of the opposite sex, then taking all the risks that went along with opening one's heart—was frightening enough. The notion of letting someone new in her life also filled her with guilt, since she was still adjusting to the fact that David was gone.

But the idea that she might be incapable of seeing people for who they really were raised her uncertainty and her anxiety to an even higher level.

When she and Harriet had both found their way to the bottom of their coffee cups and the scones had been reduced to nothing more than a few crumbs, she glanced at her watch and saw it was almost time for her cooking class.

"I'm glad to see that you're doing as well as you are," she told Harriet, still uncertain of whether to view her with sympathy or caution. "But I'm afraid I have to get going."

"I should get back to work, too," Harriet said, eyeing the stack of paper in front of her.

"I'd better pop into the rest room first."

"Be my guest. It's at the end of the hall."

Mallory was gone less than three minutes—possibly less time than Harriet anticipated. At least if the surprised look on her face when Mallory reappeared in the doorway of her office was any indication.

"Mallory! You sneaked up on me!" Harriet cried.

She was crouched down on the floor, tucking something into the bottom drawer of a file cabinet. She quickly pushed the drawer closed with such force that metal hit metal with a loud bang. Moving just as fast, she turned the small silver key in the lock, pulled it out, and dropped it into her pocket.

From Mallory's perspective, the expression on her face was decidedly one of guilt.

"I'm just trying to put things where they belong," Harriet mumbled as she stood up, brushing the wrinkles in her skirt. When she finally looked at Mallory, her face was beet red.

"Of course," Mallory agreed, studying her.

Something felt very wrong. The atmosphere in the room had changed. She suddenly felt sparks of tension, as if Harriet was disturbed over having been caught doing something she wasn't supposed to be doing.

Automatically Mallory's eyes drifted toward the bottom drawer of the file cabinet.

She's hiding something.

Yesterday, she thought, her head swimming, I spotted Harriet at an out-of-the-way restaurant with

Sylvie, a woman for whom she claimed to have nothing but contempt. Not only was she socializing with someone she'd made a point of characterizing as an enemy, she blatantly lied to me about when she'd been released from the police station and what she'd done immediately afterward.

And now this.

As far as Mallory was concerned, the police were right to consider Harriet a person of interest. In fact, from what she had seen, she appeared to be a person of *great* interest.

While Mallory was becoming increasingly convinced that Harriet was guilty, she knew perfectly well that she had yet to prove anything. Which meant she couldn't yet discount any of the other suspects on her list.

Including Gordon.

As she drove along the mountain road that took her away from Tavaci Springs, she wrestled with her ambivalence about seeing him again. After all, even though Harriet was a strong suspect herself, she had certainly made a good case for Gordon having reason to be furious with Carly.

True, Harriet could have played up Gordon's anger as a means of deflecting suspicion. Yet the fact that he had told her himself that he'd wanted to make a film about Carly's life story was troubling.

Mallory knew that even if she wanted to change her plans, she couldn't. Not only was she scheduled to meet Gordon at the Cooking School of Aspen in just half an hour, she didn't have his cell phone number with her. She couldn't simply skip the class, either, since she intended to write about it in her article.

Besides, she didn't want to believe that he could possibly be a killer. She liked him. He was fun to be with, he made her feel good, and she'd been looking forward to taking this class with him.

She drove on, mentally running down her list of other suspects.

She started with Brett. The fact that Carly was having an affair with Dusty made her husband look more guilty, not less. After all, if he'd found out about it, he could easily have flown into a jealous rage and killed her. Of course, if he really was living off Carly, the way Harriet and Gordon had said he was, he would have in essence been killing the goose that laid the golden eggs.

That led her to Astrid. Since she was having an affair with Brett, it made perfect sense that she, too, would have wanted Carly out of the picture. Since Astrid and Brett were the only ones who knew if they'd really spent the entire night together, she could have easily been the one who had gone to Tavaci Springs that night, intending to get rid of her rival once and for all.

Or maybe the lovers had both killed her, conspiring to find a way to eliminate the one obstacle to their love. Especially since Brett stood to become a very wealthy widower.

Dusty couldn't be discounted, either. No matter how Autumn tried to make his relationship with Carly sound like the best thing that had happened to him since the invention of the snowboard, the simple fact that he was having an illicit relationship with the victim made him a suspect. Being so much younger—and so much poorer—made his situation look even worse. He was someone who was forced to live simply, sharing an apartment with a bunch of other ski dudes, but who clearly had an appreciation for life's luxuries, such as Rolex watches. Which meant that even though he acted like someone without a care in the world, there were definitely other sides to him—along with reasons other than love or even simply sexual attraction fueling his interest in Carly.

And she certainly couldn't discount Sylvie, especially when even the police thought she was worth looking at. She had been counting on Carly to sell her business to HoliHealth, which would have gained Sylvie the status at her company that she so desperately yearned for. But if it turned out Carly was just stringing her along, she would have been furious that she had both wasted her time and gambled her reputation—all for nothing. In fact, it was even possible that Sylvie had been charged with Carly's murder while Mallory was busily running around town, interviewing suspects . . .

She suddenly snapped out of her ruminations and realized she was already a third of the way down the mountain road. She glanced around, surprised that she'd been driving for at least five minutes without paying attention to her surroundings.

It was at that point that she glanced in the rearview mirror and saw that another vehicle was close behind.

In fact, the mud-splattered pickup truck was a little *too* close, especially since she'd just reached the part of the road that was particularly twisty. It was also narrow, with dramatic, heart-stopping drops down the side on which she drove.

"Idiot," she muttered. "Just because locals like this jerk probably know every inch of these roads doesn't make racing along them any safer."

Besides, she wondered, doesn't the fact that I'm driving so slowly clue him in to the fact that I'm not very comfortable driving on this particularly treacherous stretch?

Or maybe it wasn't a him. She peered into her rearview mirror, trying to see the face of the individual who was exercising such bad judgment—so bad, in fact, that it could get them both killed. But the windshield was spattered with so much mud that she couldn't make out who was sitting in the front seat. From the looks of things, the driver had cleared away a space no bigger than an index card in order to see out.

She tried to speed up a bit, just to show that she was trying.

The truck sped up, too. It was still close. *Too* close.

This guy is a serious road bully, she thought, her anxiety level escalating quickly. Should I turn on my flashers? Maybe that would let him know I have no intention of going any faster and he'd back off.

But his front bumper was so close to her back

bumper—mere inches away, from what she could tell—that he probably wouldn't even be able to *see* that she'd turned on her flashers.

By this point she was fighting serious feelings of panic. She glanced from side to side, looking for a turnout or at least a stretch of road wide enough for her to move over and let the truck pass. But the road was so narrow that there was barely room for one vehicle, much less two. She contemplated moving into the other lane, but the road curved so dramatically that it was impossible to see if anyone was coming up the mountain. If being tailgated was dangerous, it was nothing compared to a head-on collision.

Realizing she was gripping the steering wheel so tightly that her hands hurt, Mallory forced herself to relax them, just a little. She glanced into the rearview mirror every few seconds, wishing she could will the imbecile who was tailgating her to stop acting like such a fool.

And then, *bump*! Mallory let out a yelp as she felt her car jerk and heard the loud thump of the truck's front bumper hitting hers.

"What the—?" she cried.

She checked the rearview mirror again, expecting the driver to slow down. That was standard procedure whenever there was a car accident, wasn't it?

Still, there was no place to stop on this narrow mountain road. Not without running the risk of being hit by any other vehicles that came along.

I can't even see the license plate, she thought.

That was when she felt another bump, this one even harder.

Oh, my God, she thought, feelings of panic instantly sending her heart racing and coating her dry mouth with a metallic taste. That nut is doing this on purpose!

I don't know who's driving, but whoever's behind the wheel is trying to run me off the road!

Chapter 14

"A good traveler has no fixed plans,
and is not intent on arriving."
—Lao Tzu

Mallory clutched the steering wheel even more tightly, resisting the urge to whimper as she fixed her gaze on the narrow road twisting in front of her. It appeared to be descending at an even more dramatic angle than she remembered.

I have to stay focused, she thought, swallowing hard. I have to keep going. And I can't speed up, or that crazy driver will hit me even harder.

So instead of accelerating, she nudged the brake and slowed down. When she dared to take her eyes off the road long enough to check the rearview mirror, she saw that the pickup truck persisted in maintaining the same minuscule distance between his vehicle and hers.

"You can do this," she whispered to herself, vaguely aware that her entire body was coated in sweat. "You're doing fine, and you don't have that much farther to go..."

She yelped as she felt another bump, this one so hard it rammed her car right up to the edge of the road. She could feel the pavement giving way to dirt, which meant her front tire had been pushed onto the three-foot-wide strip of rock-covered terrain edging the road. Beyond, she could see nothing but air.

Acting on instinct, Mallory wrenched the steering wheel to the left. She could feel the pebbles and dirt sputtering beneath her tire, and for a few terrifying moments she couldn't tell whether the car was going to move in the direction she wanted. But it finally lurched forward, the front nearly smashing into the mountain on her left. In the last fraction of a second, she jerked the steering wheel to the right, managing to maneuver the car back into the center of her lane.

Even though she had regained control, the ordeal left her shaking.

I *can't* do this! she thought, her chest heaving and her eyes burning. All I want is for this to be over!

But she knew she had no choice but to force herself to keep on going. So she gritted her teeth and drove as slowly as she dared.

A wave of relief washed over her when she began spotting side roads jutting off, which told her she was finally nearing the bottom of the mountain. Most were little more than wide dirt paths, but at least they provided a way of getting off the main road. Still, while she derived some comfort from knowing she had other options, she was afraid that if she turned off onto one of them, the pickup truck would simply follow.

And the last thing she wanted was to find herself cornered by the driver who had already made three attempts at sending her barreling off the side of a serious mountain.

"*Yes.*" Mallory breathed when she saw a car that was traveling in the opposite direction pass by. Trundling a few hundred yards behind it was a truck. She was filled with gratitude that she was no longer alone, since having other people around made it less likely that the nutcase who'd been trying to run her off the road would try again.

Sure enough, after she passed one more unpaved road, she glanced into the rearview mirror and watched the pickup turn onto it abruptly. It sped up once it hit the dirt, its dust-covered tires sending mud splattering up into the air like a geyser.

As she watched the vehicle disappear into the woods, for a fleeting moment Mallory considered following him. But the idea of driving straight into a second dangerous situation when she'd barely escaped from the first held no appeal. All she wanted was to get off the mountain.

Once she reached flat land, she felt totally depleted. The sweat that covered her body had turned her skin clammy, and she couldn't keep her hands from shaking.

She was also struck by the harsh realization that while she'd managed to get off the mountain safely, her ordeal wasn't over.

She knew precisely what the harrowing car chase

down the mountain had been: a warning. And that meant there was undoubtedly more to come.

Even though Mallory had managed to get off the mountain safely, her knees still felt wobbly and her mind was clouded. After she parked in downtown Aspen, she sat in her car for a few minutes, getting her bearings.

The fact that someone had just tried to send her plummeting down the side of a mountain intensified her lingering uncertainties about seeing Gordon again.

It *couldn't* have been him, she thought when she finally dragged herself out of her car. No matter how she tried to picture him as a killer, she couldn't.

Then again, she'd been wrong before.

But when she spotted him waiting for her in the spot they'd agreed upon along the Hyman Avenue Mall, the melting feeling in her heart reinforced her belief that there was no way Gordon could possibly be capable of killing anybody.

"Gordon!" she cried, breaking into a jog as she grew near.

She expected him to turn and smile. Instead, he stood frozen. It wasn't until she got closer that she realized why: He was imitating the gigantic wooden bear he stood next to, duplicating its posture and even its stern expression.

Despite her confused feelings about the man, she couldn't help laughing. "I *knew* I should have brought some salmon with me!" she joked.

He continued to stare straight ahead, ignoring her.

"Gordon, this is really getting un-bear-able," she quipped, wincing at her own bad pun.

It was so bad, in fact, that even he couldn't resist groaning. Finally turning to look at her, he demanded, "How am I supposed to trick people into thinking I'm a bear if you're going to make me laugh?"

Squinting in mock confusion, she replied, "Tell me again why you want people to think you're a bear?"

"To fit in, of course! I'm in Colorado, aren't I?"

"I think you'd better try another route," Mallory suggested with mock seriousness. "Maybe you can impress the residents of Aspen with your fine cooking ability. Which means we'd better hightail it over to our class—if you get my meaning."

"Unfortunately, I do." Gordon's shoulders sagged as he returned to a human posture. "I'd try to outdo you, but at the moment I can't think of any puns that incorporate bear anatomy."

"Just as well."

"Can I give you a bear hug instead?"

She rolled her eyes. "Let's just hurry," she said as she led the way to a small building a few paces off the red brick walkway.

"This seems like a great way for a nonskier to spend an enjoyable afternoon," Mallory observed as she passed through the door Gordon held open for her.

"Any option that involves food is bound to be good," he agreed.

They stepped into a small shop that was crammed with everything a gourmet chef, or even an aspiring one, could possibly hope for. Display tables were covered with colorful enamel pots and pans from France, hand-painted casserole dishes from Italy, and bright copper kettles like those immortalized in song. Kitchen gadgets that did everything from chop to scrape were lined up on racks. Packed onto the shelves that lined one entire wall were the ingredients necessary to make a foodie's dreams come true: raspberry vinegar; cocktail onions swimming in vermouth; barbecue sauces with overly cute names, most of which emphasized their ability to make steam come out of people's ears.

Jutting off the main room was a demonstration kitchen outfitted with a tremendous refrigerator, an even bigger freezer, and a restaurant-size stove. Other wannabe chefs were already clustered inside, giggling like schoolchildren as they donned aprons and arranged crisp white toques on each other's heads.

"Looks like we're right on time," Gordon observed. "Grab an apron and let's get cookin'."

"Welcome, everybody," their instructor began, breaking into the din. He was about thirty, with dark hair and handsome features. "I'm Miguel, your instructor for today's workshop, From Soup to Nuts. First we're going to prepare a five-course meal. Then we'll learn which wines to pair with each course. Afterward, we'll all sit down together to enjoy the results. Today's menu features a pear and gorgonzola salad, seared wild salmon, and a fabulously rich chocolate dessert that looks complicated but is actually deceptively easy to prepare. Now, does everyone have an apron—and have you all washed your hands?"

Somehow, Mallory felt as if she'd time-traveled back to the third grade. Then again, that tended to happen whenever she was learning something new.

She was pondering whether that was a good point to make in her article when Gordon leaned over and whispered, "Today, we weel be making zee...how you say in Eenglish, zee hot dog? Of course, in French, we say *le chien chaud,* wheech of course *means* zee hot dog but sounds so much better *en français...*"

"Sh-h-h," Mallory warned, even though she was unable to keep from laughing. "You're going to get both of us tossed out of here!"

"*Moi?* Never-r-r!" Gordon insisted, throwing his arms up in the air. "*Sacre bleu!*"

"Is there a question over there?" Miguel asked politely.

Gordon raised a finger into the air. "I have zee question—"

"No, we're fine," Mallory insisted, poking him in the ribs.

Miguel cast them both an odd look. "In that case, we will start by preparing the salad..."

Fortunately, Miguel kept them all so busy over the next two hours that Gordon had little time to make jokes—and Mallory had equally few opportunities to take notes. Like the other workshop participants, she was too busy learning how to make a perfect roux by mixing together just the right amounts of butter and flour, how to test for perfect pasta, and how to crack open an egg with one hand.

By the time the group sat down at a row of small tables set with white linen and crystal glassware to enjoy the results, she was more than ready. Gordon, however, wasn't as optimistic.

"Do we really have to eat this," he asked, "knowing it was prepared by a bunch of amateurs—myself included?" Warily he observed the pear and gorgonzola salad sitting in front of him, so artfully arranged that it looked as if it was posing for the cover of *Gourmet* magazine.

"Now, now," Mallory replied soothingly. "Almost everybody washed their hands. And that guy in the yellow polo shirt only sneezed on the pears once or twice."

Joking aside, she wasn't surprised that the dinner was excellent. The quality of the ingredients they had used was outstanding, and Miguel had been attentive without being annoying.

As he finished the last morsel of salmon on his plate, Gordon turned to her. "You're right. It was fabulous." Sighing, he added, "A nice break, too—from the nightmare we've all been living in for the past couple of days."

Somberly Mallory put down her fork. She was embarrassed to admit that she'd been having such a good time that she'd forgotten all about Carly's murder—and that she couldn't completely rule out Gordon as a suspect.

"Carly's murder has really thrown Aspen for a loop," she commented.

"That's for sure," Gordon agreed. "Especially since the cops seem to be looking at everybody in town. Poor Harriet, of course, even though from the looks of things she was the most loyal and dedicated employee anyone could hope for. Then there's that corporate-type from California who kept bugging Carly about selling the company." He frowned. "If you ask me, the person they should be trying to track down is Carly's ex."

Mallory blinked. She realized she'd been so caught up in Carly's present circle of friends and associates that it hadn't even occurred to her to look into Carly's past. "That's right. You mentioned that she'd been married twice before."

"One ex-husband dead, the other in prison." Shaking his head slowly, Gordon added, "But most of those guys don't stay locked up forever. Sooner or later they get out—and all too often, once they do they start making trouble all over again."

Mallory stared at her plate in silence as she contemplated the likelihood that Carly's felonious ex-husband might have had something to do with her death. Now that Gordon had brought him up, she realized it was an obvious possibility.

She wondered if the cops had looked at him. She also wondered what he'd been incarcerated for, as well as whether he'd gotten out of prison.

Most of all, she wondered if he harbored any hard feelings toward his ex.

The delicious meal she'd just devoured sat in her

stomach like a bowling ball. The more she thought about it, the more sense it made. After all, there was something to be said for the "once a bad guy, always a bad guy" line of reasoning. Especially where ex-husbands were concerned.

She couldn't forget what Harriet had told her about Gordon's thwarted plans for a movie about Carly's life. Was it possible he was going out of his way to cast suspicion on someone else as a means of diverting attention away from himself, just as she suspected Harriet had?

"Do you know anything about the man?" Mallory asked lightly. "His name, what he was in prison for . . . ?"

Gordon shook his head. "Every time he came up in conversation—which wasn't very often—Carly made it clear that her ex was one topic she didn't want to discuss. All I know is that at least part of the time they were together, they were in Philadelphia."

"I didn't know she'd lived there."

"The only reason *I* know it is that once I mentioned *The Philadelphia Story*. You know, the old Katharine Hepburn movie?"

Mallory nodded.

"We were talking about classic movies, I believe. Anyway, Carly kind of shuddered and said something like, 'Don't even mention Philadelphia to me, since that's where my creep of a husband and I were living when everything fell apart. For all I know, that's the place he went back to after they released him from jail, if they were ever dumb enough to let that jerk go free.'"

"Gordon," Mallory asked thoughtfully, "do you happen to know the years that Carly was married to him?"

Grinning, Gordon teased, "Don't tell me you're playing Nancy Drew."

She could feel her cheeks burning. "Not at all. I'm just curious."

"My impression is that it was pretty soon after she dropped out of college."

Mallory's eyebrows shot up. "I had no idea she'd dropped out. Then again, I don't know anything about what happened to her after high school."

"That was another piece of her past she happened to mention in passing," Gordon said. "I seem to recall that her parents shipped her off to some women's college. Somewhere in New England, I think. They felt she'd be much more likely to do well academically in a place like that. One where there were no men around, I mean. I take it Carly wasn't exactly class valedictorian back in high school."

"Not unless they were giving out A's for cheerleading and being elected Homecoming Queen," Mallory replied. "When she was voted Most Likely to Succeed, it was because of her good looks and her outgoing personality, not because of her grade point average."

With a little laugh, Gordon said, "Not a bad call, since she seems to have done pretty well for herself." Almost to himself, he added, "She could have done pretty well for a lot of us if she'd only been a little more flexible."

Mallory drew in her breath sharply. When Gordon

glanced over in surprise, she said, "Wow, that meal was really heavy. I'm starting to wish we'd made Alka-Seltzer for dessert instead of chocolate lava cake."

"Tell you what," he suggested. "How about taking a stroll around town? We can work some of it off."

When they stepped through the door of the cooking school, Mallory was surprised to find that it had grown dark. There was also a chill in the air she hadn't noticed earlier. A heaviness, too, as if some mischievous weather system had started acting up while they were busy dicing and slicing.

"Let's do a little window-shopping," Gordon suggested. "It's not the best exercise in the world, but at least we won't pull any muscles. Rack up any credit card bills, either, since most of the stores are closed by now."

It was true that most of the shops had shut down, leaving only a few dim lights shining in their windows to combat the darkness. The two of them were the only ones around as they strolled back to the main walkway, then stopped in front of a jewelry store.

But as she admired the baubles and beads in the window, Mallory felt a prickling behind her neck. She thought someone was tickling her until she realized that whatever she felt flicking against her skin was ice-cold.

"It's snowing!" she cried.

"So it is," Gordon agreed.

"But it's April!"

"I ordered it especially for you, my dear," he said with a teasing smile. "I wanted to make sure you had the total Aspen experience."

As more and more fat white flakes floated down from the sky, he tucked her arm under his. "Let's duck under that awning."

Mallory had just begun walking with him when she unexpectedly encountered a slippery spot. As her feet slid out from under her, instinctively she grabbed onto his coat, meanwhile hurtling her body against his to keep from falling.

"Whoa!" she exclaimed once she'd regained her footing. "Sorry about that!"

"I'm not," he replied, grinning. "In fact, that's the best thing that happened to me all day."

He turned to face her, then gently pulled her closer. "At least so far."

And then he leaned forward and kissed her.

Before she knew what she was doing, she was kissing him back. For a few moments, all she was aware of was the delicious feeling of his lips melting against hers.

And then a warning voice inside her head broke in.

Don't do it! it warned. It's dangerous. *He's* dangerous.

You don't know that, she thought stubbornly. Just because Harriet planted the idea in your head that he might have . . .

But as she stood in the cold night air, surrounded by a lovely dusting of snow that had been custom-ordered for her by the man who held her in his arms, she found it impossible to believe she'd misjudged him so badly. Once before, she'd doubted her own instincts, letting her fears about someone special get in her way.

She didn't want to let that happen again.

Of course it made sense to play it safe. But the simple fact was that she just didn't want to. Not when kissing Gordon—and being kissed by him—felt so good.

But there were other factors to consider. Other emotions. Specifically, the ones that popped up whenever she even entertained the idea of letting a man other than her husband David into her life. It hadn't even been two years since he had died, and she still wasn't sure she completely grasped the idea that he was really gone.

She was the one who broke off the kiss.

"I should really get back to the hotel," she said, reluctantly stepping back.

Gordon reached up and stroked her cheek. "How about if I come with you?"

She shook her head. "I can't."

He hesitated for a few seconds before saying, "Okay. Not that I'm not disappointed. It's just that I know better than to push people too hard." With a little shrug, he added, "They used to say that was one of the things that made me a good director. Back in the day, that is."

She stiffened at his mention of his past success as a movie director. It served as a harsh reminder of his recent attempts at regaining the status he had once enjoyed—which in turn led to the accusations Harriet had made.

"I think I'll call it a night," she said, aware of the awkwardness that had suddenly sprung up between them.

"At least let me walk you back," he insisted.

"Thanks, but I'll be fine alone. I...I want to do some thinking. Good night, Gordon."

Before he had a chance to respond, she turned and walked away, taking care not to slide on any invisible patches of ice. Since her initial slip, she'd done her best to keep her balance.

And that was something that she didn't want to change.

Despite the chill in the air, Mallory was in no hurry to get back to her empty hotel room. And it wasn't only because the wintry night was so beautiful. She was also trying desperately to sort through the confusing assortment of emotions whirling around inside her head.

Here she had thought being chased by a faceless killer in a pickup truck had shaken her. But it turned out that the feeling of being out of control that *that* episode had elicited was nothing compared to her reaction to kissing Gordon Swig.

Do I feel something for this man? she wondered as she scuffed through the half inch of snow that had already drifted onto the sidewalks. *Should* I feel something for this man?

Answering questions that should have been simple was beyond her.

When she neared Main Street and realized that the Jerome was only a few hundred yards away, she purposefully headed in the opposite direction. She'd been meaning to visit the John Denver Sanctuary, and the novelty of checking it out at night struck her as something that might add a nice touch to her article. The snow had stopped, and a pale round moon had put in an appearance, glowing dimly in the otherwise dark sky.

Mallory decided to forget all about Gordon and Carly and everything else that was troubling and instead, at least for a few minutes, to think like a travel writer. Shortly after she passed a sign that said RIO GRANDE PARK she spotted a tremendous skate park. It was made up of perfectly smooth concrete bowls that no doubt constituted heaven for young people who could conceive of nothing more thrilling than having wheels attached to their feet.

Seeing it brought her back to Jordan's skateboarding phase. It also made her remember all the times he'd been chased out of parking lots and schoolyards in his ongoing search to find a place to enjoy his hobby. She was pleased that the town of Aspen had recognized the need for such a facility. Then again, given the town's dedication to enabling people to take advantage of gravity in the name of having fun, she supposed it wasn't all that surprising.

She made her way along a path that meandered along a shallow creek edged with white stones. Even in the darkness, she could see that it had a wild look that she decided captured the Colorado spirit. As she walked a little farther, she noticed that jutting up ahead were granite stones with rounded tops. The configuration looked like a pint-sized version of Stonehenge, minus the symmetry.

Once she got close, she saw that the collection of rocks included several that were engraved with the lyrics of Denver's songs: "Rocky Mountain High," "Sunshine On My Shoulders," "Annie's Song," and half a dozen others. But the most prominent one looked chillingly like a headstone. It was engraved with some lyrics from one of his songs that included the phrase. "I sing with all my heart."

She brushed away the light coating of fluffy white snow to read the rest. Centered below were the words:

JOHN DENVER
Composer, Musician, Father, Son, Brother, Friend

Underneath were the dates of his birth and death. Born 1943, died 1997 ... Mallory did a quick calculation and realized he'd lived only fifty-three years.

She knew from her research that John Denver had not only lived in Aspen, he had been one of its greatest admirers. And every October, fans continued to gather in this spot to celebrate him. In 2007, the tenth anniversary of his death, the event had gone on for five days, with tributes, films, and concerts. That same year, Denver's song, "Rocky Mountain High," had been chosen as Colorado's state song.

Mallory found the simplicity and naturalness of the sanctuary moving. Curious about where he had actually been born and raised, she opened her guidebook, holding it up to her nose as she tried to find the section that described the sanctuary. But she couldn't make out the tiny print on the page, given the small amount of light afforded by the starless sky.

As she closed the book with a sigh, she also noticed how dreadfully cold it had gotten. Shrugging under her jacket and pulling it tighter, she glanced around and realized she was the only person foolish enough to be wandering around a cold, dimly lit park this late at night.

But instead of finding her solitude comforting, it occurred to her that walking alone in a deserted place like this might not be such a good idea. In fact, the looming rocks suddenly struck her as threatening, and the silence that surrounded her seemed menacing instead of tranquil.

She jumped when she heard what sounded like a footstep—then told herself she was merely a victim of her own overactive imagination.

It's just the wind, she told herself. A tree branch or something else blowing around . . .

She heard the sound again. And this time, it definitely sounded like a footstep.

Oh, my God, she thought, her heartbeat instantly speeding up. If somebody attacks me, do I have anything to fight him off with?

Trying not to panic, she mentally reviewed the

contents of her pocketbook. Wallet, credit cards, room key, tissues...

And then she remembered that she did have something that could be useful. Moving slowly, without making a sound, she opened her purse and with trembling fingers reached inside.

Chapter 15

"We wander for distraction, but we travel for fulfillment."
—Hilaire Belloc

Mallory fumbled around until her fingers made contact with smooth metal. Grateful that she had something that at least vaguely resembled a weapon, she grabbed the can of room spray she'd bought for Amanda the day before and forgotten to take out of her purse. Grasping it tightly, she whirled around, poised to attack.

Her finger froze in the split second before it pressed the aerosol button.

"*Sylvie?*" she cried, blinking at the figure cowering in front of her. The fact that her would-be attacker was dressed in a pale pink ski jacket, its hood trimmed with fluffy white fur, made her look more like the Easter Bunny than the Abominable Snowman.

"Don't shoot!" Sylvie cried, defensively holding her hands out in front of her. They were swathed in a pair of fuzzy white mittens that made her look even more harmless. Squinting in the darkness, she demanded, "Is that Mace?"

"Room spray," Mallory admitted sheepishly, lowering the can. "Organic, made with green oolong. The worst thing it would do is make you smell like a tearoom."

A look of confusion crossed Sylvie's face. But instead of asking why Mallory was carrying around such a thing in her purse, she demanded, "What are you doing out here?"

"Research, of course," Mallory replied indignantly. "For the article I'm writing. I was visiting the John Denver Sanctuary."

"At *night*?"

"There's a lot I need to see here in Aspen," she explained. "I'm having trouble fitting it all in."

Especially since I'm spending so much of my time investigating a murder, she thought ruefully.

That thought reminded her that the woman she was talking to happened to be a prime suspect.

Uneasily, Mallory asked, "What about you, Sylvie? What brought *you* out here?"

"I had to get out of that hotel room," Sylvie insisted, shaking her head as if trying to brush away something unpleasant. "Mallory, I feel like a caged animal. Would you believe those cops who showed up in my room this morning told me not to leave town?" Snorting contemptuously, she added, "As if I would ever resort to violence. For goodness sake, I have a Harvard MBA!"

Ri-i-ight, Mallory thought. As if no one with a degree from an Ivy League school has ever committed a serious crime.

"I can't believe their audacity!" Sylvie continued. With an arrogant toss of her head, she added, "Imagine *me,* of all people, endangering everything I've worked so hard for. And the idea of doing something that stupid because of someone like that... that small-time operator who got lucky because she turned out to have a flair for self-promotion... The whole thing just makes me crazy!"

Once again, Mallory was struck by the irony of Sylvie's words.

How about the fact that you're so angry at the woman—not to mention so disdainful—that in your own words, it makes you crazy? Isn't *that* enough for the police to think you might have been driven to kill her?

"I'm sure they'll find the real killer soon," Mallory said soothingly, trying to appease her. "And then all this will be nothing but a terrible memory."

A gust of wind suddenly made her feel as if icy fingers were encircling her neck.

What am I doing, standing alone in the dark with this woman? she wondered with alarm.

For all she knew, Sylvie had noticed that Mallory was a little too interested in Carly's murder and had followed her here with the express intention of doing her harm. In fact, it was possible that the prospect of spray in her eyes—even organic spray that probably tasted absolutely delicious—was all that was keeping the person who had sneaked up on her from following through on her plan.

"You know, Sylvie, you were right about coming out here at night being a silly idea," she said as calmly as she could. "In fact, I'm so cold right now that my fingers are numb. Why don't we both go back to the Jerome where it's nice and warm?"

She was relieved when Sylvie fell into step beside her, walking at the same brisk pace.

But as they headed out of the park, another thought occurred to her.

"Sylvie," she said in a conversational tone, "what do you think will happen to Rejuva-Juice now that Carly is gone?"

"I've always thought her husband had more sense than she did," Sylvie replied, her voice tinged with bitterness. "At least when it came to business. Carly had emotional ties to the company that he never had. After all, she's the one who created it. Now that Brett's in charge, I'm hoping that once and for all we can get this settled."

"I see."

The wheels in Mallory's head were turning with alarming speed.

So not only is it possible that Sylvie became enraged by pushing and pushing without getting anywhere, she thought. Another scenario is that rightly or wrongly, Sylvie might have decided that while Carly wouldn't sell the company, her husband was likely to be more willing.

Which gave Sylvie a second motivation for killing

Carly—and Mallory another good reason to move her even further up on her list of suspects.

As she let herself into her hotel room, Mallory was still pondering the question of whether mere coincidence or something much more sinister had been responsible for her unexpected encounter in the park with Sylvie. She kicked off her shoes, hoping the fact that she was dog-tired would enable her to get a good night's sleep instead of spending a good portion of it ruminating about Sylvie and all the other suspects in Carly's murder. But as she headed toward the bed, she noticed the red light blinking provocatively on her phone.

Amanda? she thought with a concerned frown. She picked up the receiver and dialed the code printed on the instruction card next to the phone.

As soon as she heard Trevor's voice on the recorded message, she realized she'd had such a long, busy day that she'd completely forgotten that her boss was in town.

"Where have you been all day?" Trevor's recorded message demanded. "And why haven't you been answering your cell phone? I thought—I *hoped*—that we'd be able to, I don't know, do some sightseeing together. Call me, Mallory. It's been too long since I've heard from you and I'm worried."

Guiltily Mallory pulled her cell phone out of her purse—and saw that the battery had died. Even though it was late, she decided she owed him a return phone call. Especially if he was as anxious as he sounded.

"Trevor?" she asked when he answered the phone in his room.

"Mallory?" His groggy voice told her she'd woken him up. "Where have you been all day? Are you okay?"

"I'm great," she insisted. "I've just been busy." Wanting to assure him that everything was fine, she added, "It turns out that learning everything there is to know about a place in only three and a half days requires being a nonstop tourist." Particularly when you're also trying to learn everything there is to know about half its residents, not to mention its visitors. Lightly, she added, "How about you? Have you had a chance to see much of Aspen?"

"Sightseeing wasn't my main reason for coming," he pointed out. "Look, I know it's late, but how about meeting me somewhere for a drink?"

Mallory hesitated. Here she'd wanted nothing more than to climb into bed and sleep. Still, Trevor was her boss. And he *had* come all this way to make sure she was all right.

"A quick one," she said, already cramming her feet back into her shoes. "I'll be downstairs at the J-Bar in five minutes."

As soon as Mallory combed her hair and smeared on some lipstick, she felt energized. True, her first reaction to the idea of an impromptu late-night rendezvous had been to view it as an annoyance—as in I'm only doing this because Trevor is my boss. But as she checked her appearance in the mirror before heading out the door, she found herself looking forward to what now struck her as sort of an adventure.

While Trevor was the man she worked for, she couldn't deny that she enjoyed his company. Of course, she rarely saw him, since they did most of their communicating with phone calls and e-mail. But their e-mails had become increasingly chatty over time. Longer, too. Their exchanges through cyberspace may have started out with nothing more personal than Trevor's editorial comments and the details of Mallory's upcoming trips, but they invariably turned into conversations that went back and forth far past the time the two of them had accomplished whatever was needed.

Despite her reluctance to admit it, Mallory thought Trevor was charming. She was also eternally grateful to him for having faith in her at a time when she had virtually none of her own. The fact that he'd made certain assumptions about her abilities, not only as a writer but also as someone centered enough to handle whatever came up on a press trip, had prompted her to find the inner strength required to keep from disappointing him.

That didn't mean he liked the idea of her sticking her nose into criminal investigations. As she rode down in the elevator, Mallory promised herself that tonight she wouldn't say a word about her involvement in Carly's murder.

Like the rest of the hotel, the J-Bar embodied the spirit of the days when Aspen was known for its silver mines, rather than as a gold mine for anyone in the ski business. The cozy hideaway was tucked into a front corner of the hotel, facing the street to increase its accessibility. While a few tables were crammed into the compact space, the focus was the wooden bar. Given its rustic look, it was hard to imagine approaching it any way besides bellying up to it.

Tonight, however, Mallory opted for one of the small tables. She'd barely had a chance to sit down before Trevor appeared in the doorway. His dark hair was slightly disheveled and there was a distracted look in his hazel eyes. The white shirt he wore with a pair of jeans looked so wrinkled that Mallory could picture the heap it had undoubtedly been lying in before he'd grabbed it off a chair five minutes earlier and pulled it on.

"You're looking good," he commented as he sat down opposite her.

"I wish I could say the same for you," she replied with amusement. "You look like somebody who was fast asleep ten minutes ago."

"Don't forget, I'm still on East Coast time," he replied, clearly doing his best to look more alert. "I have a very good excuse for not being the life of the party."

Frowning, he added, "Besides, I might have been in bed, but that doesn't mean I wasn't tossing and turning."

Mallory was relieved that the bartender chose that moment to slide a couple of cocktail napkins in front of them and cheerfully ask, "What'll you folks have?"

"I'll try the house drink," Mallory told him. "The Aspen Crud."

"Always doing research, huh?" Trevor teased.

Mallory laughed. "Drinking a milkshake that's spiked with bourbon isn't exactly hard duty."

"Whoa. Who came up with that combination?"

Flippantly she replied, "You'll just have to read my article to find out."

After he ordered his own drink, Trevor turned back to Mallory. Frowning, he said, "I'm glad the terrible thing that happened to your high school friend didn't put a damper on your enthusiasm for this trip. Or for Aspen."

"I won't say it hasn't affected me," Mallory admitted. "But I like to think I'm a professional. No matter what, I have to get the job done."

"Even if the job involves throwing down a couple of those?" Trevor joked as the bartender plopped what looked like a normal milkshake in front of her.

"No one appreciates how demanding this job is." She took a sip. "Wow. Now this is what I call dangerous."

"As long as drinking milkshakes is the worst thing you get involved in," Trevor commented, picking up his drink, "I'll be able to sleep nights."

"Talking to a few of the people who were close to Carly isn't much more dangerous than sucking up a zillion calories," she mumbled.

As soon as she saw the look on Trevor's face, Mallory kicked herself.

No sooner do I have two sips of this deceptive drink, she thought, *and I'm spilling the beans, telling* him the one thing I was determined not to let slip out.

"What did you say?" he demanded.

"Nothing!" she insisted. "I just meant that in the course of getting in touch with her again, naturally I've run into some of the people who—"

Trevor banged his drink down on the table. "You've launched a murder investigation of your own, haven't you?"

Mallory was silent for a few seconds. "It's complicated, Trevor," she finally said, staring into her milkshake. "Someone I met my first day here, a woman I was convinced was innocent, asked me for help. It all started when the police called her in—"

"The police!" Trevor exclaimed. "Mallory, have you lost your mind? Why on earth would you get involved in something like this?"

As she tried to come up with a short answer, she realized this wasn't something that was easy to explain. So she simply told him, "Like I said, it's complicated."

He sighed. "Mallory, you can't blame me for being worried. After what happened in Florida . . . and now this . . ."

"Trevor, I can take care of myself," she told him gently. "I appreciate that you're worried. I really do. But this is something I have to do."

"Look, the last thing I want is to sound heavy-handed," he said. "I'm just concerned." He hesitated before he thoughtfully added, "In fact, I find myself worrying about you—and just generally thinking about you—a lot more than just about anybody else in my life right now."

As she looked into his eyes, only inches away across the small table, she saw an intensity in them that she hadn't seen before. She was also aware of a spark of electricity flying between them that set her heart pounding.

And then he leaned over and kissed her.

Almost as quickly and unexpectedly as it happened, he jerked away.

"Oh, my God!" he cried. "Mallory, I—I don't know what came over me! I'm so sorry!"

I'm not, she thought, surprised by her own reaction.

But since Trevor seemed to regret what had just happened, she wasn't about to admit to her true feelings. In fact, he was suddenly so flustered that she actually felt sorry for him.

"I—I don't know what to say!" he said, unable to make eye contact. "Believe me, that's the *last* thing I ever intended to happen. I mean, I don't want you to think that I'm sexually harassing you. Or doing anything at all to make you uncomfortable or put you in an awkward position—oh, wait. That didn't come out the way I meant it to. What I mean is—"

"I know what you mean, Trevor," she assured him. "You're my boss and we're on a business trip together."

Even though your being here wasn't part of the original plan, she thought. *Which brings me back to the question of what you're even doing here in the first place.*

"But honestly," she continued, "I promise that whatever happens in Aspen stays in Aspen."

"Thank you," he said, his facial muscles still tense. "I appreciate that you're being so understanding."

Even though the creases in his forehead had yet to disappear, he looked relieved. Still, she hoped the uncertainty on his face meant that he was at least a little disappointed that she hadn't—well, ripped off her clothes or pushed him to the ground and thrown herself at him or declared that she felt the same attraction he did . . .

But she didn't feel it.

Or did she?

Oh, my, she thought, suddenly even more flustered than Trevor had been. *Am I attracted to Trevor? Have I felt that way all along?*

It was possible that she'd simply been reluctant to admit it to herself—or even that her perceptions had been clouded by the fact that he was her boss. Then again, she couldn't deny that the teasing banter that had become their normal way of talking to each other wasn't exactly the kind of interaction she would have expected to have with someone who was purely her employer.

And what about all those e-mails and the way they'd moved way beyond matter-of-fact exchanges of information long ago? She couldn't deny that they'd taken on a flirtatious tone shortly after she'd started writing for *The Good Life.*

While she'd told herself all along that the fact that he believed in her was all that was behind the engaging tone of his constant communications, she couldn't deny that the two of them clearly liked each other. Somehow, they seemed to have been on the same wavelength since the very start. Or maybe it was just that he seemed so comfortable with himself that she, in turn, found herself feeling just as comfortable with herself.

"If you don't mind, Mallory," Trevor finally said with an air of resignation, "I'm going to bed. Uh, to my room, I mean. Alone. Of course alone. I didn't mean to imply that you thought that I thought—"

"Good night, Trevor," she told him calmly, amused to see that for once in his life, Trevor Pierce had lost his cool. And struck by the fact that *she* was responsible.

A few minutes later, as she slid into her own bed, relishing the sensation of slipping between cool, silky smooth sheets, Mallory suddenly started to giggle.

Wow, she thought, suddenly overcome by a crazy, wonderful giddiness. Two kisses in one night. From two different men.

The only other time that had happened, according to her recollection, was when she was fifteen.

Somehow, it seemed even sweeter the second time around.

Chapter 16

"Half the fun of travel is the esthetic of lostness."
—Ray Bradbury

The next morning, Mallory lay in bed for a long time, savoring the delicious groggy state that always enveloped her as she awakened. Her brain was still so firmly encased in cotton batting that she didn't know whether the feelings waiting for her on the other side of semiconsciousness would be good or bad.

But as the cotton batting began to fall away, she gradually remembered that both feelings were lurking in the wings.

The good feelings, of course, were the result of having been kissed by two different men the night before. Two *divine* men, if she dared use a word that sounded like something out of Sandra Dee's vocabulary.

But as she grew even more awake, she remembered that her luscious role as femme fatale was also clouded by negativity. While Gordon Swig elicited plenty of good feelings, at the same time he elicited some bad ones. After all, she still wasn't completely convinced that he wasn't Carly Berman's killer.

Impossible! Mallory thought, finally opening her eyes to a room that positively glowed, thanks to the bright early morning sunlight streaming in through the windows. As she replayed the night before in her head, she found that she couldn't believe Gordon capable of any crime—that is, aside from stealing someone's heart.

Then, of course, there was Trevor. Sweet, shy, down-to-earth Trevor, she thought, unable to keep from smiling. She and her boss had both been jolted into recognizing that they had feelings for each other, and as a result she was glowing with the same intensity as the early morning sun.

After weighing the pluses and minuses, she decided that on balance she deserved to be happy about what had happened. What *is* happening, she corrected herself. Yesterday was just the beginning.

She finally dragged herself out of bed and busied herself with her first task of the day: calling room service and ordering breakfast. Doing so signified that she was now officially awake, which meant it was time to stop lolling about like the heroine in a romance novel and get busy with the day's To Do list.

So while she waited for breakfast to arrive, she grabbed the small pad of paper printed with the hotel's logo and did some quick calculations. Then she turned on her laptop and went on-line to look up the number of the state of Pennsylvania's government offices.

By the time Mallory had worked her way through half a pot of coffee, she was ready to get serious. After checking her watch to make sure it was late enough on the East Coast, she dialed the phone number for the Office of Vital Records. She was pleased that an actual government employee answered, instead of a machine.

"I'm wondering if you can help me with kind of an unusual problem," Mallory began, hoping the woman on the other end of the line would turn out to be as friendly and helpful as her greeting had made her sound. "I'm going to my high school reunion next month, and for the life of me I can't remember the name of the guy my best friend from back then ended up marrying. I know I'll run into both of them there, and I'm going to be really embarrassed if I don't know what to call her husband when she and I start reminiscing about gym class and prom night!"

"Have you tried looking through your yearbook?" the woman suggested. "That might jar your memory."

"My friend and her husband didn't meet until later," Mallory explained. "That's why it's so hard to remember what the heck his name was. Is there any way you could look it up for me?"

"What year did your friend get married?"

Mallory's heartbeat sped up. This was looking promising...She glanced at the pad of paper on which she'd figured out the year Carly had most likely married her first husband. Based on what Gordon had said, she'd figured Carly had probably been around twenty.

After telling the woman the year she'd targeted, she added, "I'm not positive that's the correct year. It's close, but it could actually have been a year or two before or after that."

"Give me the exact spelling of her name and I'll see what I can find," the woman said kindly. "Do you mind if I put you on hold for a few minutes?"

"Not at all. Her name is Carly—that's C-A-R..."

While she waited, Mallory's heart pounded so hard she was glad she wasn't a hypochondriac. It was only then that she realized how badly she wanted it to turn out that Carly's wayward ex-husband was the culprit. She certainly didn't want it to be Gordon. Harriet, either. Or even Sylvie, for that matter. If the reason for Carly's murder was that a terrible mistake she'd made more than twenty years earlier had come back to haunt her, her death would still be just as terrible—but at least it would let all three of the people Mallory had gotten to know in Aspen off the hook.

"I found it!" the woman at the end of the line announced triumphantly less than five minutes later. "The man your friend married is named Clive Darnell. Let me spell that for you."

After thanking the woman profusely, Mallory focused on her laptop once again. Her heart was still pounding as she did a search for the state of Pennsylvania's corrections department. Once she found it, she did a prisoner search for the name Clive Darnell.

Then she held her breath for the few seconds it took the system to search. "No Name Found."

"Okay, there are still forty-nine more states to try," she muttered, unwilling to be discouraged. "Just because Carly's ex spent some time living in Pennsylvania doesn't mean he never got into trouble somewhere else."

She tried Ohio, then Indiana. When both states' corrections department Web sites failed to turn up anything about a Clive Darnell, she hesitated, wishing she'd paid closer to attention in geography class. She finally Googled a map of the United States, then started checking the Web site of every state in that part of the country.

"Yes!" she cried when Clive Darnell came up on the Iowa corrections department Web site.

But her momentary elation over finding the information she'd been looking for turned to something else when she read the rest of the information the Web site supplied. Clive Darnell had been released in March, exactly three weeks before Carly's murder.

"Oh, my God," she breathed. "He's out."

Which means he could very well have killed Carly.

She was agonizing over whether she could figure out how to use the Internet to find out if he owned a forest green Ford pickup when her cell phone rang. She rushed to her pocketbook and pulled it out.

She just assumed one of her admirers was calling, and she was anxious to find out which one. So she was actually disappointed when the number of the caller ID screen told her that one of her children was calling.

Squelching the feelings of guilt that instantly arose, she answered, "Hello, sweetie," even though she didn't know which of her two sweeties it would turn out to be.

"Why haven't you called?" Amanda immediately demanded, her tone accusatory.

Where should I begin? Mallory wondered.

Aloud, she said, "Sorry, honey. I've been busy. You know I'm only going to be here for a few days but there's still so much I have to get done—"

"You know I worry about you when you're on the road," Amanda countered. "Traveling in a strange place all by yourself..."

If only you knew, Mallory thought, smiling to herself.

"As a matter of fact, that hasn't been a problem," she assured her daughter.

"I've been thinking," Amanda continued, barging ahead as if she wasn't really listening. "Maybe I'll just hop on a plane and fly out there myself. To keep you company, I mean."

"Please don't!" Mallory cried. *Believe me,* she was thinking, *the state of Colorado is already crowded enough.* But since she didn't want to sound as if she wasn't grateful for her daughter's concern, she quickly added, "Honestly, Amanda, there's no reason to worry about me. I'm just fine. Besides, I don't want you missing any of your classes."

"But Mother, I hate to think of you stuck out there all alone!"

"I'm not exactly alone," Mallory finally told her. "My boss flew out here last night."

"Trevor Pierce?" Amanda asked, surprised.

"That's the one."

"Now *that* makes me feel a lot better," Amanda said. "It must be comforting to have someone you know out there with you."

I don't know if comforting is the right word, Mallory thought. Confusing, maybe. Or discombobulating... but in a *good* way.

After hanging up, she distractedly grabbed her coffee mug and realized the coffee had gotten cold. She plopped it back down on the tray and turned back to her laptop.

Where was I? she thought. But she quickly remembered precisely where she'd been: making real progress in her Internet research about Carly's first husband, but growing frustrated over all the questions that still remained unanswered. And the most important one of *those* was the nature of the crimes that had put him behind bars.

Thank heaven for Google, she thought, typing in the name of Carly's ex-husband once again. But this time, she added a few more search words, including "arrested."

She held her breath while she waited for Google to work its magic. Within seconds, a page of entries popped up, with Clive Darnell in bold in every one of them.

She clicked on the first entry and found an article

from a local newspaper in Iowa, right below a short article requesting donations of cakes and other baked goods for the Methodist church's annual bake sale. Its date was July 13, 2005.

Downingville Man Arrested
for Check Fraud

Clive Darnell, a 44-year-old resident of Downingville, was arrested yesterday on suspicion of check fraud.

He was apprehended while trying to purchase a big-screen TV at an electronics store in Davenport. His arrest ended an eight-month investigation into a series of thefts dating back to 2003.

According to police, Darnell stole the checkbook from someone's briefcase, then wrote a check for $2929.50 and attempted to use it to buy a 46" Sony flat-panel LCD HDTV. When the store's employee asked for identification and he was unable to provide any, he alerted police.

Darnell was booked on suspicion of theft and forgery.

Check fraud? Mallory thought frowning.

It was a terrible crime, of course. It just wasn't the type she'd imagined Carly's ex-husband committing. Frankly, she'd been expecting something more along the lines of armed robbery or assault with a deadly weapon.

In other words, something violent. Something that would make him look more like the type of person who was likely to track down his ex-wife and kill her in cold blood. Maybe even someone whose behavior had pointed to psychopathic tendencies.

You've been reading too much Jonathan Kellerman, she scolded herself. The criminal world isn't characterized by that level of drama. Or by such quirky personalities, either. All it would take for Carly's ex to have acted that way would have been extreme jealousy or a desire for revenge...

With a sigh, Mallory pushed her laptop away. The information she'd found was disappointing. True, the scenario she'd been hoping to construct—one in which Carly's ex-husband hightailed it over to Colorado to track her down the moment he was let out of prison—was still a possibility. It was just that deep down in the pit of her stomach, she wasn't even close to convinced that it was a strong enough possibility to clear the names of all the other suspects.

Which meant she still had more work to do. And that work had to be done where Carly's killer most likely lurked: right here in Aspen, within the circle of people who had been closest to her.

As she contemplated what to do next, Mallory mentally ran through her list of suspects. She realized that questions about Dusty still nagged at her. She supposed she shouldn't have been surprised that over lunch at the top of Aspen Mountain he'd denied being Carly's paramour. But what interested her even more was that Autumn had insisted he was.

Then there was the fact that he had insisted Autumn was his girlfriend while she claimed to be his ex. What's *that* about? Mallory wondered.

She remembered Dusty mentioning that he and his household full of ravenous roomies lived on Waters Avenue. According to her map, it was tucked away on the edge of town.

A few minutes later, she found herself strolling down the quiet residential street, trying to look casual instead of like someone who was scoping it out. Not surprisingly, most of the buildings she passed were well-maintained condos whose proximity to the base of Aspen Mountain undoubtedly meant they were the weekend getaways of the wealthy. One building, however, stuck out like the proverbial sore thumb. The dilapidated three-story structure, covered in wooden shingles instead of sturdier materials, looked unloved, as if it was silently begging for a new coat of paint and the services of a competent window cleaner. Its tired appearance, combined with the fact that it was wedged between two considerably tonier complexes, made Mallory wonder if its owner was counting the minutes until he could knock it down and put up something that would justify higher rents.

Once she'd zeroed in on the building she was certain had to serve as Dusty Raines's castle, she retreated to a small espresso joint she'd noticed on the corner. The last thing she needed at this point was more caffeine. Her nerves already felt as if someone who'd time-traveled into town from the Spanish Inquisition had stretched them on a rack. But she needed a place that could serve as headquarters for her stakeout.

So she went inside and ordered a cappuccino.

"Make that a decaf," she added at the last minute, figuring that at some point in her life she might actually want to sleep.

While most of the tables were empty, she headed for one of the stools at the counter lining the front window of the storefront. What the seating arrangement lacked in comfort it more than made up for in the first-rate view it afforded her of Dusty's street. At least the end of it, a point he had to pass through if he was going to leave home sweet home.

Mallory only had a chance to sip half her coffee before she spotted her prey, dressed in the same sloppy jeans that in her mind had become his trademark. She stuck the plastic lid back on and stepped outside, trying to act casual even though her heart was pounding so hard she wondered if the barista had surreptitiously slipped a few milligrams of caffeine into her cup.

She was out on the street quickly enough to see Dusty turn right. She strode down the street after him, walking at a speedier pace than just about anybody else in Aspen. Then again, she still had half a cappuccino in her hand, which she hoped would offer an obvious explanation to anyone she passed who thought it strange that she was moving so fast.

Mallory took care to lag far enough behind that she could keep an eye on Dusty without him realizing he was being followed. When he disappeared inside a doorway, she quickened her step. The leftover coffee sloshed around in the cup, threatening to erupt through the tiny opening in the plastic lid. She was still debating whether to chuck it or hold onto it as a valuable prop when she saw that the place Dusty had ducked into was a small grocery store. She tossed her cup into the nearest trash can, then followed.

Peering through the storefront window, she saw that the shop sold basics to condo dwellers, staples like blue corn tortilla chips, vitamin water, and cartons of limited-edition Ben & Jerry's flavors. But as she was about to step inside, using the same door through which Dusty had disappeared, she realized that not only was it practically empty at this hour, it was small enough that he was nearly guaranteed to spot her.

Instead, she loitered outside on the sidewalk, debating what to do next.

But before she'd had a chance to come up with a plan, the door opened and Dusty emerged. Mallory stepped back against the building, cursing herself for standing in such an obvious spot. But luck was with her. He turned to walk in the opposite direction without even glancing in her direction.

She also saw that he was no longer alone. Walking alongside him was a woman.

But she didn't appear to be Dusty's age, even from the back. Mallory could see she was wearing a tailored jacket made of fine, expensive-looking wool and a pair of shiny patent leather high heels. She carried a Coach purse and her hair was meticulously styled into a neat pageboy, dyed blond and subtly interlaced with silver streaks.

In short, she looked rich. And not at all like a person who was part of Dusty's demographic—that is, someone who would enjoy whiling away the day eating pizza and playing Grand Theft Auto.

Another lady friend? Mallory wondered.

She picked up her pace, trying to keep far enough behind to go unnoticed but close enough to hear some of what Dusty and his Coach-clutching companion were saying to each other. The two activities, it turned out, were mutually exclusive. Unless she dared to hover dangerously close to them, she would never be able to hear a word of their conversation.

She was still struggling to come up with a solution when the woman suddenly threw back her head and laughed loudly. "Oh, Dusty!" she cried. "I don't know *what* I'd do without you!"

Is he that clever? Mallory mused, thinking that she must have missed something.

She trailed them a little farther, noticing that by that point the three of them had reached the outskirts of town. Here, the streets were still lined with buildings, but most were clusters of condominiums.

Mallory realized that if Dusty and his companion went inside one of them—for example, if it turned out that Ms. Coach lived in this part of town—she wouldn't have learned a thing.

Mallory's heartbeat speeded up again when they turned into a small park that separated two of the condo complexes.

Actually, it was more like an alleyway—that is, if the chic town of Aspen could have within its boundaries anything as base as an alleyway. Mallory broke into a jog, suddenly afraid she'd lose them. If they headed down a long, narrow passageway, especially one that veered off in another direction, she knew she ran a terrible risk of being spotted—and that if she was, she'd be hard-pressed to come up with a reason for why she was pursuing them.

But as she stopped a few feet before the turnoff, inched her way along a brick wall, and finally peered around the corner, she saw that the alleyway was only about twenty feet long. It was also filled with garbage pails. Not surprisingly, the residents of Aspen seemed to prefer to keep their trash out of sight.

This hardly struck her as the mostly likely place for a romantic interlude.

From where she stood, she could see that Dusty and his female companion were standing amidst the collection of plastic trash bins with their backs to her. But she still had a good enough view that she saw Dusty slip his friend a small plastic bag filled with something white. As soon as he did, the woman handed him a wad of bills, which he unceremoniously jammed into the back pocket of his jeans.

"You're the best, Dusty," the woman told him, grinning. "And so is what you're selling."

Cocaine? Mallory thought, astonished. *Dusty is a dealer?*

The realization hit her like a bolt of lightning.

She didn't dare wait around a moment longer. Her heart pounded with jackhammer speed as she quickly turned and hurried back in the direction from which she'd come. She veered off onto the next side street she encountered, anxious to keep Dusty from spotting her as he and his happy customer emerged from the alley.

As Mallory half walked, half jogged away, her mind raced even faster than her feet or her heart.

If Dusty is *this* middle-aged woman's friendly neighborhood drug dealer, she thought, does that mean his relationship to Carly was the same?

It would certainly explain what he and Carly were doing all that time Juanita reported they spent behind closed doors. It also gave her a good idea why Carly would have been anxious to keep her association with him a secret from her husband. As for Autumn—who Mallory believed really was Dusty's girlfriend—Mallory suspected that the girl was simply covering up for him, feeling it was safer for people to think Dusty was motivated by an active libido rather than to figure out he was selling drugs.

The more Mallory thought about it, the more sense it made. As she continued along the sidewalk, by now slowing her pace, she remembered something else that had struck her about Carly: her high level of energy. Mallory could picture how she'd looked the night she gave her talk at the Wheeler Opera House. Her eyes had been bright, her cheeks flushed. But rather than simply seeming excited, she'd appeared almost manic.

At the time, Mallory had thought all that energy was simply proof that Rejuva-Juice really was the wonder drug Carly claimed it was.

Now, it occurred to her that maybe a different drug had been responsible.

The more she thought about it, the more sense it

made that Carly's relationship with the twenty-something ski dude had had nothing at all to do with sex.

But as she mulled over what to do next, one question plagued her: If Dusty was Carly's dealer, rather than her lover, did that make him less of a suspect in her murder or more? After all, drug deals were notorious for going bad. And if Dusty was helping himself to his own wares, that could have contributed to erratic behavior—and perhaps even resulted in the impulse to kill.

Chapter 17

"It is not down in any map; true places never are."
—Herman Melville

The more Mallory pondered her hypothesis about the true nature of Carly's relationship with Dusty—one which cast everything she had learned so far into a totally new light—the more eager she was to find out if it was correct. And if there was one person who had known Carly well enough to verify her newfound belief about the true source of Carly's sparkle, it was Harriet.

The fact that Harriet also happened to hold a very high ranking on her list of suspects made Mallory wary of seeking her out to ask about Carly's secrets. But at the same time, she was glad to have an excuse to talk to her again. Mallory was anxious to see what Harriet's reaction would be when she confronted her with her findings about what Dusty Raines was selling besides ski wax and goggles.

She rifled through her purse until she found Harriet's business card, then dialed her office number at Tavaci Springs.

"Come on, come on," she muttered. "Answer, Harriet!"

After the twelfth ring, she gave up.

Where else would she be? Mallory had barely asked herself the question before she answered it: *at home.*

It was certainly the most likely possibility. The only problem was that she didn't know where Harriet lived.

Her first impulse was to call Cass-Ber and ask Juanita over the phone. But given the Bermans' housekeeper's attitude, she decided she had a much better chance of getting what she wanted by talking to her in person.

As she drove up the mountain road, keeping an eye out for the turnoff, she pondered the best way of ferreting out the information she was seeking. By the time she pulled into the driveway, she decided to play up to Juanita's vanity—namely, the key role she had played in the Bermans' life. If there was one impression she had formed about the woman, it was that she wanted to be treated with respect.

"What you want?" Juanita demanded, looking her up and down suspiciously as she stood in the doorway, guarding the entrance to the Bermans' home. Tucked under one arm like a giant football was Bijou. The poodle's eyes were bright and her tail wagged nonstop, as if she was thrilled to see someone who wasn't too busy moping around the big, silent house to play with her.

Just as Mallory had feared, Juanita didn't seem to feel the same way. In fact, she looked about as happy to see her as if she were a door-to-door salesman.

"Hello, Juanita," Mallory said evenly. "I dropped by because I hoped you'd be able to give me Harriet Vogel's home address."

The housekeeper narrowed her eyes suspiciously. "I don't geev out information to nobody!" she insisted. "Meester Berm, he ask me questions. The cops, they come to the house and *they* ask me questions. But I say the same thing to all of them: I don't know nothing—"

"The police questioned you?" Mallory asked, thinking, Of course they did. If there's anybody who knows about everything that ever went on around here, it's Juanita.

"Sure," Juanita replied with a proud toss of her head. "They come here. But I don't say nothing. I answer their questions, because I don't want no trouble. But I don't tell them nothing else."

For someone who prides herself on saying nothing, Mallory thought crossly, Juanita certainly says a lot.

"What did the police ask you?" she asked, curious about what the cops had managed to get out of her.

"Ees like on TV," Juanita replied. She still showed no sign of budging from the doorway long enough to let Mallory inside. "Where I was when poor Mees Berm is killed, where Meester Berm was that night . . ." Narrowing her eyes, Juanita added, "I tell them I don't know nothing 'bout Meester Berm. I was in my room with the door closed the whole time.

"But when I try to tell them I have my own ideas about who killed Mees Berm, they don't want to hear." She snorted before adding, "I think the police are not so interested in what a housekeeper thinks."

"*I'm* interested," Mallory told her eagerly. "Juanita, who do you think is the murderer?"

Juanita held up her hand. "I don't say noth—"

"Juanita," Mallory said in a low, even voice, "what you think—what you *know*—may not be important to the police, but it's important to me. After all, you were one of the people who was around Carly the most. You knew her very well, maybe better than anybody else. You saw and heard everything that went on around here."

"Ees true," Juanita agreed. Mallory was glad that her expression had softened. Her voice, too. "Ees like I am invisible. When I come into the room, most of the time people don't even notice."

"Exactly," Mallory said firmly. "When in fact what you are is knowledgeable. Which is why I'm really interested in hearing what you think." Taking a step closer, she added, "Maybe I can come in so we can talk."

Juanita finally moved aside to let Mallory in. As she did, she seemed lost in thought.

The two women were silent as Mallory perched on the edge of the woolly white couch. Juanita finally released Bijou and lowered her substantial frame into one of the wooden chairs with leather cushions. The poodle glanced back and forth between Juanita and Mallory several times, obviously trying to decide which one was more likely to pay attention to her. When she chose the newcomer, Mallory complied, reaching down and scratching the dog's ears.

"Now," she said, fixing her gaze on Juanita. "Tell me what you think."

"As soon as I hear what happened, I know who killed Mees Berm," Juanita said, nodding enthusiastically. "I was here—right in this room!—when I hear the whole thing the other night."

Mallory stiffened. "What 'whole thing'?"

"The big fight."

"Between Carly and her husband?" Mallory asked. She remembered only too well the argument she had overheard outside the dressing room at the Wheeler Opera House. Carly and Brett, yelling at each other...

"No. Those two, they fight all the time. Like cats and dogs. But they always make up. I talking about the big fight between Mees Berm and that accountant of hers."

Mallory's heart pounded furiously. "You mean Harriet?"

"They have beeg fight, Harriet and Mees Berm." Juanita reported. "Yelling and screaming...I hear all of eet. Thees time, I don't turn on the TV."

"And what were they fighting about?"

Juanita shrugged. "I don't hear every word. And sometimes, when people talk fast, my English ees not so good." Her eyes burning into Mallory's, she added, "But there ees one word even I understand. *Lawsuit*."

Mallory gasped. "A lawsuit? I had no idea anything like that was going on!"

Juanita nodded smugly. "That's right. And whenever people get lawyers involved, ees always bad news."

"What exactly were they saying about this lawsuit?" Mallory persisted.

"I hear Mees Berm say something like, 'If thees and that happens, then I have no choice but to go through with thees lawsuit.'"

"And you're certain it was Carly—Mrs. Berman—who was making that threat, and not Harriet?"

"Of course!" Juanita replied indignantly. "I know her voice, even eef they are yelling like—like wild coyotes. Eef there ees one thing I am good at, ees listening in on other people's conversations!"

I don't doubt it, Mallory thought.

But her thoughts were racing. "And you're certain that Carly was talking about suing Harriet and not someone else?"

"Like I say, I don't understand every word. But I know from what they are saying that they are very, very angry weeth each other." Juanita sighed. "The next thing I know, Mees Berm is dead."

Mallory felt as if the room was spinning. "Juanita, when did this fight take place?" she asked.

"A few nights before you come here for dinner. Two, maybe three."

In other words, Mallory thought, not long before Carly's murder.

Which meant the timing was right.

Still, Mallory wasn't one hundred percent convinced that Juanita's theory was correct, even if the conviction with which she presented it certainly went a long way in making her lean in that direction.

But she was determined to find out for sure.

"Juanita, I really need Harriet's home address," she said. "I want to talk to her myself."

"What, you think I am wrong?" Juanita asked indignantly.

"As a matter of fact, I think you're probably right," Mallory told her. "But I want to see if I can find evidence that she's guilty. Do you know where she lives?"

Juanita hesitated for a few seconds. "I never been to Harriet's house. But I theenk I know where Mees Berm keeps her address book."

I'll just bet you do, Mallory thought as Juanita scurried off to retrieve it. After all, her sense that Juanita didn't miss a trick was turning out to be right on.

And Mallory was finding the housekeeper's revelations most illuminating. After all, learning that Carly had planned to initiate a lawsuit against the quiet accountant certainly provided Harriet with a motive. That, combined with the angry note from Harriet that even the police thought implicated her, made for pretty strong evidence that she was the killer.

Now, all Mallory had to do was prove it.

By the time Mallory got back into her rental car, she was clutching a sheet of cream-colored stationery embossed with the name Tavaci Springs. Neatly handwritten on it was Harriet's home address.

Next stop, she thought ruefully, glancing at it as she backed out of the driveway.

As she drove down the mountain road, she contemplated the fact that so much of what she'd learned about what had happened in the days before Carly was murdered pointed to Harriet. And the note the police had found, insisting that an urgent matter be cleared up right away, was just the beginning. Even more compelling was Harriet's strange behavior after she was released from police custody—namely, going out to lunch with someone she had sworn she despised, rather than contacting Mallory, whom she'd treated like her only means of salvation. Then there was the guilty way she acted as she hurriedly locked something away when Mallory came back to her office more quickly than expected.

And now this. Juanita was one of those individuals who seemed to have been born with eyes in the back of her head. And that made her report that she had heard Carly and Harriet heatedly arguing about a lawsuit just a few nights before Carly was killed all the more believable.

Harriet really played me for a fool, Mallory thought bitterly. She *is* the murderer—yet she was crafty enough to talk me into investigating the murder and trying to pin the blame on someone else.

She held the steering wheel tightly, furious with herself for being duped. Still, as preoccupied as she was, she made a point of checking her rearview mirror every few seconds to make sure no diabolical pickup trucks were following her down the narrow, twisting road.

She was still gripped with rage as she turned on Harriet's street. She purposely parked half a block away from the house she identified as the accountant's, glad that rental car companies specialized in the blandest vehicles imaginable. Then she walked down the street, trying to act casual. When she reached the house, she saw there was no fence around the property, no BEWARE OF DOG signs, and no other obstacles that might make it difficult for her to approach the front door.

The small, two-story Victorian house was modest but well maintained. While its owner hadn't exactly gone overboard with making it seem homey, there were a few personal touches that made it welcoming. Half a dozen flower pots edged the wooden steps that led to the front porch, where a wooden swing with what looked like a fairly fresh coat of paint swayed gently in the early afternoon breeze.

Mallory recognized the Ford Escort parked in the driveway as Harriet's. But there was another car right behind it, one she didn't recognize. That one also had Colorado license plates. The fact that it blocked Harriet's car led Mallory to believe that the visitor didn't expect to stay long.

As she lingered in front of the house next door, planning what she would say once she rang the doorbell, the front door suddenly swung open, banging against the shingles loudly. Mallory slipped behind the thick trunk of a large tree, her eyes widening as she peered around the side.

"A deal is a deal!" she heard Harriet cry.

"Not when the terms change," a man grumbled.

He was stocky and dressed in clothes so wrinkled they looked as if they'd spent the night balled up on the floor. His head was completely shaved, and he wore a single gold earring. The glint of the metal matched the glint in his eyes.

"Keep your voice down," Harriet insisted. "Or do you want every one of my neighbors to hear us?"

"I don't give a rat's ass what your stupid neighbors think," the man growled. "I want more money. This job turned out to be a lot dirtier than I thought. I had no idea this was going to end up all over the news!"

Mallory grabbed onto the tree trunk to steady herself. Was it possible that Carly's murder had been the result of a contract killing? Had Harriet *hired* someone to kill her employer?

Her head was spinning from what she had just seen and heard.

But she was sure of one thing: Confronting Harriet to find out what she could learn about either Carly's real drug of choice or the lawsuit no longer seemed wise.

If Mallory was going to find out what it was all about, she was going to have to do it herself— *without* Harriet knowing.

The other times Mallory had come to Tavaci Springs, the secluded spa had seemed like a glamorous enclave for those who possessed too much time, money, and vanity. Now that Mallory was here alone, however, it struck her as downright eerie.

The isolated grounds were silent except for the chirping of birds, and the large windows that linked the indoors with the outdoors seemed to be staring at her blankly. As she walked through the property, her shoes crunched loudly against the gravel, causing her to look around nervously, hoping no one was watching her.

From what she could see, she was completely alone.

She held her breath as she tried the door of the back building, hoping that the events of the past few days hadn't prompted the staff to change the security codes. But as soon as she punched in the numbers she remembered Harriet using, 5–5–2–2, she heard a beep. When she tried the knob, it turned easily in her hands.

She hurried through the dark hallway, glancing from right to left. But the building was even more silent than the outdoors, with no birds singing and no gravel colliding against the soles of her feet.

As she stole into Harriet's office, her heart pounded so hard she felt nauseated. She could hear the blood throbbing in her temples as she prepared to do something she found painful.

I really like Harriet, she thought miserably. *The last thing I want is to find out that she actually is a murderer.*

But not only did she want justice to be served. She was also desperate to know whether she had been set up from the very start.

Mallory was reluctant to turn on any lights, so she was glad there was enough natural light coming through the window. Her goal was to find out what Harriet had been so anxious to hide the day before—and to get out before anyone spotted her. Then, once she had seen enough to convince her that Harriet was indeed the killer, she planned to go to the police. As for the details of how she would convince them, she had yet to work that out.

At the moment, however, she had a more immediate concern: how to break into the metal file cabinet. Unlike the front door of the building, it didn't open with a code. It required a key. And the only key Mallory had seen was the one Harriet had slipped into her pocket.

But she figured it was unlikely that Harriet carried the key to her file cabinet with her at all times. It was more likely it had a special place right here in the office.

Still, while the room wasn't very big, it was extremely cluttered. Just glancing around at the stacks of folders, office supplies, boxes, envelopes, and all the other accoutrements required to run a business made her feel as deflated as a balloon the day after the birthday party.

How will I ever find that key? Mallory thought, remembering how tiny it was and contemplating the thousands of places Harriet could have stashed it.

She wondered if there was a simpler way to open the drawer. After all, in books and movies people were always picking locks using hairpins.

Desperately she glanced around, even though she

was aware that it was unlikely that she'd find a hair-pin on Harriet's desk. After all, fussing with her hair didn't exactly strike her as Harriet's style.

Yet she was heartened when she noticed an item that struck her as close enough: a paper clip. She grabbed a large one that had been left on the desk, pulled it apart to turn it into a thin metal stick, and plunged it into the lock.

"Come on, come on..." she muttered as she poked it around inside the tiny hole.

The truth was that she didn't have a clue as to what she was supposed to be doing. All she knew was that in the movies, this technique always looked so easy. Then again, it was possible that hairpins possessed some magical property that paper clips just didn't have.

When she heard a click, it was all she could to keep from crying out in triumph. That is, until she realized that what she'd heard was the sound of the paper clip snapping in two.

"Great," she mumbled, tossing it into the trash.

She decided to return to Plan A, which was hunting down the key. She began by opening drawers, feeling under stacks of papers and rifling around in containers filled with more paper clips, pennies, and erasers. Then she ran her finger along shelves and even the top of the door. Finally, in a last desperate attempt, she dumped out the contents of the pencil mug sitting on the desk.

Mallory let out a cry when there, among all the pens and pencils, she actually spotted a small silver key that looked very much like the one she'd seen

Harriet use. Still, it wasn't until she shoved it into the lock and felt the perfect fit that she realized she had, indeed, found exactly what she was looking for.

She glanced around furtively, remembering Harriet saying that she sometimes thought the walls had ears. For all Mallory knew, they also had eyes. But once she had assured herself that at least it didn't appear that anyone was watching her, she pulled the drawer open.

Mallory's heart pounded furiously as she peered inside. Despite all the chaos outside the cabinet, inside this particular drawer there was only one thing: a thick manila folder.

Written neatly on the outside in large capital letters was a single word: *LAWSUIT.*

Surprise, surprise, she thought wryly. Juanita was right.

Tentatively Mallory opened the folder and read the top page: *Harriet Vogel, plaintiff, v. Rejuva-Juice Corporation, defendant.*

It's backward, Mallory thought, puzzled.

But her cloud of confusion cleared as she realized that while Juanita had been correct about the lawsuit, she'd apparently gotten the details wrong. Carly wasn't suing Harriet; Harriet was suing Carly.

So much for Juanita's supernatural eavesdropping powers, she thought wryly.

But *why* was Harriet suing Carly? she wondered. And if it was Harriet who had initiated the lawsuit, why would that make her angry enough to kill Carly? It should have been the other way around.

She sat cross-legged on the floor and perused the

contents of the folder, page after page of dense legalese. She stopped when she came across a thin notebook with a soft cover and stapled sides. As soon as she flipped it open she realized it was a journal of some sort. Actually, it was more like a log, one in which somebody had recorded events in a straightforward, factual way.

How am I ever going to make sense of all this? she thought with dismay.

But she forced herself to focus on the first page, holding the tiny, handwritten notes close as she tried to decipher them.

"April 12, 2004," the first entry began. "Realized I could use the Internet to pursue my interest in health tonics after finding an article about nontraditional treatments. Decided to explore possibilities."

Mallory scanned down the page, glancing at the entries that followed. One read, "Found more than ten articles on health benefits of folic acid. Must learn about its mechanisms in the body." Another said, "Exciting new developments at Life Sciences Institute in Amsterdam. Contact for permission to visit." A third said, "Set up appointment with Dr. Marilou Moschetti re: discoveries about body's ability to rebuild."

As she read on, Mallory wondered if perhaps she'd stumbled upon a log that Carly had kept.

After she'd skimmed several pages, she turned over a page and found a single sheet of paper, folded in half and stuck inside the book. Frowning, she opened it. Carefully printed on top were the words "HEALTH DRINK."

Below, written in the same handwriting as the journal, was what looked like a recipe.

As Mallory skimmed it, she immediately recognized the names of some of the ingredients. Açaí berries, goji juice... she remembered that those had been mentioned in that *New York Times* article. She seemed to recall Carly being quoted as saying that they were well-known as restorers of youth and vitality. The other ingredients that were listed had equally strange names.

A wave of intense heat ran through her as she realized what she was looking at. It was the recipe for Rejuva-Juice. The original recipe.

But why would Harriet have the recipe and Carly's journal? Mallory flipped through the other pages in the folder, various notes and letters, some with Harriet's scribbled signature. And that's when the truth dawned on her. The recipe was written in *Harriet's* handwriting and stuck into *her* journal.

Almost as if Harriet, and not Carly, had developed the magic potion that had given birth to a multimillion-dollar enterprise. One for which Carly, and not Harriet, had received both accolades and lots of money.

But Mallory was still confused. If Harriet is the real inventor of Rejuva-Juice, she thought, then why is everyone acting as if Carly invented it? And if Carly stole it—and if Harriet actually initiated a lawsuit over ownership—why would Harriet have worked for her all these years, cheerfully going along with the charade?

She was still puzzling over what she had found and

what it meant when she heard another click. A loud click, one that had nothing to do with a paper clip snapping in two.

In fact, she had seen enough movies in her day to know exactly what she was hearing. So she wasn't all that surprised when she slowly turned her head and saw that the click had come from a gun.

Or that the person holding the gun was Harriet.

Chapter 18

"No one realizes how beautiful it is to travel
until he comes home and rests his head
on his old, familiar pillow."
—Lin Yutang

Hello, Harriet," Mallory said, trying to sound matter-of-fact instead of letting on that she felt as if her heart was about to explode in her chest. "I see you have a gun."

Harriet nodded. "I've had it for years. I got it ages ago, just in case I ever felt threatened."

Mallory found herself unable to stop staring at it. Somehow, letting it out of her sight seemed unwise, given the fact that it was pointed right at her.

"But it's only me," she said, her voice catching. "Surely you don't feel threatened right now."

"I'm not sure what I feel," Harriet replied, her voice just as uncertain. "I thought we were friends, Mallory. I thought I could trust you. But instead I find you sneaking into my office, breaking into my file cabinet... At this point, I don't know what to think."

Join the club, Mallory thought morosely.

She held up the journal with the recipe sticking out of the pages. "All I wanted was to find out the truth," she said. "And I did. At least, I think I did." She took a deep breath. "Harriet, are you the person who really invented Rejuva-Juice?"

Mallory watched as Harriet's face reflected one emotion after another. Shock, anger, relief... and finally resignation. "Yes," she replied simply.

"Does that mean Carly stole it from you?"

"She didn't steal it!" Harriet insisted. In a much quieter voice, she added, "Not at first."

"Harriet," Mallory said, speaking in a low, gentle tone, "maybe you should put that silly gun down and tell me the whole story."

"I'll tell it to you," Harriet said without moving the gun from its original position, "but I'm still not sure if I can trust you."

What about me? Mallory thought. *It's not easy to trust someone who insists on talking to you from the other end of a gun.*

"You can trust me, Harriet," she assured her. "What matters now is the truth. I have a feeling that Carly Berman has been living a lie for the last few years, one that affected you very deeply."

Harriet nodded. "You're right—it was a lie. The whole thing. I did invent Rejuva-Juice. Just like I told you, I got interested in health because I've had such serious problems of my own. That's why I started doing research and traveling around the world, trying to find out what people could do to hold onto the most important thing they have."

"But if you came up with the formula," Mallory asked, "why on earth did you let Carly pretend she was the one who developed it?"

"Because she was the one with the charisma," Harriet replied bitterly. "The beauty, too." She glanced down and made a sweeping gesture at herself with her free hand, adding, "Look at me, Mallory. Who would ever believe that I was someone who had discovered the fountain of youth? What kind of spokesperson—what kind of *symbol*—could I have ever been for a product that was capable of keeping people young and vibrant—and most of all, healthy?"

"So you just handed it over to Carly?" Mallory asked, incredulous.

Harriet's eyes widened. "Of course not! I'm a businessperson, remember? Carly and I had an agreement. She was going to popularize Rejuva-Juice, and once she started making money with it, we were going to divide up the profits. But she kept putting me off." She laughed coldly. "Even though I was her accountant, she kept trying to convince me that we weren't making a profit. She was always coming up with different excuses. She had to expand Tavaci Springs; she needed to hire a better and more expensive public relations firm; her market research told her she should start using a more upscale bottle that would cost more..."

With a deep sigh, she said, "Mallory, you probably think I'm naïve or just plain dumb, but for years I accepted whatever she told me. If there was one thing Carly was good at, it was making people believe whatever she wanted them to believe. Including me. But finally enough time went by that even I began to doubt her. So I went out and hired a lawyer. Of course I felt bad about suing Carly, but I had no choice.

"Besides, I was confident that I'd be able to win back the rights to Rejuva-Juice," Harriet continued calmly. "So was my lawyer. He was also certain that we'd get a big portion of the fortune she'd made over the past few years. All we had to do was make a jury believe that I was the one who invented Rejuva-Juice, not Carly."

"But she was so convincing!" Mallory exclaimed. "I completely bought into her presentation at the Wheeler Opera House. All those photographs of her traveling to the most remote destinations in the world—"

Harriet snorted. "Nothing but a fairy tale. A total fantasy. It was something she and I dreamed up to make the story behind Rejuva-Juice sound enticing."

"But what about all those shots of Carly standing in the rain forest and in those little villages in the Himalayas?"

"The wonders of computer technology," Harriet snapped. "Carly used Photoshop to superimpose pictures of herself over stock photos of the most exotic corners of the world. In fact, she even made up most of the names of the places she supposedly visited in her quest to create her own version of the fountain of youth."

"You mean there's no village called Mongo-Bongo in New Guinea?" Mallory was disappointed. She'd already considered pitching Mongo-Bongo to Trevor—maybe a piece on whether a diehard vegetarian can have fun in a place where cannibalism still prevails.

"If anyone did any traveling," Harriet continued in the same biting tone, "it was me. I went all over the world, doing research. But I didn't go trekking around primitive villages or any other exotic locales. I did my research at libraries and medical research institutes."

Mallory still wasn't sure that Harriet was telling the truth. But it certainly sounded as if she was. And the fact that she was still holding a gun on her had nothing to do with how convincing she was.

That didn't mean there weren't still some loose ends.

"What about Sylvie?" she demanded.

Harriet looked startled. "What *about* Sylvie?"

Mallory took a deep breath. "Harriet, I saw you having lunch with her right after the police released you. Even though you swore the two of you were enemies—"

"But we're not!" Harriet insisted. "In fact, I was hoping that Sylvie would testify on my behalf."

"Testify?" Instead of the whole scenario becoming clearer, it seemed to Mallory that it was just getting more confusing.

Harriet nodded. "Before that jury I had to convince." Gesturing toward the booty Mallory had found stashed in the locked file drawer, she explained, "I have the handwritten recipe, of course, along with all my notes. But in the end, it was going to be my word against Carly's. That's where Sylvie came in. She'd had enough dealings with Carly to know that she didn't really know very much about the product she had supposedly invented. Carly wasn't exactly a chemist, you know. Sure, she was great at the fluff, but when it came to the real interaction of Rejuva-Juice's ingredients with the human body, she never understood any of it."

"But wasn't Sylvie determined to buy the company?"

"Yes, she was. In fact, I figured she might even have to be subpoenaed as a hostile witness. Which is why I wanted to do everything I could to ingratiate myself."

"And Gordon?" Mallory asked. "What about the movie he wanted to make about Carly's life?"

"Hah!" Harriet cried. "How could he possibly make a movie about someone's life story when it was all a lie? He didn't know it, of course. But Carly certainly did! And so she knew she could never sell the rights to him. It was one thing to tell her adoring customers that she had traveled to New Guinea and the Himalayas and all those other exotic places. But it was something else to tell a whopper like that on as grand a scale as a full-length feature film! That doesn't mean she didn't adore the attention. She loved being courted by a Hollywood director, even if he wasn't exactly on the A-list anymore."

The more Harriet spoke, the more confused Mallory became.

"Harriet," she finally said, "if all this is true—and I believe that it is—then why did you hire that man to kill Carly?"

Harriet's mouth dropped open. "What are you talking about?"

"That man I heard you arguing with at your house! It was less than an hour ago. Isn't he the person you hired to kill her?"

"I still have no idea what man you're—" The creases in Harriet's forehead smoothed slightly as she said, "Now I get it. You must mean Micky Mitchell, the process server."

"That man you were fighting with is a process server?"

Harriet nodded. "He's the guy I hired to serve Carly with the papers for the lawsuit."

"In that case," Mallory asked, sounding as doubtful as she felt, "what did you two have to fight about?"

"Money," Harriet replied matter-of-factly. "After Carly was killed, we switched gears and served Brett, since as Carly's spouse he would inherit everything. And given all the news coverage the Bermans were suddenly getting, Micky decided he deserved to be paid more money than the amount we'd originally agreed on. Do you believe he was even talking about hiring a ghostwriter so he could write a book about his version of the events?"

Mallory had to admit that, like everything else Harriet had told her, that explanation made perfect sense. Which still left her puzzled about Harriet's motive for killing Carly.

"Okay, so you didn't hire that man to kill Carly," she said. "But all that means is that you killed her yourself. What I really want to know is *why*."

Harriet's voice was at least two octaves higher than usual as she cried, "But I didn't kill Carly!"

Before Mallory had a chance to say the words, "Of course you did," she heard a thump in the hallway. At exactly the same moment, she and Harriet swiveled their heads around to see who had come up behind them.

"Of course she didn't," Brett Berman's voice boomed. "I did."

As soon as he stepped into the doorway right behind Harriet, Mallory saw that he, too, was holding a gun.

Out of the corner of her eye, she noticed that Harriet quickly tucked hers into her skirt pocket.

"And now," Brett said calmly, holding his gun up to the accountant's head, "I'm going to kill *you*."

Mallory noticed that even now, Brett looked as if he was posing for the cover of *GQ*. Every strand of his thick silver hair was in place, and his deep tan made the color of his electric blue eyes even deeper. And he was wearing the same beige suit she'd seen him checking out at the designer boutique.

Mallory was wishing she could climb into the file drawer and hide when he glanced in her direction. "You, too." With a smirk, he added, "That'll teach you not to go around digging up old friends from your past."

"I understand that you feel you have no choice but to kill us, Brett," Harriet said matter-of-factly. "But surely you're not going to do it here."

"Why not?" Brett demanded gruffly.

"Because you'd get blood and all kinds of other stuff all over the company's financial records, which you'll need once you're the owner," she explained. Glancing at Mallory slyly, she added, "You're much too smart for that."

"Ri-i-ight," he agreed uncertainly.

Mallory stared back at Harriet, trying to telepathically communicate, *You have a gun! Use it!*

But Harriet wasn't showing any signs of fighting back. Mallory wasn't sure what she was up to, but she suspected that someone as clever as Harriet had to have something up her sleeve. And whatever it was, it was probably related to the gun that, at least for the moment, was stashed away in her pocket.

So when Harriet suggested, "The hot tub, Brett. That's a much better place," Mallory chimed in, "But Harriet, that way Brett can clean off all his fingerprints!"

"Quiet!" he cried. But she could practically hear the wheels turning in his head. "Okay, you two. Into the Hydro-Salon."

"That's what we call the hot tub," Harriet noted.

"I told you to be quiet!" Brett repeated. To emphasize his point, he jabbed his gun into Harriet's ribs. "Now start walking!"

Hanging her head meekly, Harriet stepped into the hallway. Mallory shuffled after her, aware that Brett was following close behind. She suspected he was still gripping his gun, but at least he resisted the urge to poke her with it.

Harriet led the way along the hallway, making the turn that led the threesome to the back wall of the spa building. For a fleeting moment, Mallory hoped the fact that it was made entirely of glass would make them visible enough that someone, *anyone,* would notice what was going on and call the police. But then she remembered that Tavaci Springs was located in the middle of nowhere.

Her stomach lurched when she spotted the sunken hot tub surrounded on three sides by mountain views. The first time she'd seen it, she thought this unbelievably scenic setting was the height of luxury. Now, she nearly sobbed over the likelihood that here in this breathtaking spot she was about to meet a fate that was horribly similar to that of her high school acquaintance.

"Stand over there, right in front of the hot tub," Brett barked, gesturing with his gun.

Dutifully Mallory headed in that direction, taking baby steps. Harriet scuffed along behind her.

"Brett," Mallory asked, trying to buy herself some time as she turned to face him, "I can't help asking you why you killed Carly. Even if you didn't care about her, she was responsible for the fabulous lifestyle you've been enjoying."

"The only reason you're saying that is because you have no idea how uncertain our financial future was," he grumbled. "The woman had such a huge ego that it completely got in the way of whatever minuscule amount of business sense she happened to possess."

"What do you mean?" Mallory asked. "I didn't really know her as an adult, of course, but from what I could see she'd done really well."

"Hmph! Except that she was too stupid to recognize a good thing when she saw it. A reliable thing—one that would have set us up for the rest of our lives."

"What was that?" Quickly Mallory added, "You might as well tell me. You have nothing to lose at this point."

"HoliHealth, that's what!" he replied angrily. "They were dying to buy Rejuva-Juice—but that idiot had no intention of selling, even though it would have made us multimillionaires." With a contemptuous snort, he added, "She saw the stupid company she created as her baby and she intended to hold onto it. In fact, we had a big fight about exactly that, right before I decided I had no choice but to take matters into my own hands."

"You mean that night Carly gave her talk at the Wheeler Opera House?" Mallory asked without thinking.

"Yeah, that's right." A look of surprise crossed Brett's face. "How did you know?"

"I overheard you two arguing," she admitted. "I was on my way to the dressing room to wish Carly luck. When I heard what was going on, I backed off and went back to my seat."

"That's when I decided to kill her." Brett sounded

almost proud. "After all, I knew I'd inherit everything. And the first thing I intended to do as soon as the funeral was over was sell Rejuva-Juice to that pushy woman from HoliHealth."

"But I thought you planned on running the company yourself!" Mallory protested. "That's what you told me in that store."

"I lied," he sneered. "I didn't want people to know how anxious I was to get rid of that stupid business. I thought admitting that would give me too obvious a reason for killing Carly.

"But selling the company is what all this was about," he continued angrily. "Unloading it on HoliHealth for a nice chunk of change would have put me on Easy Street for the rest of my life. Why would I want to worry about the ups and downs of running a company? Frankly, I can think of much better ways of spending the rest of my life."

As if you'd know what running a business demands, Mallory couldn't help thinking. *It sounds as if the most challenging thing you ever did was sharpen a few pencils. That, and spend the profits as fast as they came in.*

"I knew exactly what I was going to do," Brett went on. "The first step was getting her estate settled. I knew that wouldn't take too long, since it was all spelled out in her will. Then I was going to move Astrid into that flashy house Carly built for us. Next I was going to buy myself a Ferrari. The Rolls is great, but I need a car that really tells people who I am. After that, I was going to get myself a serious yacht, along with a nice little weekend place somewhere in the Caribbean where I could keep it." Scowling, he added, "At least, that was the plan. Everything changed as soon as I was served by that barracuda first thing this morning."

"I believe he's referring to Micky Mitchell," Harriet muttered, casting Mallory a meaningful look. "The process server I mentioned."

"Damn right," Brett agreed. "As soon as I looked through those papers and saw what they were about, I knew my work wasn't done." Glowering at Harriet, he added, "If some jury realized that it was you and not Carly who invented Rejuva-Juice, it would take them about two seconds to sign away the entire company to you. Even if they just awarded you a piece of the action—meaning you and I had to make decisions together—I knew it wouldn't work." His lips curled into a sneer as he added, "You probably don't know this about me, but I've never been very good at sharing."

I bet it even says that on your kindergarten report card, Mallory thought ruefully.

Suddenly a lightbulb went on in her head.

"That phone call for Sylvie, the morning after Carly was killed," she said. "What was that all about? Who was calling her?"

"HoliHealth, of course." Brett's lips stretched into a sneer, revealing two rows of gleaming, perfect teeth. An image of the Big Bad Wolf popped into Mallory's head. "They called to tell her to up the bid. When they heard Carly was gone and that she wouldn't be screwing them around anymore, they figured it was finally time to get what they wanted.

They told Sylvie to sweeten the deal even more in the hopes that whoever stood to inherit Carly's company—that would be me—would bite. And it would have worked—at least if the company had simply passed to me, without Harriet mucking things up.

"What all this means is that I have no choice but to get both of you out of my way, just like Carly," Brett continued bitterly. Turning to Mallory, he added, "I was about to head over to Harriet's when Juanita mentioned that you'd just come by the house to get her address. She told me everything you'd said. All those questions you asked, the fact that you were so interested in Carly's murder . . . Of course, I'd already been keeping an eye on you. I couldn't help being suspicious about the fact that all of a sudden, when Carly was at the peak of her success, you were suddenly anxious to be her friend again. I had a feeling you were up to no good. There had to be *something* you wanted from her."

How about an acknowledgment that even though I never made the cheerleading squad at JFK High, I'm still a valuable person? Mallory thought morosely.

"Then I noticed you were running around town questioning everybody who knew Carly. Even that lowlife drug dealer."

Mallory's eyebrows shot up. So Brett *had* known! And from the way he sounded, he hadn't cared. In fact, as long as Carly kept the money coming in, he didn't appear to give a hoot about what she did.

"The fact that you seemed just a little too interested in figuring out who killed Carly made me realize it might not be such a bad idea to keep you from getting in my hair, too," Brett continued. "I thought the most efficient way to get rid of you was by running you off the road. But it turned out you're a pretty decent driver. Especially for somebody who lives in a place that's completely flat.

"Anyway, when that didn't work, I knew I had to try something else. I was still trying to figure out what to do when Juanita's compulsive nosiness actually turned out to be a good thing. When I found out the two of you were going to be together, I rushed off to Harriet's, figuring I'd be able to kill two birds with one stone. But no sooner did I pull into her street than I saw that cheap rental car of yours take off. Not long afterward, Harriet followed." He shrugged. "Same plan, different place. I'm flexible that way."

Juanita and her big mouth, Mallory thought angrily. If it wasn't for all the information blabbed by a woman who claims she doesn't say anything, none of us would be here right now.

"When I saw that you'd both come up to the spa and realized that nobody else was here," Brett went on breezily, "I knew I'd just stumbled upon the perfect opportunity. It'll be a piece of cake to get rid of you both and then get on a plane before either of you have even been missed. You know, Europe has some seaside towns that are much nicer than anything you'd find in the Caribbean. Monaco, Nice, the Costa del Sol . . . And skipping the country will be no problem. Thanks to Astrid's willingness to lie in order to give me an alibi, I'm not even on the cops' list of suspects."

With a smirk, he added, "And they say there's no such thing as the perfect crime."

Brett took a step closer, still holding the gun on Harriet. Mallory's head buzzed as she realized he was on the verge of putting the finishing touches on what he considered "the perfect crime"—"finishing" as in finishing them both off. She knew she had to do something, and she had to do it *fast*.

"Oh, my God! Look out behind you!" she screamed at Brett, pointing at some vague spot beyond where he was standing.

Instinctively he turned. She took advantage of the split second he was off guard by stepping forward and striking his arm as hard as she could.

It turned out to be hard enough that he let go of the gun. In fact, he jerked his arm with such force that he flung it in the direction of the hot tub.

"Hey! What do you think you're—?"

He lurched toward the edge of the tub just in time to join Mallory in watching the gun drop to the bottom of the tub of water.

"What the—!" he growled.

For a fleeting moment, a look of such fury crossed his face that Mallory winced, expecting him to strike her. Instead, he leaned over the edge of the hot tub to retrieve his weapon. Mallory started to dash away, but not before seeing the muscles of his face tighten as he looked down and realized that the tub was just deep enough that he would have to climb inside to reach the bottom.

Mallory had gotten less than ten feet away when she noticed that Harriet had taken full advantage of the few seconds in which Brett was distracted. She reached into her pocket and pulled out her gun, then pointed it directly at Brett.

"Maybe it's not such a perfect crime after all," Harriet announced, her eyes flashing with fury. "Especially since Mallory is going to dial nine-one-one on her cell phone and it'll take the police about fifteen minutes to get up here and arrest you. That is, if you're smart enough not to do anything that gives me a reason to use this thing."

"You don't have the guts to shoot me," Brett sneered.

Harriet had barely had a chance to open her mouth to reply when he stepped to one side, clearly intending to flee. But water from the hot tub must have splashed onto the floor, because his foot instantly slipped across the smooth tile, causing him to lose his balance. Quickly he grabbed onto a tall display case to steady himself. But instead of holding him up, the force with which he grasped the glass shelving was enough to send a hundred glass bottles of shampoos, lotions, and soaps flying off the shelves, crashing to the ground and sending rivulets of thick liquids oozing across the floor.

He ended up sprawled on his back anyway, still clinging to a shelf that at this point was nothing more than a large glass shard. He lay with his arms and legs flailing, bug-style, splattered with magic potions that emitted a peculiar mixture of fragrances.

Mallory was able to identify honeysuckle, orange, and cinnamon.

Harriet stepped closer, still gripping the gun. As she held it to his head, she demanded coolly, "Still think I don't have enough guts, Brett? Why don't you try pulling yourself up from the slime to attack me and we'll both find out? Huh? Go ahead, try it!"

In response to her goading, a look of intense rage crossed his face, making his eyes gleam like those of some evil character in a horror flick. But he seemed to realize quickly that the mousy accountant was turning out to be a lot more of a tiger than he ever would have anticipated, since instead of fighting back, he held his hands up in front of his face.

"Don't shoot me!" he begged. "Please, Harriet! All those years we worked together, I never did a thing to hurt you, did I? I thought we were friends. We were practically *family*!"

"Mallory," Harriet barked without taking her eyes off the giant cockroach splayed in front of her, "hurry up and call the police, will you?"

Mallory didn't bother to reply. She was too busy dialing 911.

"The way you handled yourself in there was amazing," Mallory said admiringly as she followed Harriet through the front door of the Hotel Jerome.

"I even surprised myself," Harriet admitted. "I had no idea I'd turn out to be a gun-toting mama." Glancing over her shoulder and grinning at Mallory shyly, she added, "Maybe it's a sign that I've been in the West too long."

Mallory was about to ask Harriet if she had any idea where else she might like to live—and what she might like to do once she got there—when she stopped in her tracks.

When she'd invited Harriet to come back to the Jerome to recover from all the excitement of not only fingering Carly's murderer but also handing him over to the police, she'd envisioned nothing more than a soothing cup of tea. She certainly hadn't expected a crowd of reporters to lunge at her from across the lobby the moment she walked inside. Some carried notebooks, some brandished cameras, and a few balanced gigantic video cameras on their shoulders.

"Did some movie star just check in?" she wondered out loud.

She'd barely had a chance to remind herself that this was Aspen, where movie stars were as common as snowflakes, when one of the bellmen rushed over to her.

"Sorry about all this, Ms. Marlowe!" he exclaimed. She immediately recognized him as the young man who'd helped out during her silk scarf ruse, which she'd used to locate Sylvie's room. "We usually ensure our guests' privacy here at the Jerome. But this story is just too big."

"How did you know Brett Berman was the killer?" one reporter cried out as he headed in Mallory and Harriet's direction with frightening determination.

"How did you catch him?" another demanded.

"Ms. Vogel, what are you going to now?" a third

asked. "I understand that you've initiated a lawsuit against the Bermans, and that you're the actual creator of Rejuva-Juice. What are you going to do if you gain ownership of the company?"

Goodness, they know a lot, Mallory marveled. Somebody must have been talking to Juanita.

Before either she or Harriet had a chance to formulate answers to any of the reporters' questions, the bellman whispered, "In here!"

She glanced over and saw that he was gesturing toward a small side parlor that was closed off from the main lobby by tall potted plants. She wasted no time in dashing in that direction. Harriet was right behind her.

But instead of finding respite, she immediately saw that she'd been catapulted out of the frying pan and into the fire.

"Gordon?" she cried. "Trevor? What are you doing here?"

The two men sat side by side on a red velvet couch with ridiculously ornate legs, looking about as comfortable as two cowpokes who'd just come into town for the very first time.

"Waiting for you, of course," Trevor replied anxiously, rising to his feet. "I wanted to see for myself that you were safe. Good God, Mallory, what happened at that spa today?"

She glanced at Harriet ruefully. "Let's just say that Harriet and I have turned out to be the Butch Cassidy and the Sundance Kid of the twenty-first century."

"Sounds more like Wyatt Earp and Doc Holliday,"

Trevor insisted. "But at least you both got out of there without being hurt."

"I would never have managed without Harriet." Turning to her, Mallory said, "What happens now? What *are* you going to do once you own Rejuva-Juice?"

Harriet smiled shyly. "Actually, I've been doing quite a lot of thinking about that very topic. Now that the truth about Brett has come out, I'm more confident than ever that I'll manage to gain control of the company. And I'd bet the secret recipe for Rejuva-Juice that I can do a better job of running it than Carly ever did.

"The only thing I'm missing of course, is a spokesperson, one who's as attractive and charismatic as Carly was. But I think I've come up with someone."

"Who?" Mallory, Trevor, and Gordon asked in unison.

"Sylvie," Harriet replied happily. "It's something she and I talked about over lunch at the Pine Creek Cookhouse. She's decided to leave HoliHealth and become my Director of Marketing. Maybe she's not as flashy as Carly, but she's got real style. I think she'll do a great job of promoting both Rejuva-Juice and Tavaci Springs."

"She's a great choice," Mallory agreed sincerely. "And I'm sure she'll be much happier working for you than she was at HoliHealth."

No more Flax or Bulgar, at least. Those two sounded as if they were enough to give anybody indigestion.

Gordon chose that moment to come over to Mallory and take hold of her hand. Looking into her eyes earnestly, he said, "Thank heavens you're all right—and that Carly's killer has been caught. But once you've recovered from your heroism, I'm hoping you and I can paint the town red."

"Funny," Trevor piped up, "I was thinking the exact same thing."

Harriet glanced over at Mallory with a look of merriment in her eyes. Even though she didn't say a word, Mallory knew exactly what she was thinking.

And just as Harriet had pondered her future as head of the Rejuva-Juice empire, Mallory had done some thinking of her own.

"I'm sorry, Gordon," she said. "But while I've really enjoyed our time together, I think I'm going to spend the twenty-four hours I have left in Aspen with Trevor."

A look of surprise crossed Trevor's face. But he didn't waste any time before lumbering over, wearing a cat-that-ate-the-canary grin.

"So I finally get to spend some time with you," he said, "even though I had to fly two thousand miles and wait two days to do it."

"Sorry about that," Mallory said. "I've been busy."

"In that case," he replied, "we'll have to squeeze in all the sightseeing we can manage. Which leads to the question, Is there anything for a nonskier like me to do in Aspen?"

She smiled. "It just so happens you've asked exactly the right person."

IT'S ALL UPHILL IN ASPEN

By Mallory Marlowe

When it comes to the world's best ski towns, Aspen, Colorado, ranks high on the list with such luxurious spots as St. Moritz, Innsbruck, and Chamonix. But while this enclave of the rich, the famous, and the well-coordinated makes a great destination for skiers, what about travelers who prefer admiring mountains from afar to sliding down them?

The good news is that Aspen is big enough and diverse enough to keep just about anyone entertained—even flatlanders. Once a center for silver mining, today Aspen offers cultural activities, first-rate accommodations, historic sites, and fabulous shopping—especially for those with humongous limits on their credit cards. And while the entire town occupies less than four square miles, it boasts more than eighty restaurants.

Here's just a sampling of ways that even a nonskier can have fun in Aspen:

Soar to the top of the world. To feel like you're on top of the world, take a ride to the top of Aspen Mountain on the Silver Queen Gondola. While the main purpose of the fifteen-minute trip is to transport skiers, the cable car runs to the 11,200-foot summit year-round. The view of the Rockies is spectacular, and visitors can enjoy their scenic surroundings while lingering over tandoori chicken at the mountaintop restaurant, the Sundeck. (Silver Queen Gondola, http://www.aspensnowmass.com/summer_rec/gondola.cfm.)

✳ **Enjoy a concert or play.** Back in the late 1800s, silver baron Jerome Wheeler dreamed of turning the rough-and-tumble town of Aspen into a cultural center. His legacy includes the Wheeler Opera House, which combines the Wild West with European elegance. Today, visitors can enjoy plays, concerts, opera, ballet, films, and lectures while luxuriating in this Aspen institution's old-fashioned red velvet seats and enjoying the sleek wooden balcony and airy blue ceiling. (Wheeler Opera House, 320 East Hyman Avenue, Aspen, Box Office: 970–920–5770, www.wheeleroperahouse.com.)

✳ **Gorge on fabulous food.** Aspen's extensive list of restaurants starts with 1950s-style diners and ends with world-class eateries. Montagna at the Little Nell resort features "farmhouse food" that incorporates local ingredients. (Don't be overwhelmed by the sixty-nine-page wine list, since the sommelier is happy to make recommendations.) The jury is still out on the eighteen-dollar chocolate tasting, which includes four minuscule but marvelous desserts. (Montagna, 675 East Durant Avenue, Aspen, 888–843–6355 or 970–920–4600, http://www.thelittlenell.com.) For a truly unique experience, take the half-hour drive to the Pine Creek Cookhouse. The adventure begins by traveling from the parking area to the restaurant by horse-drawn sleigh. Once inside the rustic log cabin nestled in the mountains, guests can enjoy such Colorado fare as buffalo meat loaf and the Wild Game Mixed Grill, made with caribou, antelope, and homemade wild game sausage. The setting, replete with knotty pine, light fixtures fashioned from antlers, and incredibly scenic views, provides the perfect opportunity to enjoy a Rocky Mountain high. (Pine Creek Cookhouse, 314 South 2nd Street, Aspen, 970–925–1044, http://www.pinecreekcookhouse.com.)

Luxuriate in top-of-the-line accommodations. In addition to building the Wheeler Opera House, Jerome Wheeler constructed the opulent Hotel Jerome. While the hotel has undergone multiple renovations, it still has a historic feeling. Upon entering the lobby, visitors will instantly be transported back to the Wild West. Ornate dark red wallpaper covers the walls, thick Oriental carpets cushion the wooden floors, and the old-fashioned lampshades and overstuffed couches are edged with silk fringe. Be sure to try the J-Bar's house drink, the Aspen Crud, a milkshake spiked with bourbon that reflects the fact that during Prohibition, the bar became a soda fountain. (Hotel Jerome, 330 East Main Street, Aspen, 970–920–1000, http://hoteljerome.rockresorts.com.)

 Pay tribute to a musical icon. John Denver's love of the Rockies prompted the singer-songwriter to make Aspen his home from the 1970s until his death at age fifty-three in 1997. Well-loved songs such as "Rocky Mountain High," "Annie's Song," and "Sunshine On My Shoulders" made him one of the five top-selling artists in music industry history, earning him eight platinum and fourteen gold albums. Today, Denver is honored at the John Denver Sanctuary near the Rio Grande Park, a tranquil spot marked by boulders engraved with the lyrics of his songs.

Become a gourmet chef. Eating in Aspen's great restaurants is enough to inspire anyone to learn their way around a kitchen. So what better place to live out that dream than the Cooking School of Aspen? Classes include "From Soup to Nuts," in which participants prepare a five-course meal, learn which wines to pair with the food, and then sit down to enjoy the fruits of their labors, resulting in an experience that's not only fun but delicious. (Cooking School of Aspen, 414 East Hyman Avenue, Aspen, 970–920–1879, www.cookingschoolofaspen.com.)

Spend some of your hard-earned dough. When it comes to shopping, the streets of Aspen may not be paved with gold, but having a little in your pockets certainly wouldn't hurt. The fact that downtown still retains its Wild West feeling, rather than an ambience of glitz and glamour, makes browsing through shops that sell cashmere sweaters and Gucci purses a wonderfully incongruous experience. But there is truly something for everyone. Even at Amen Wardy, where the merchandise includes rubber gloves decorated with ruffles, fake flowers, and a rhinestone ring for forty dollars, a discriminating shopper can find bargains like organic room spray made with green oolong tea and orchids—a product that turns out to have many varied uses. (Amen Wardy, 210 South Galena Street, Aspen, 970–920–7700, www.amenwardyaspen.com.) And be sure to check out the Explore Booksellers and Bistro, where book lovers are guaranteed to find a home away from home. (Explore Booksellers and Bistro, 221 East Main Street, Aspen, 970–925–5336 or 800–562–READ (7323), http://www.explorebooksellers.com.)

✺ **Learn to relax with yoga.** One of the best ways of getting in touch with your body is by taking a yoga class at one of the many studios in town, such as the Earth, Wind, Fire, and Water Sanctuary for Mind, Body, and Spirit. Experience Vinyasa Flow Yoga, Iyengar, Ashtanga, Bhakti, and Jivamukti—one of which is bound to pave the way to a more peaceful existence. (600 West Main Street, Aspen 970–555–5353, www.EarthWindFireWater.com.)

✺ **Mellow out with a spa treatment or in a hot tub.** Nothing is as relaxing as a massage—except, perhaps, unwinding in a hot tub. The Remède Spa at the St. Regis Aspen Resort raises the concept of pampering to an entirely new level. Visitors can luxuriate in the one-of-a-kind grotto, a wonderfully serene pool surrounded by three waterfalls that cascade down its rough stone walls. Just beyond is a stone-enclosed hot tub with a cold plunge pool. (Remède Spa, 315 East Dean Street, Aspen, 970–429–9038, http://www.remede.com.)

Another spa worth checking out is the unique hideaway on the outskirts of Aspen, Tavaci Springs. Many of the treatments that are offered feature a magic potion that's been touted as the fountain of youth in a bottle, Rejuva-Juice. While this health drink's effectiveness is still up for debate, there's no denying that the spa is paradise for anyone looking for pampering. And the extremely private facility is gorgeous, tucked away in the mountains and surrounded by outstanding natural beauty. (Tavaci Springs, P.O. Box 1712, Aspen, CO, http://www.tavacisprings.com.) Please note: At the time of this writing, Tavaci Springs was undergoing a management change.

About the Author

CYNTHIA BAXTER is a native of Long Island, New York. She currently resides on the North Shore, where she is at work on the next mystery in the *Murder Packs a Suitcase* series. She is also the author of the *Reigning Cats & Dogs* mystery series. Visit her website at www.cynthiabaxter.com.